T0129384

INDIAN KEY

C. Lee Harrison

iUniverse

Indian Key

This is a work of fiction. All of the characters, names, incidents, organizations, and dialogue in this novel are either the products of the author's imagination or are used fictitiously.

iUniverse books may be ordered through booksellers or by contacting:

iUniverse
1663 Liberty Drive
Bloomington, IN 47403
www.iuniverse.com
1-800-Authors (1-800-288-4677)

Because of the dynamic nature of the Internet, any web addresses or links contained in this book may have changed since publication and may no longer be valid. The views expressed in this work are solely those of the author and do not necessarily reflect the views of the publisher, and the publisher hereby disclaims any responsibility for them.

Any people depicted in stock imagery provided by Thinkstock are models, and such images are being used for illustrative purposes only. Certain stock imagery © Thinkstock.

ISBN: 978-1-4401-8791-9 (sc)

Printed in the United States of America.

iUniverse rev. date: 01/27/2015

CHAPTER ONE

THE PLANE WAS LATE, as usual, arriving at the Fort Lauderdale airport, Nick Jensen gathered his carry-on, preparing to leave the plane and face the evening rush hour traffic on I-95. Nick made his way along the corridor to the doors leading to the parking lot, where he had left his Mercedes convertible.

Nick had made a quick trip to Baltimore to see his younger brother, Jonathan. Nick had been a father to his brother ever since their parents were killed in a home invasion. His parents, both lawyers, were beaten and shot by gang members in retaliation for prosecuting their leader. Six year old Jonathan had hidden in a closet upstairs while the brutal murders were being committed. Jonathan, now 20 years old, 6'1" with wide set blue eyes, blond hair, 210 lbs., almost a twin version of his 38 year old brother.

Nick shed his leather coat as he got into his car. The Fort Lauderdale sun was much warmer than December in Maryland. As Nick drove along U.S. 1 towards home in Pompano Beach, he recalled his conversation with his brother. Jonathan had been having a rough time in college, he had always been a slow student, and Nick thought that Jonathan should take a break from school, come back to Florida and move back in with Nick.

Jonathan, remembering when he was a teen and the rules that his older brother imposed on him was hesitant about the idea. After much debate, Jonathan agreed to pack his belongings in his Chevrolet Silverado and drive south to Nick's place. Nick planned on putting Jonathan to work in his home Improvement business and maybe he could be helpful when Nick had a client for his Private Investigation Company. Jonathan was pretty handy with a camera.

Nick drove into the driveway, he noticed that the lights on his boat were on and the cover had been removed. He parked, leaving his luggage in the car he went down to the dock and peeked into the cabin.

Sara, his seventeen year old neighbor, was at the table wrapping Christmas presents. Sara was the daughter of his ex-fiancée.

Nick and Laurie had been together seven years before they split over Nick not being able to commit to marriage. They remained friends, at least until the past six months, when Laurie had become close to Jason Sanders.

Jason was dark, well built, with movie star features. He was a fitness expert and loved to show off for both Laurie and Sara, usually within sight of Nick. of course, was extremely jealous of Jason, and hated that Sara also seemed smitten by Jason.

Nick walked onto the boat and into the cabin. "Nick!" Sara yelled. "Boy, am I glad to see you!" "What are you doing on the boat?" asked Nick. "Oh! Me and my mom had a big fight, and I moved into the boat for the week." "Yeah, what was the fight about?" "She thinks I am still a kid. She thinks I pay too much attention to Jason" "So do I" "Oh, Nick, I am not a kid, I'm seventeen." "Sara, I think that you should make up with your mother." "Oh, Nick, can't I stay? I just want to finish my wrapping, then I'll make up with mom."

"Yeah, sure. Are you hungry? I am going to grill a steak, I can just as easily put two on the grill." "Hey! Make that three," said Laurie, as she walked in the door.

"Welcome home, Nick. I was just going to suggest a fishing trip to the Keys, for a day or two. The weather has been just beautiful." "Great, when do you want to leave? Tonight? We can get there late and be early bird fishermen." "No, let's leave early tomorrow morning. I want a steak now. ""You got it" Nick said, as he fired up the grill, then went to get the steaks from the fridge. While Nick was grilling the steaks, Laurie made a salad and steamed broccoli for a side dish. Later, as they sat down to a dinner Nick wanted to know if the girls had made up.

Laurie said, "Oh yes, it was just a mother, daughter disagreement" Nick said, "Sara said it was over Jason." Laurie answered, "It wasn't *over* Jason, it was *about* Jason .Sara is in her final year of high school, and I don't want too many distractions for her. Jason can be a bit full of himself at times, and he tries to impress Sara in numerous ways."

Nick quietly cleared the dishes, not commenting. He knew that if he was critical of Jason, it would make Laurie angry, and he did not want to screw up the planned fishing trip.

Early the next morning, Nick prepared the boat for the trip to the Keys. After leaving a note for Jonathon, he cast off the boat and the three of them were on their way. It was a pleasant trip down the Inttercoastal waterway to Biscayne bay, then into the Beautiful blue/green waters of the Keys. As they neared Islamarada, Nick cut back the speed and they broke out the fishing gear. Nick had taught Sara to fish when she was a child. Sara loved to fish, especially with Nick. She loved to beat him by snagging the biggest fish. By early evening, they had caught enough to cook for dinner plus a few to take home and freeze for later.

While Nick cleaned the fish, Laurie and Sara prepared the meal. Nick watched both of the girls at work in the galley. Sara had inherited her mother's beauty and lovely body. Both women were blond, with blue/green eyes, with a lovely oval shaped face and a playboy body. Sara and Laurie were often mistaken for sisters. Both had a playful personality. Sara could be a bit bolder than her conservative mother.

After the dishes were cleared, Sara went up on the front deck, while Nick and Laurie drank a couple glasses of wine and danced on the back deck to music on the radio. Nick pulled Laurie closer and started to kiss her neck. At first Laurie resisted, but eventually the wine, music and the magic of the warm Florida night changed her mood. A little kissing led to more and than instead of Laurie sharing the master suite with Sara as planned, her and Nick ended up in the large bed making love. Laurie pulled Nick into her and surrendered to her emotions. Sara, after hearing their sounds of passion, went into the second cabin and tried to sleep.

The next morning, Nick was laying awake next to Laurie His leg was over her warm, naked body and Nick was enjoying the morning sunrise. He suddenly was aware of a movement by the bed and turned his head to See Sara, naked, she slid into bed next to him. *God , he thought, she is as lovely as her mother! What the hell is she up to, what am I going to do?* Laurie was still sleeping as Sara started to playfully to kiss his back and rub his thigh. Nick gently removed her hand. Sara resumed rubbing, gradually moving higher on his thigh. He again removed her hand and quietly slid out of the bed so as not to wake Laurie.

He went into the galley and started to make coffee. Sara followed. "What's wrong Nick? Don't you like me?" asked Sara. "Sara, put some clothes on, do you want your mother to kill both of us?" "Oh Nick, I thought we could do a trio. I thought you would like my body." "Sara, I don't see you that way. You and I have a special relationship, I would not want anything to ruin that." Sara pulling on shorts and a t-top, asked "Don't you think I am pretty?" "Sara you are a beautiful young lady, but I love your mother and probably always will."

"Well you should do something about it before Jason does." 'You, young lady, should be careful of Jason. He is a dangerous man." "Oh poo, I can handle him, he just likes to look at my body, especially when I am wearing my Bikini."

Laurie entered the cabin with a cheery good morning. She started making breakfast, Sara helping. After they all had enjoyed breakfast ,Nick said "What a wonderful night, Laurie, I love you, I think we should talk about getting back together." "Forget it Nick it was just the wine and the moonlight." "Oh no, it was more than that, you felt it, you know that you did." "Nick, we have been over this before. You and I want different lives." "I am not going to discuss it any longer. Let's head home." said Laurie.

Nick, still grumbling, started the motor, as he was pulling up the anchor, he looked up towards the front deck.. Sara was standing facing Nick, when they locked eyes, Sara removed her top, stretched and waved at him, then turned her back on him and lay on the deck sunning herself. Nick glanced quickly at Laurie, busy clearing the breakfast dishes, did not appear to have noticed Sara's antics..

Five hours later, they entered the canal leading to Nick's. When Nick pulled the boat along side of the dock, Laurie jumped to the pier, as she waved goodbye, Nick yelled "This is not over Laurie." Laurie yelled back "Yes it is Nick, you just won't admit it. Nick and Laurie continued to argue for another fifteen minutes. It became heated until Laurie turned her back on Nick, said "Good Night!" and stormed into her house. Sara stood on tip toe and gave Nick a kiss. "Goodnight Nick, I'm sorry, you know that *I* love you." Then she ran to join her mother.

Nick went into the house. Jonathan had not arrived from Baltimore. He must be taking his time, thought Nick, it doesn't take more than a day or two for the drive. Nick drank a couple of shots of bourbon. Sara knocked on the door, "Are you decent?" She asked. "Yes, Sara, what do you want? I am tired and going to bed." "Oh I just wanted to get the gifts that I had wrapped this afternoon." "Yeah, sure, do you need any help?" "No, I'll be fine, you go on to bed, I'll close the door behind me." She kissed him, softly, "Good night." Sara was out the door. He watched her walk across the lawn, *what a great kid, I sure hope she has enough brains to stay clear of Jason.* Nick went to bed, tomorrow was a work day.

CHAPTER TWO

NICK JENSEN WAS A happy man. He lived alone in a three bedroom house with a Florida room overlooking a canal in Pompano Beach, Florida. Nick and his partner John Daily ran a profitable lawn care/home improvement business. Nick also did some private investigating for the law firm of Lawson and Lawson. His dream was to open his own detective agency, he just needed financing and the right partner. Nick loved living in South Florida, he enjoyed the warm weather and the abundant sunshine. Nick had a nearly new BMW convertible, and a 38 foot Bayliner tied at his dock. It was modest by South Florida standards but he was a satisfied man. He had it all. Life was sweet and uncomplicated. Just the way he liked it.

It was Friday night, the end of a tough week following the Holidays, a beautiful January south Florida evening. Nick and his partner John Daily had stopped for a couple of drinks before heading home. It was the perfect way to unwind. They went to Rick's on Ocean Boulevard in Pompano Beach. He had his favorite bourbon, Jim Beam and John a Coors Light. They had sat at the bar and discussed the projects of the past week, their progress and some future contracts. John always thought that the home improvement portion of the business was always behind schedule. Nick said well it's not like cutting grass, you have unforeseen problems. You always think that the customer can change the plans at the last minute and nothing will be delayed.

John, the business manager, was 5' 11' with red hair and matching beard. He was married to Charlotte, his college sweetheart. Nick and he had both dated her with John, much to his amazement, winning her favor. Charlotte explained to John, I want to be married, Nick is never going to marry anyone. John asked about Nick and Laurie,he wanted to know if they had patched up their differences. Nick said that it looked pretty bleak, and related the events of the fishing trip in December.

John exclaimed "Sara climbed into bed with you!" "My God, what is she, fourteen?" "No, she is seventeen, she was just showing off" "Well she has a body to show off, I don't care how old she is", John said." Yeah, sure, said Nick, by the way how is Charlotte these days, you know, your wife. ""She is fine wise guy, and as a matter of fact, I had better be getting on home." "Ahh, come on" said Nick, "Have one more for the road. "

John agreed and they ordered another round of drinks and just sat and watched the people in the café.

After finishing their drinks, John headed home to his wife and Nick, thinking about John going home to his wife drove home, than decided to walk to Mulligan's bar and restaurant in Lauderdale by the Sea. It was a convenient place to have some drinks for Nick. He lived about four blocks up the road. He could walk home if he had a couple too many, and he often did.

While savoring his 2nd Jim Beam, Nick had noticed a lovely, dark haired woman, She was dressed in a snug, pink blouse and white shorts. Her legs, were smooth and tan, anyone could see that she spent her free time at the beach. Sitting next to her was a woman that looked almost exactly like her, except she had red hair and a fairer complexion. This woman was wearing a short crop top blouse and a pair of pink shorts. Together, the two women were stunning. It was still during the early evening, the two women had not yet been beseeched by the vultures. Jimmy Buffet called them the land sharks, and these girls were the right kind of bait.

Nick walked over, to the women, introduced himself, asked "Can "I buy you ladies a drink?" "Sure, cowboy, sit down," said the dark haired woman. "I'm Kristie Ryan and this is my sister Katie." "What are you ladies drinking?" "Oh, cosmos, please."

He sat down ordered their drinks and another for himself. Nick asked Katie, "Don't I know you, I guess that sounds lame, but you do look familiar." Kristie, gave Nick a closer look, thought for a minute, she said, "Yeah, I remember, you don't know me, you know *about* me. You followed me once for my ex-husband." "Is that how you got to be ex?" "Yeah!" "Oops, sorry." "No Nick, I got a decent settlement, although not as much as I could have if you hadn't taken those pictures." "Sorry again." "Hey, but they were knockout pictures. She smiled, "You *do* remember." "I would have a hard time forgetting that assignment, you gave that guy quite a work out, I almost ran out of film." "You needed that many pictures, did you?" "Well, I like to be thorough" smiled Nick.

"How long have you girls lived in south Florida? " "Oh about five years, we're from Marquette Michigan," answered Katie. "Man, its cold up there, that's right around Canada." Kristie answered, "actually some parts of Canada are south of Marquette". Nick said, "Well I like it here, where it is always nice and warm, and you ladies certainly enhance the scenery."

Katie said, "I have to go, I have a date and I'm late." As she stood, Nick asked "Was it that corny line?" "No," she laughed, "But it was pretty lame." "I really do have a date. It was real nice meeting you, Nick." "You, Kristie and I will have to get together one day. "She kissed her sister on the cheek, brushing her body against Nick as she did." Don't be too late, little sister," than she left.

" She is such a wise ass", said Kristie. "Just because she was born three minutes before me she plays big sister. Until I introduce her as my older sister, that is." Nick laughed. "Well would you like another drink?" "Yes, but I really like the Margaritas at Aruba's." "So, let's go, would you like dinner also?" "No, but I might want dessert later."

They walked down the street to Aruba's on the beach. It was a pleasant night, the barman in Aruba's had opened the sliding doors that faced the ocean.. A soft breeze blew in off of the ocean. Sitting at the bar, they sipped their drinks and watched the moon shinning over the water. Kristie sighed, "What a beautiful night." "Yes, how nice to share it with a beautiful girl." "Nick, how sweet." They danced to a couple of tunes, and after another round of drinks, they left the club, Nick paid for the drinks, leaving a generous tip. "Let's go to Bootleggers on the Intercoastal." Nick said, "You'll like it." "Oh, I know that place, great, let's go."

As they walked out, Kristie grabbed hold of Nick's arm, and moved closer to him.. Nick said "We will have to take your car, mine is at home. ""Sure, I like to drive, anyway. "Bootleggers, a very popular cafe with the boating people, was crowded and noisy. Kristie and Nick danced on the outside dance floor. Some time around one, Nick asked, "Are you ready to leave? ""Sure," said Kristie, "Where do you live?"" You drive, I'll give directions,"

Kristie drove Nick home. She pulled the car into the driveway, Nick asked "Want to come on in for a while?" "Sure I told you that I wanted dessert later." Nick leaned over and kissed her. Kristie kissed back. She said "Let's get inside, now, I can't wait any longer." She started kissing him and fondling him as they came through the door, stripping her clothes off, she quickly bared all. Kristie than quickly stripped off Nick's shirt and pants, and proceeded to do everything he had hoped she would. Kristie had a great body and knew how to use it. She also knew what to do with his, after two or three hours Nick fell asleep, exhausted.

Later, Kristie as woke up, she heard muffled voices and moaning through The open window. She thought, *the people next door must be having a party,*

It sounds like a pretty good party. She got out of bed. Nick was still asleep, she smiled, *I think I wore the guy out.* Kristie left her business card on the table. *Coastal Real Estate* with her name Kristie Ryan and a phone number. Written in pencil was her Pompano Beach phone number, and the words, *Great night, call me we'll do it again. Soon!*

Kristie, pulled on her blouse as she went outside. It was dark and deserted that time of morning, it gave her the creeps. She would have stayed until morning, but she had an early Saturday appointment. Kristie got into her car, as she pulled away, she noticed a dark sedan parked on the side of the road. It just caught her attention because it was not in a driveway, like the rest of the cars were. I'm letting the darkness get to me, it's just a car. Oh who cares? She drove home, she was tired. Kristie thought about being with Nick. *Hmm, I guess he kind of wore me out also. It was a really pleasant evening*, she thought, *Nick is a nice guy.*

CHAPTER THREE

FRIDAY EVENING JASON SANDERS, Laura and Sara were having dinner at Laura's. The subject of conversation was when, or in Laura's thoughts, whether the wedding would take place. , As always, Jason was impatient and arrogant with Laura.

"What are you waiting for, Laura? We have discussed this for weeks. Are you still waiting for Nick Jensen to decide whether he wants to commit to marriage or are *you* getting cold feet?" "I don't know, Jason, I think I would like to have Sara settled in college before a wedding takes place." Jason's face darkened, "You baby her too much, she can take care of herself, she probably has sex more than you do." "Jason! Stop that, she is right in the next room, she will hear you. There is no need to talk about her in that way.

Besides, what difference does it make how often I have sex?" "Because you and I don't see eye to eye on how often you should. I am a sexy, passionate guy, and I don't like being put-off by a woman, any woman." "Yes, Jason, I know, that's one of my concerns about us. Maybe we should just remain as we are until I am more comfortable with this arrangement." "Fine, Jason snarled, you just keep stringing me along and see what happens. I dumped better women than you."

"Jason, maybe you better leave, we can have this discussion at another time." "Suites me, baby, some day you are going to be sorry you messed with me." "Good night, Jason." Laura said as she hurried to her room

Sara had been listening at the door and she whispered to Jason, "You are still coming back later, right?" "Yeah baby, I'll be back, you just wait for me."

Sara gave him a soft kiss as she opened the door, than quietly Closing it, she took Jason's hand and lead him into her bedroom. Turning to him, she kissed him passionately.

"Can't wait can you baby? said Jason as he started to remove her clothing. Sara and Jason quickly undressed and climbed into bed. They began pleasuring each other, Sara responding with raw passion.

They were so engrossed in each other, that neither heard Laura call to Sara. "Sara, did Jason leave? Are you in bed already? I want to talk to you." she said as she opened Sara's door. Laurie saw Sara naked, having sex with a man.

"Sara! What are you doing?" Laurie thought *Is that one of Sara's boyfriends? She then realized that it was Jason!* My God is that Jason?" "Jason, you bastard, get out of my house! Go! There is not going to be any wedding now or ever! I never want to see you again! "Jason hurried gathered his clothing and ran towards the door. "You haven't seen the last of me bitch, I want my share" he yelled as he left.

Sara looking at her mother, make no attempt to cover her body. Said "He loves me, mother, not you. We have been doing this all summer. We are going to go away together once we told you. Jason thinks I am a beautiful and sexy woman, not a kid. I have money, my father told me where it is. I will find it and Jason and I will share it. I haven't told him yet, I wanted to see if he really loves me. I don't think he could love me like he does if he didn't love me."

"Oh Sara, you are just a kid, you can't cope with the likes of Jason, the only person he loves is himself. He is a selfish and violent man, he will leave you as soon as he gets his hands on *your* money, as you call it. That money is stolen, it belongs to the police. As soon as yo

u touch that money, if you find it, you will be a fugitive from justice." "I am not a kid! You are just jealous of me!" Sara screamed as she dressed. "I am leaving, you can't treat me like a child." Sara rushed out of the house.

Jason after leaving the house, called his partner from a cell phone. "Where are you? Something went wrong, her mother caught me and the little bitch. After you get the information, you will have to take care of them. Know what I mean? OK, OK, I'll pay, I'm good for it. Maybe we can frame Nick Jensen, the Ex-boy friend, he's a neighbor. How soon can you be here? Hurry, I need an alibi, maybe I'll drive down to the Keys. Call me when you get the information."

Carter Melman worked by contract, usually for people who wanted revenge or information. This contract was given to him by the old man in Miami, the boss. Jason had given the old man information about the hidden money, and thought that he was a big shot, but he was just an expendable piece of the puzzle.

Melman called Miami to find out if he should really kill the women. The boss answered, "No loose ends, Melman, do it!

Carter was good at what he did, mainly extracting information for unscrupulous people. He wasn't a hit man, but he could do the job. By the time he finished extracting information, many wished that he had killed them.

Melman arrived at Laurie's house, went to the side door, turning the knob, he found the door unlocked. He entered the house. Rex the dog met him, growling and baring his teeth. Carter had brought a supply of drugged dog treats with him" Here doggie, nice doggie, you will like these, good dog. Rex gobbled the treats and shortly became groggy. Well, now for the work at hand. It was time to start.

The man walked through the house, surprising Laurie in her bedroom. "Who are you, get out!"she screamed. Laurie fought with Carter, scratching and punching Him. Carter grabbed her, punched her hard in the face and overpowered her. He then pulled the phone cord out of the wall and tied her hands to her sides. Carter then tapped her mouth with duck tape. He had his tools, but he needed a weapon from the house. Carter went to the kitchen and removed a medium size butcher knife from the rack. This will do nicely .Then he went into the Laurie's bedroom. He smiled. Laurie looked at him, fear in her eyes, she kept shaking her head, no.

He grabbed the quilt and dragged her into the garage. Carter taped her wrists to water pipes along the garage wall. Then he sliced the phone cord, pulled her pajama bottoms off, and slit the tops with the knife. She was a beautiful woman lying there on the floor. Laurie was shaking.

He said, "I don't want your body. Relax." "I am going to ask you some questions, move your head yes or no, understand?" .She nodded her head. "That's right, good girl Now, where did Reggie hide his money?" .Laurie shook her head. He sliced her across her breasts and stomach with the knife. She moaned loud enough to be heard through the tape. "Laurie, tell me where the money is!" Another head shake, this more desperate, her eyes pleading. He made a few more slices, he opened his bag and took out a rain coat, it was starting to get messy. Tears were running down Laurie's face, "The money, Laurie? Behind the tape, she was moaning, "Please!". He slapped her, than he threw some water in her face. She came too. She looked at him with an unspeakable fear. He said, "Laurie, I am going to take the tape off of your mouth. If you scream or make any noise, I'll have to get rough, you understand?" She nodded her head, slowly. He removed the tape. "Do you want some water?" He asked. "No, she whispered. What do you want?" I just want to know where is the money?" "I swear, I don't know, he never told me, honest."

He cut her swiftly with the knife, across her body. She whimpered, "Please, please, stop." "Please, she said, If I knew I would tell you. Oh God! Sara What have you done to Sara? Don't hurt her, please." "She doesn't know anything about the money, she was just a little girl." "I won't Carter said, just tell me about the money." "I don't know, God, I don't know." "I'll find out what you know."

He taped her mouth, and once again used his knife. Laurie lay still. "Laurie, he said. Can you hear me.?" She slowly opened her eyes. They were dull with pain, her beautiful face was twisted with pain, her body raked with open wounds, she wasn't very pretty now. One more time, "Laurie, where is the money?" "Maybe Sara put it in the safe at the pottery shop, I noticed papers in there. Take it, but please stop and please don't hurt Sara, we don't want it."

"Sorry Laurie, the less people know about the money the better for us." He swiftly brought the knife across her throat. The blood spurted, and he watched the life slowly leave her eyes. He packed up his tools and carried them into Sara's room. She was not there. *Oh dammit, where is the little bitch? I don't have time to look for her, I have to get out of here.* He left the house by the side door and returned to his car. Discarding the rain coat and his gloves, he put them in the trunk Later, he could safely dispose of them. After Carter finished his business he sat in his car, thinking, so the directions to the money could be in the safe at the pottery shop, I am going look into that.

Melman noticed a woman leaving Nick Jensen's house. He checked the clock on the dash, it was 4:30 a.m. She was a looker, dark hair, nice, lean body. The woman came out of the house, got into her car and drove away. Carter was right behind her, he saw from her license tag that she worked for a Real Estate company. He followed her home, observing the surroundings, the number of houses on the street, the bushes, the lighting.. *This lovely lady should fit nicely into his plan to frame Nick Jensen. When the plan was ready, for this young lady He would arrange for her to show him a house. But it was no sense rushing it.*

CHAPTER FOUR

SARA AWOKE AT DAYBREAK, dressed quickly and walked up the road to Shop for breakfast. As she passed her house, all was quiet. She was going to go in and wake her mother and ask her to join her. Sara thought, *Oh, I'll wait until she is awake or she will be grouchy. Then we can make up and be friends.*

As she walked a black pick-up truck pulled along side of her. Sara ignored it. The driver gave a quick beep of the horn. Sara, annoyed, looked over at the truck, the driver waved at her and yelled, "Hey Sara, where are you going?" She gave the driver a closer look, than ran over to the window. "Jonathan, what are you doing here? Wow, it's been five years since I've seen you, come give me a hug." Jonathan got out of the truck and hugged her tight. "Wow , have you grown up!" he said, as he looked at her. "Man, you are a beauty! What happened to that little girl?" "Well, you know, little girls and boys grow up. You look great Yourself. You and Nick could go for twins, except you are younger and a little leaner.

Jonathan asked, "Where are you going?" "Oh, I am going to get breakfast, why don't you join me, later we Can see my mom and Nick. We will have a reunion!" "Sounds good, I have been driving all night, I'm starving, jump in." They drove to Mulligan's on A1A and had a long breakfast, sitting at the outside tables. They were so engrossed in the conversation, time just slipped past. Jonathan couldn't keep his eyes off of her, *she sure is a beauty, I wonder if she is seeing anyone,* he thought. Sara watching Jonathan, forgetting about Jason, was thinking the same thing

A soft breeze was coming off of the Intercoastal, and the sun was just peeking over the rooftops. Nick pulled the covers to his chin and buried his head further under the pillow, trying to ignore the cold, wet nose poking him as he tried to sleep. Last night had been a long, long night involving a string of clubs, bars and a woman, but he could not quite recall the last hours. He pushed the dog away for the third time, and gave in, finally rolling over and struggling to sit up.

He was surprised that he was alone, he didn't think he went to bed alone. Finally the big red retriever, known to his friends as Rex, had his way, pushing his nose insistently against Nick's leg, prodding him to move. Rex was not really a retriever, he was reddish with sort of long hair and he had never actually retrieved anything. But he was big, and lazy and lovable and didn't know anyone who was not a friend. Kind of like me, Nick thought, as he rubbed the dog's big head.

He grabbed his t-shirt and jeans and pulled them on while the dog tugged at his pant leg and growled. What's this all about! Rex was not even his dog. He belonged to his neighbor, Laurie, and her daughter, Sara. Rex played "Lassie" pulling and pushing Nick to get him to open the door and go outside. Shaking his head at the dog's behavior, Nick obliged and pushed open the screen door while Rex ran ahead, coming back to hurry Nick along as he walked. Whatever had Rex upset, he was eager to share it with Nick.

He crossed the lawn connecting his house with Laurie's, and rapped loudly on her screen door. The sound echoed hollowly through the empty house. No answer. It was still pretty early, he thought, maybe Sara and Laurie are still sleeping. He didn't want to bring the wrath of Laurie down upon him. He tapped one more time.

Walking around the house he felt the first heat of the sun, it would be another beautiful January day. The girls could be out in their skiff doing some early morning fishing. Rex probably just wanted Nick to feed him and keep him company until they returned. The dog kept whining and fussing and running up to the house and back.

Nick went to the dock, the boat was neatly tied and covered. He headed toward the garage. Rex became more excited as they got closer. Nick tried the handle, it was unlocked. He raised the overhead door. The dog's whine became a low continuous howl that grew louder and longer as Nick opened the door.

Nick stared in horror at the sight of Laurie lying in a pool of blood. She was stretched out on a bedspread on the floor of the garage, her hands tied to water pipes along the wall. Her pajama top was open and soaked in blood. The bottoms were missing. She was staring straight ahead, with the look of fear and horror still on her face. He staggered out of the garage, pulling Rex with him.

The ground seemed to rush up at him; he was dizzy and nauseous Nick had seen some terrible sights, but nothing had prepared him for this. Laurie! *My God, who could have done this?* He sat on the driveway, trying to collect his thoughts. Nick stood up tentatively as his head cleared, and he checked out the garage,

Laurie's Mustang convertible was still here. The small pottery workshop she had set up in a corner showed no signs of struggle. Whoever did this must have brought her from the house.

Oh My God! Sara! Where's Sara? He ran over to the house, where he found the back door unlocked. Careful not to touch anything, he let himself inside. Walking through the house, it appeared that Laurie had been forcibly taken from her bed and out of the house. The sheets had been pulled off of the bed and lay across the floor, a lamp and a chair had been knocked over and the phone ripped out of the wall. Nick hurried into Sara's room. Sara was not there. Nick checked all of the other rooms, no Sara, *Where the hell is Sara? What happened here? Some one had tortured Laurie and Sara was missing.*

Did they kidnap Sara? Nick wondered, why the torture? Was it just a deranged killer, or was there a reason for this. They were wonderful, beautiful girls. Laurie was a very young thirty-six, with a gorgeous face and a body to match. She could pass for Sara's older sister, and did. Why would anyone want to kill Laurie? Why would anyone want to torture her? Nick slowly walked through the house.

The rest of the rooms were neat and orderly. Laurie had last night's supper dishes stacked on the drain board. Nick noticed that there were three plates, cups, saucers, etc., so they must have had company for dinner, either one of Sara's friends or Laurie's boyfriend, Jason. He looked in the den, Sara's computer was on, but the only thing on the screen was a screen saver. Not really anything of interest there. It appeared as though they had gone shopping, probably at Sara's favorite, the Galleria. There were pieces of clothing, with tags still attached, piled on the living room chair. Had someone followed them home from the mall? Rex kept looking at him, panting and whining. Come on Rex, let's get out of here.

Back at his house, he fed Rex some Dog Chow, put on a pot of coffee and poured himself a stiff shot of Jim Beam. He needed to steady himself. Nothing could help those Laurie now. I need to get myself together. Since he had discovered the bodies, and he had a relationship with Laurie, he would be the number one suspect.

Nick recalled that there had been a woman with him last night. He knew that they came back to his house in the early morning hours. What was her name? Karen, umm Kristie, that's it, Kristie. The next thing Nick remembered feeling was Rex's cold, wet nose, and that was no way as warm as the other things that had rubbed him last night. The coffee was ready and Nick poured himself a cup. On the kitchen table was The business card of a Real Estate company with the name Kristie Ryan and written in pencil was a Pompano Beach phone number, with the words, *wow, great night, call me we'll do it again soon..*

Nick guessed that Kristie had left early this morning. It was getting near ten, he had better call the cops. Nick had worked out in his head, a story for last night. At least he had one that made sense. Kristie, could vouch for him all night. Nick finished his coffee, finally called 911. After the usual 911 questions, they finally got it into their heads that he wasn't a nut or a fraud and they dispatched a patrol car. Nick wondered how they ever got to anyone in an emergency. It's like everything else, by the time the powers that be set up the rules and regulations it's becomes pretty much useless.

The cruiser they sent was from The Lauderdale by the Sea, Police Department. It was probably one of three that they possessed. Lauderdale by the Sea is a very small town, consisting mainly of motels, restaurants and bars along a mile and a half strip of A1A.The biggest job they had were dealing with a tourist That had too much to drink. The police sure were not experienced for what they were about to encounter. *I hope they send a seasoned officer, and not some kid earning money for college.* Nick thought.

Nick met the two young officers in front of Laurie's house. The driver, a tall, blond guy, got out and approached him, while the other one waited in the cruiser. "What's the problem, Sir?" "Maybe you should look for yourself, in the garage." "Yes sir, but what's the problem?" "Son, there is a young women in that garage with her throat cut and her seventeen year old daughter is missing" "Yeah! Right!"

The big cop turned to the other, "Josh, get out, come with me." Turning to Nick, he said, "Stay where you are sir." They went to the garage, turned the door handle. The door rose, revealing the body, along with the odor of blood and by now, a stronger odor that needed no description. Rex, once again began to howl. The younger cop, turned away, covering his mouth and ran for the patch of nearby grass and lost whatever had been breakfast or lunch or both.

The blond cop looked at Nick. "Who found them?" "I did." "How?" "The dog woke me and led me to them." The blond cop picked up his radio, called dispatch. "Get some help over here from Broward county. The crime Lab, some homicide cops and the Coroner. Yeah! We have a homicide and a missing person. No I am not kidding."

About 10 minutes passed, than two Broward County police cruisers and a plain dark sedan pulled up, followed shortly by a truck with Crime Lab. on the side and a plain black van. A man about 5' 10", sort of stocky and the face of a cop who had seen it all stepped out of the sedan. He walked into the garage, looked down at the body, The cop addressed one of the Broward officers. "Get some uniforms canvassing the neighborhood. Knock on every door, question everyone, get some guys to search the area, trash cans, flower beds, everything." "Yes sir, said the patrolman, What are we looking for?" "You'll know when you see it. Is this your first day on the job? Move!"

He looked over at Nick." I'm detective George Gabriel, pointing to his badge. "Who is missing?"" The woman's seventeen year old daughter." "Did you find the body?" "Yes!" "Who are they?" "Laurie Richards and her daughter Sara." "She have a husband?" "No. they lived here alone. ""Who are you?" "Nick Jensen, I live next door." Gabriel looked at the CIS crew, "Do your thing guys." He walked over to Nick, pulling a notebook out of his pocket.

After taking Nick's name, address, occupation, etc., he looked up and asked. "Haven't I seen you around?" "Yeah, I do some investigating for Lawson and Lawson."" Oh yeah, the ambulance chaser or I should say the husband chaser." "Well, it's a living." "Hmmph. How did you come to discover the body?" "The dog, woke me up this morning, and led me over here." "What time was this?" "Oh I guess about seven or so." "Seven! And you just called this in, it must be 10:30!""I was trying to get myself together." "Why would you have to get yourself together?" "I just found the body of someone I cared for a great deal" "What is you relationship with the deceased?" "We were just neighbors." "That's it just neighbors?" "Well, we used to date steadily, but haven't for past eight months." "But the dog came into your house this morning and led you over here?" "Right. ""How did the dog get in?""The sliding door was ajar, I had the opened the windows to let in the ocean breeze." "So you were still friends." "Yeah." "Do you have keys to their house?" "No." 'How did you get into the garage?" "It was unlocked.' "So you just decided to open the garage to see what was inside. ""Yes, the dog kept sniffing and whining at the door."

'Did you go to the house?" "Yes. But no one answered." "Did you go into the house, Mr. Jensen?" Nick hesitated. "Mr. Jensen?" "When I saw Laurie, I went to find Sara." "So you did go into the house?"" Yes, I had to know what happened to Sara." "Did you touch anything?" "I don't think so."

"Hey George, we're ready to move the victim." Gabriel hurried into the garage. The body was laying on the concrete floor with the ME looking over her. He stated she had been stabbed in the throat, cutting into the artery causing death, actually bleeding to death. "It doesn't look as though she was sexually molested, but we will have to check further to be sure." "What's the estimated time of death?" Gabriel asked. "My guess is between 4 am and 5 am." "Mr Jensen, where were you at that time of morning?" "Sleeping, where were you?" "I'll ask the questions, thank you. Can anyone verify that?" "Yes. I got home around 2 a.m. or so, I had a young lady with me. We spent the better part of the morning together." "What time did she leave?" "I don't know. It had to be around 4 or 5 am." "I woke up and she was gone." "Did you hear anything suspicious this morning?" "No, I didn't hear anything until Rex woke me up." "Rex?" "The dog."

" Well you'd better come on down to the precient to make a statement." "Let me put Rex in the house, he's kind of lost. I'll get him settled down. I'll be there in half hour or so." "That's Ok Mr. Jensen, we'll be happy to give you a ride." "Russell, Take Mr. Jensen down to 115th St., station will you?" The blond cop looked over at them, walked over to Nick asked Gabriel "Should I pat him down and cuff him?" "No., No. just give him a ride." The cop looked disappointed. Nick got into the cruiser, and they pulled off with the lights flashing. "You think you need the siren too?" asked Nick The cop ignored him.

Sara and Jonathan drove up to the house, passing a couple of police cars. "I wonder what's going on" said Sara, nothing ever happens here. "As they drove closer to the house, they noticed police and other people coming out of Laurie's house. Sara jumped out of the truck and ran to the house. "Where is my mother! What's happened? Somebody tell me what is going on" she screamed.

The officer guarding the door, stopped her "You can't go in there right now." "It's my house! Where is my mother? Please tell me what has happened." A man, about 40 years old, husky build with dark hair tinged with gray and the face of a man who has seen all the worse that the world had to offer approached Sara. ."I'm detective George Gabriel, are you the daughter?" "Yes, where is my mother? Let me see her!" The detective, pointing at Jonathan, asked "Who is this?" "I'm Jonathan Jensen, my brother lives next door." "Why all of the questions? Where is my mother, damnit?"

'Miss, I am afraid that your mother is dead. She was killed last night." "What! What? My Mother... Sara fainted, Jonathan catching her as she fell. "You better take her into the Jensen house, we need to find a relative to be with her for a while." said Gabriel .

Jonathan carried Sara into the house and put her on the sofa. She started to regain conciousness, she looked at Jonathan, "Where is Nick?" "My God, my mother I want to see her, where is she?" "I am afraid she has been taken to the morgue, you can see her there. Miss, I am afraid you can't go into the house for a while. Where were you last night?" asked Gabriel. "Last night? Why I...we were having dinner with Jason...then my mom and I had a fight and I slept on Uncle Nick's boat." "You mean Nick Jensen?" "Yes, where is he?" "I am afraid Mr. Jensen is a suspect in this case, we took him in for questioning." "What!" Sara and Jonathan said at the same time.

"Who is Jason, Where can we find him?" asked Gabriel "At his house, I guess, he lives up in Boca" said Sara. "Do you have any relatives close by, Miss?" "Yes, my mother's sister, she lives in Jupiter. "We will send for her, meanwhile, I'll get a doctor over here to give you a sedative." 'I don't want a doctor, I want to see my mother" said Sara. She started to cry hysterically, than she fainted again. Jonathan put Sara on the sofa.

Gabriel turned to Jonathan "Where were you last night? "Me. I just got here, I was driving all night, I just got in from Baltimore." "Anybody with you, how did you and the girl end up together this morning?" "I was just getting in, when I spotted her walking along the road." "What time was this?" "I guess it was maybe six, the sun had just come up." "So the girl was walking along the road at six in the morning? where was she going?" "She said she was on her way to get breakfast, so we went together." "Where did you two go?" "We went to Mulligan's" "So you had breakfast until, what ten?" "Yeah, we hadn't seen each other for years, we had a lot to catch up".

"Ok," said Gabriel, "Don't leave and see if Sara can stay here, I'll send the doctor to give her a shot." The doctor gave Sara a sedative and a prescription. "Get this filled, you will need them the next two weeks. They will keep you calm." Turning to Jonathan the doctor said, "Try to get her to rest or sleep for a while, call me at this number if she needs me." Jonathon made up the bed in the guest room, as Sara ignoring Jonathan ,slipped out of her clothes and into bed. Jonathan, seeing her naked was taken by the beauty of her body. He quickly covered her with a light blanket, and left the room. Rex, the dog positioned himself at the foot of Sara, while Jonathan unpacked his things and put them in the third bedroom. He wondered down to the boat, went into the cabin. Jonathan ran the latest happenings through his head. *None of it made sense, where was Nick? How could Nick be a suspect in whatever happened? Nick loved Laurie, Always had, since the day that they met. What happened to Laurie? Was it a robbery? Did it have anything to do with her ex-husband? Was Sara safe? Jonathan thought about Sara, boy she is beautiful and fun to be with. I wonder if her and I can hook up after all of this mess is over?* Suddenly exhausted from his drive and the events of the morning, he stretched out in the master bedroom and fell into a deep sleep.

CHAPTER FIVE

LATER IN THE DAY, Carter Melman drove back to Nick's place. Parking out of sight of two cops that were posted at Laurie's door, he walked to Nick's house and tried the door it was unlocked. His intent was to hide the murder weapon at Nick's house to further incriminate him. Entering the house, he was confronted by Rex. Again he used the drugged dog treats to fend him off. Looking through the house, he noticed Sara sleeping in the bedroom. He was tempted to wake her and force her to go with him, but he wasn't going to try it with the two cops guarding the house. He would have to wait until another time. There was no rush, no one seemed to think that she was in danger. Carter walked through the house, looking for a place to plant the knife He decided to tape it the trailer that held the mowers in Nick's garage. Then he quickly left the house, *The cops will be sure to find it after they get a search warrant.*

Jonathan was awakened, by a noise he heard, either on the boat or from the direction of the house. He pulled on a pair of jeans and looked around the boat. No one was there, than he heard the gravel of the driveway crunching. He looked out in time to see a stranger walking away from Nicks' garage. Pulling a T-Shirt over his head he hurried into the house. Jonathan went into the bedroom to check on Sara. Rex the dog was sound asleep on the floor, Sara was breathing evenly, she appeared to be OK. He gently awakened her, Sara looked at him sleepily, "What do you want, is something wrong?" "I am not sure." He answered. "I saw a strange man leaving the house and I wanted to check on you." Sara, suddenly aware that she was naked under the sheet, grew embarrassed. "Let me get my clothes on and I'll meet you out in the living room." "Sure, I'm sorry." said Jonathon as he started to leave.

"By the way, how did I get this way, did you undress me?" "Oh, No!" Jonathan answered. "You took your clothes off and got into bed. "Sara smiled, "Did you watch?" Jonathan cleared his throat. "I'll see you in the living room." When Sara joined him, he had made a cup of tea for her. Sara took the tea and thanked him. After taking a couple of sips, She said "I am famished, is there anything to eat?" "I don't know.

Sara, is there someplace that you can stay?" "You are welcome here, but I think that you are in danger." "What do you mean, in danger?" "Well, Rex is still sleeping, it looks as if he has been drugged. I think that someone was in this house and I think it has something to do with your mother. "Do you know of anyone who would want to hurt you or your mother?" Sara suddenly felt a chill run through her body. "What's wrong, Sara, what is it." "I...I don't really know, but Jason was asking me about the money that my father had hidden, and he and my mother had a terrible fight Friday night."

Jonathan asked, "Isn't that the guy your mother was going to marry? " "Yes...but, I don't know how to say this, but Jason and I were lovers, I thought he loved me...now I am not so sure." Jonathan looked at Sara, "You were lovers?" "Yes, he seduced me last summer and we have been intimate ever since. He said he wanted to marry me, not my mother. We were going to tell her when the time was right. I thought that if I could find the money my father hid, Jason and I would be happy. It sounds kind of sleazy now, I am so confused" Sara broke into tears. "Now my poor mother is dead, and I think that I might have caused her to be killed." "Nonsense!" said Jonathan "Did you ever tell Jason that you knew where the money is hidden?" "No, the fact is, I really don't know where it is. I didn't even tell Jason about it, he seemed to know that it existed"

"Sara, I don't want to hurt your feelings, but maybe Jason knew about the money and got close to you and your mom to find out if you knew where it is." "I don't know, Jonathan, I don't think he could fake his feelings for me without my realizing it." Sara answered. "Sara, money and sex make men say anything that women want to hear. "Sara was crying uncontrollably. Jonathan went to her, holding her shaking body close to his, rubbing her back and arms.

"Easy Sara, easy. The most important thing we have to do is to make sure that you are safe. Is there somewhere that you can stay, that no one would know that you would be there?" Sara wiped her eyes and looked up at Jonathan. "My mother and father had a small cabin in the Keys, we haven't used it for a couple of years. Maybe I could go there, would you take me?" Jonathan answered "That's a great idea, get some things together, we'll leave as soon as you are ready." Sara, suddenly aware that Jonathan was holding her close, started to move away, then reached up and quickly kissed him warmly on the lips. Sara broke away and said "I'll get some things from the house, be right back." Jonathan, a little shocked, gathered his clothes together and went to his truck. He thought, *What a warm, lovely kiss, what was that about?* Sara meet him at the truck, she had packed a bag and a make-up and toiletry kit, and tossed them in the truck, turned to Jonathan, "Let's go.

"Nick and the cop drove to the station, he ushered him inside and put him in an interrogation room. It was a bleak room, gray concrete block walls, gray tile floor. It was furnished with a metal table and four steel folding chairs. There was a mirror on the wall, presumably one that someone could see though from the other room. Nick sat at one of the chairs. Presently Gabriel and another detective joined him.

" This is detective Clarence Davis" said Gabriel They sat across from him, Davis was a black guy with corn rows in the hair, he wore a better suit than Gabriel. Davis said "You want to write down where you went and who you were with last night?" "Look, I was with a girl named Kristie Ryan, she works for Coastal Realty. The number is on her card on my kitchen table." Gabriel: "What was your relationship with the deceased?" "Like I explained before, we are neighbors, sometimes we have a cook out together. Sometimes we go fishing." Davis: "You're neighbors say that you are lovers. That you spend a lot of time together, that you and the girl are close. ""We were at one time, but not lately." Gabriel: "What's lately? How long since you were together? Why did you stop seeing each other?" "Eight months or so, it just would not work out. Laurie wanted more than I wanted to give. Like Marriage."

Davis :said, "The neighbors say she had a new boyfriend that you didn't like. said you and the guy had a disagreement." "So we had a disagreement, so what?" "What about?"" I thought he paid as much attention to Sara as he did Laurie the kind of attention a guy his age should not be paying to a girl her age. "Davis: "Are you the girl's father?" "No. She is… just a nice kid." Davis said, "Your neighbors said that you and Ms. Richards had an argument, last week end, they said it got pretty loud." "Yes, we did." "What about?" "We had taken a fishing trip to the Keys, last week. Things got kind of intimate and I realized that I loved her and wanted to get back together."

"She didn't?" "No, she said she wasn't ready to discuss it." "Did that make you mad?" "No, just frustrated." "What do you mean, frustrated?" "Well if you won't discuss something, you can't very well settle anything." "So you were mad." "No, frustrated." "Did your frustration lead to anger?" asked Davis. "No, I just wanted to sit down and talk about us." "But she would not do that, so you were mad, right?" "I wasn't angry with her." "Were you mad enough to kill?" "I did not kill anybody!" shouted Nick.

"Take it easy, you two" said Gabriel. "Mr Jensen make your statement and you can go. We will be in touch, just don't go anywhere." Nick arrived home around eight Saturday evening. Rex was sound asleep *.Man that dog can sleep* thought Nick. He saw a note from Jonathan on the table, next to Kristie's card. *Nick, Sara is safe, she had slept on your boat Friday night. I met her on her way to breakfast this morning, we talked to detective Gabriel. She had been given a sedative and was sleeping in the guest room. I think someone was in the house, while you were gone, so I am taking Sara to a safe place. We will call you J*

Nick called the number on Kristie's card. After three rings, Kristie answered. "Hi, It's Nick Jensen. "Hi, seems like I just left" said Kristie." Yeah, I just wanted to know if you got home ok. I wanted to thank you, What a wonderful night." "Well right back at ya. When can we get together again?" "Real soon, I hope.

I might need you to verify that we were together last night. There was a little trouble around here." "What do I have to do, I don't like cops." "Just say that you and I were together from eight until whatever time you left." "I left around 4:30, I had an appointment Saturday morning that was the only reason that I left. It sounded like your neighbors were having a party, they must have been getting it on, there was a lot of moaning coming from that house." Nick felt a cold chill pass through him. *While he and Kristie were making love, Laurie was being murdered.* Nick and Kristie agreed on a dinner date. They arranged to meet Tuesday at Kristie's home. Nick carefully reread Jonathan's note. *I wonder who could have been in the house .What information did Laurie have and is Sara a part of this. Why was she on the Boat Friday night. They apparently had someone to dinner, why did she leave. Did Laurie and Jason want privacy or was there a disagreement between Laurie and Sara? What has Jason to do with all of this, I never trusted that guy .*Rex finally woke and Nick let him out for a run. When the dog returned, Nick had a sandwich and a drink. He sat in the dark, just thinking. He was exhausted from the events of the day ,he went into the bedroom and crashed

CHAPTER SIX

SUNDAY MORNING DAWNED WITH a bright sunrise, and a warm breeze blowing through the open windows. Rex was restless and anxious to go out, When Nick opened the door, Rex rushed right over to the house. Nick restrained him, snapped on the leash and walked Rex down to the water. Nick, standing on the dock watched a car pull into Laurie's driveway. An attractive woman got out of the car, walked up to the house and tried the door, finding it locked, she turned, looking around, spotted Nick on the dock and walked towards Nick. When she got a little closer, he saw that it was Laurie's sister, she must have driven from Jupiter earlier in the morning.

Nancy, an accomplished artist, shared the blond beauty of her sister. She ran a small art gallery in Jupiter. Often she would have a show featuring Laurie's pottery pieces Nancy walked over to Nick. "Hi Nick, Oh God isn't this terrible?" She collapsed into his arms, sobbing, "My big sister dead and that poor little girl Sara." "Nick, what happened? Did you hear or see anything?" "Not until Rex woke me," he replied.

"They have police tape on the door, I can't get in "I was planning on staying there." "You can stay with me this evening. Why don't we take the boat out for a while? We can go fishing, get your mind off all of these terrible things." "I don't want to get my mind off of this. I want whoever did this to pay, dearly, Nick." " The police called me, they want me to identify the body, will you go with me? I don't think I can do it alone, I'll just fall apart." "Sure," Nick said, if they let me. "You do know that I am a suspect, since I found the body and I do have a history with Laurie"

"Well, Yeah, but that's just police routine, right? I mean, you couldn't have done anything that terrible to them, you loved them both, or you did at one time." "Sure, sure, and we were still close, but you know cops. Nancy, you must be tired, from your ordeal and the drive, let's get brunch at the Sands on the Intercoastal, we'll take the boat. Rex can come with us." "Oh, Ok, I could use a Mimosa." Nick fired up the twin Mercury inboards, let them warm a while, then cast off the lines and eased away from the dock As they were pulling away, he saw a sedan drive up.

Davis and Gabriel got out and approached Laurie's house. They looked his way as he slowly cruised up the canal. Nancy and Nick pulled along side the pier at the Sand's, an attendant help them with the lines and fenders. Nick escorted Nancy to a table and ordered two mimosas. They sat outside on the patio, enjoying the soft breeze, a waiter brought the mimosas. Nick told Nancy the news about Sara, she is safe, Jonathan and her went somewhere, he will call me today. "Now bring us two orders of eggs benedict, and two black coffees," ordered Nick. "That should help you through the day, Nancy."

"You are a dear, Nick. I was so devastated when the police came to my door." "They just blurted it out! I couldn't believe what they were saying." "Nick, do you think it was a robbery or a prowler? ""We don't get many prowlers in that neighborhood. The Lauderdale by the Sea police keep a close watch on people going through this area that don't belong here." Nancy asked, "You think it was someone that knew them?" "Who could have done such a terrible thing?"

" Reggie has spent a lot of years in jail. He could have made some powerful enemies." "Oh, Nick! Reggie will be heartbroken. He adores Sara." "This could kill him, he is not well." "Well, we don't know anything. Let's hope the cops can find the person that did this. "They finished their breakfast, each had another cup of coffee, and Nick paid the bill.Nick ordered two orders of bacon to go." Rex is probably hungry" he explained .Nick gave Rex his treat, untied the boat and they headed for home.

Davis and Gabriel watched as the boat pull away from the dock. "That was Jensen with a woman, she might be the sister, that we planned to meet here. "I wonder where they are going?"

A crime investigation truck pulled into the driveway. Gabriel wanted the crime scene analyzed more thoroughly. "Ok, look around carefully, look for anything that might help us learn who was in here." "How did they get in? Check the door, windows, how did they get past the dog?" " Do the usual checks of prints and hairs. Just be a little more thorough, we want this guy, bad. He's a monster." Davis said, "He also is a pro, this was torture, he wanted something, maybe revenge. "We know one of the kitchen knives is missing, and we are assuming that it was the murder weapon." "Scour the house, the yard, and let's check that boat."

While the investigators got to work, Gabriel started going through the papers in the dining room desk. The house was typical a Florida style, with a living room, a dining area, connecting with a hallway leading back to two modest size bedrooms, and a den. The master bedroom had an attached bath, the others had a bath across the hall. Off of the dining area was the kitchen with a Florida room at the back.

Davis sat at the computer, started to browse, "It looks as if the kid enjoyed using the Internet, this has a high speed hook up and had been used often." "She had many conversations with many different people. It appears that they were all high school students." "I don't see a threat there." "As long as they were really high school kids," Gabriel answered. "Yeah! I'd better take this back to the lab and let the techs do some research."

While they were looking through the house a muscular, dark haired man drove up in a blue Mustang convertible. He stopped, got out, looking around, walked up to the house." Who are you?" he asked, Gabriel. "Detective George Gabriel, homicide," he answered, flashing the badge. "What! Homicide! What happened? Where is Laurie? ""Where is Sara?" "Who are you?" asked Gabriel. "I'm Jason Sanders. Laurie's fiancée, "Where the hell is Laurie, What happened?" I am afraid I have some very bad news for you Mr. Sanders, Laurie has been murdered." " What! Murdered! When? How? Oh my God!" Sanders leaned against the car his head down." Is there someone we can call, Mr. Sanders?" "No, No I'll be Ok in a minute, let me get myself together." Davis approached Jason,

"Mister Sanders, where were you on Friday evening?" "Why I was here, for a while. I, we had dinner, a small cookout. Then I left, I had business in the Keys…on Islamorada , Saturday. I wanted to get there and be fresh for the meeting.." "What time did you leave? Did anyone see you?" "What? I guess ugh… guess about seven or so, I didn't see anyone." "So you would have gotten to Islamorada about 10:30, or 11" asked, Gabriel. "Yeah, somewhere around that time, Why?" Davis, looked at him, "where did you stay? Were you with anyone?" "Hey! See here! I didn't do this, I want to see Laurie. ""Look Mr. Sanders, Gabriel said, we are trying to establish a time line here. You may be the last person to see them alive. We understand this is difficult."

Jason answered, "I stayed at a small motel on Islamorada, the Sea Breeze .I checked in Oh, maybe 2 or 3 in the morning." So, Davis said, "you left at seven and did not check in until three, traffic?" "No, I stopped at a bar for some drinks to unwind, look, I want to see Laurie I am not the killer." "Maybe you should check the guy next door." "You mean Nick. Jensen?" asked Davis. "Yeah! That guy didn't like the idea of me being with Laurie, he was pretty pissed when she dumped him." "Did he cause any trouble, did he threaten Ms. Richards or you?" "Well no, but he was always finding ways for the three of them to do things. If you want my opinion, he was sweet on the young girl."

"Mr. Sanders, Do you know whose car is in the driveway," asked Gabriel "That looks like Nancy's car, Laurie's sister. here is she?" "We don't know, it looked like she may have been on Nick Jensen's boat. It was pulling out when we arrived." "That figures, He's always around a female" "We want her to identify the body." "Why does someone have to identify the body, you know who they are" said Jason." It is procedure, Mr. Sanders." Davis said, "Jensen's boat is back. They are docking now." The two detectives walked down to Jensen's dock "Good morning, Mr. Jensen, Ma'am" said Gabriel. "Are you Ms Richard's sister?" "Yes, I am Nancy Johnson," she said, extending her hand. "I am Detective George Gabriel, this is detective Davis." "Clarence Davis, miss, pleased to meet you". They shook hands, Gabriel asked, "will you come down to identify the body? ""Yes, of course, detective."

The building housing the morgue was on S.E. 41st Street in Fort Lauderdale. It was a square, cinder block, three story building. This Sunday it was quiet, there were only a few people in the building. The detectives and Nancy took the elevator down to the ground floor. As the elevator doors opened, the odor of chemicals, blood and formaldehyde hung in the air. Nancy was shown into a viewing room with TV monitors. She stopped, turned to Gabriel and said, "detective, I want to see her, I want to see the body, I don't want a TV monitor between us." "All right, if you insist, but it is not pretty."

They went into the cool, almost cold autopsy room. The stainless steel tables were clean and empty. One of the attendants led them over to a row of numbered drawer. The attendant pulled the first drawer open. Nancy was shocked, the body wasn't even covered by a sheet. Nancy starred at Laurie's naked body. Nancy was not prepared for the raw brutal sight of the body. The autopsy scars were red and raw. The wounds of the torture and murder were so prominent. Nancy could barely recognize her as Laurie, she staggered forward, than collapsed into Davis's arms. He led Nancy away sobbing, "That's her, that is Laurie Oh God!"

She looked at the detectives, tears running down her face, her hands shaking.. "You find him! You find this monster!" The detectives and Nancy went to see the medical examiner in his office. The detectives led Nancy inside, once she was seated, the examiner approached Nancy. "Ms. Johnson, I am Mel Brown, I am sorry for your loss, here have some of this." He handed her a cup of black coffee, laced with a shot of whiskey. She sipped a little and coughed. "Well that will get the blood circulating again," she said.

"Doctor Brown," Gabriel asked, "do you have any of the toxology reports back? I know it is Sunday, but I was hoping that we might be lucky." "No, not really, but we know the cause of death was from the carotid artery being severed on Laurie Richards. Her body had been badly mutilated, as though she had been tortured." Nancy shuddered at this. Dr. Brown looked over at her, "Should I proceed?" He asked. "Yes, I'm sorry, I'm alright…please go on." "Mrs. Richards had not been raped, there was no semen present. As I said, there were signs of torture. "She also had bruises on her neck as though she had been choked. The body had restraints on the legs and arms, true, there were signs of a struggle, but considering the condition of her body, the cuts and burns would have caused her to struggle against the restraints." Nancy asked, "What caused the burns? "Brown hesitated. "Tell me, Doctor, I need to know." "It appears there was some sort of electrical device, I would not say it was a cattle prod, smaller, but something along those lines. Probably something the killer constructed himself, designed to deliver maximum pain. "Oh God!" said Nancy.

"Are you all right, should I go on asked Brown?" "Yes, just give me another sip of that coffee." "What was the cause of death asked Detective Gabriel?" "She was stabbed in the neck. Furthermore, from the forensics, it appears that the daughter had Recently had intercourse in the bed, there was fresh semen on the sheets. "Are you saying my niece had consensual sex with the killer?" "I don't know, but a very strong possibility exists, that she knew the killer and had sex with him, before whatever went wrong." "There always the possibility the mother discovered them having sex and may have caused a scene, but that doesn't account for the torture of mother." It appears that Sara or possibly both knew the killer."

"What does all of this mean asked Nancy? ""Who knows what transpired in that house that night? We can only hope to piece together using forensic evidence and skillful police work to find the truth. I'm almost positive that they knew their attacker." We need to talk to Sara, but she seems to be missing again said Gabriel ".Nick's brother, Jonathan and her went somewhere, he is supposed to call Nick today said Nancy.

"Laurie's body did show some signs of a tranquilizer drug. I am sending a report to her doctor to see if she was on prescription drugs." "Thanks doctor, said Gabriel, turning to Nancy, he said let me take you back to your car, Ms. Johnson. Where are you staying tonight?" "Oh I guess I'll stay at Mr. Jensen's, he offered to put me up in his extra room until I get every thing squared away." "What do you know about your sister's relationship with Jensen" asked Davis." Well they went together for a few years, there was never any trouble, you know, violence." "Nick is a nice guy, I think Laurie wanted to marry and have one more chance at a child."" I don't think a child was in Nick's plans, although he adored Sara." "Do you think Nick ever had any sexual intentions with Sara?" "Oh no, I can't imagine. I mean, she is only seventeen. What kind of man, would seduce a seventeen year old?" "I don't know, but we have managed to get voluntary DNA samples from Sanders and Jensen, those may tell us something." "Oh God! Nancy said, I have had enough, please take me home."

CHAPTER SEVEN

STORM CLOUDS WERE GATHERING Sunday afternoon, the wind had shifted to the Northeast, and a cool breeze was blowing off of the ocean. Since Nancy was planning to stay for a couple of days, Nick went to the Publix on A1A across from the Sea Colony. He bought steaks, chicken, fresh vegetables, fruit and stocked up on wine and beer .Nancy arrived shortly after he had everything put away and had started the grill. Nick put the steaks on hoping they would be finished cooking before it started to rain.

"How did it go asked Nick?" 'It was terrible, Nick, her body was… Oh my!" "Yeah, she was pretty bad." Nancy said "Nick, have I time to take a shower before dinner?" "Yeah, sure." Nick having already put fresh sheets on the bed, remembered that he haven't been able to give the house a good cleaning since before Christmas. He hoped that everything is clean enough, no one had been in the spare bedroom, so it shouldn't be too messy.

After her shower Nancy relaxed in the Florida room. Nick opened a bottle of wine and set up the table overlooking the canal. He made a fresh salad to serve with the steak. As they ate Nancy filled him in on what happened at the morgue. When she got to the information about Sara and the consensual sex, his blood ran cold. Suddenly he was very uneasy, some facts were becoming obvious. Had Sara and Jason been intimate

Nancy asked, "Nick do you think that young girl could be having sex?" "Oh I know that she could, but knowing Sara, do you believe it?" Nick mentioned that he thought Sara had been overly friendly with him around the holidays. He described the cruise last week, and the early morning visit by Sara, it was embarrassing, he did not give any more details Nancy was stunned. "You and Laurie had sex last week?" "Well, yeah." "God Nick, didn't you know that she was engaged?" "What?" "No, to whom?" "Jason, he asked her on Christmas day, Laurie called me with the news." "Laurie didn't say a word to me, neither did Sara" Nick said. "What did Sara think of this?" Nancy replied, "She seemed Ok, after all she couldn't do anything to stop it." Nick said, "I don't think much of Jason. I think he paid too much attention to Sara." Nancy laughed, "Oh, and her playing with your dong is OK" ."No it wasn't Ok! I put a stop to it." "Yeah! After she rubbed that young body against you and kissed on you." "Well I was shocked. I mean her mother was lying next to me." "Right laughed Nancy. She was naked too." "Honestly!" "Do you think Laurie knew what happened?" "I don't know, she was very quiet in the morning." "I am not sure whether it was because of the night before or what happened that morning" Nancy said "Never a dull moment on the Jensen boat.". Nickfell silent. He did not want to discuss either Laurie or Sara with Nancy ."That was something that just happened, we were drinking." "Oh Nick, I don't know why you didn't stay with her, you two were so good together." "Sara adored you. I never could figure what Laurie saw in Jason, he wasn't her kind of a Man, he paid too much attention to other women." "Yeah and he was a big show off too said Nick. He was always strutting around the yard without his shirt." Nancy laughed, "God Nick, you sound like a teenager. Well, I am going to bed, I am tired." "I put your things in the guest room, you have clean sheets and fresh towels. Good night Nancy" "Good night, Nick, thanks for letting me stay, I know I could not sleep in that house tonight. The steaks and salad were delicious, thank you." Nancy bent over and gave Nick a kiss on the cheek. After Nancy went to bed, Nick got the bottle of Jim Beam and a glass. He went out to the Florida room, poured the bourbon into a glass, over ice and sat and watched the storm build in the east. His thoughts went back to Laurie, how they met six to seven years ago. He had been working construction up in Stuart. Nick had stopped in a bar after work. He had been staying in a trailer until the job was finished, and he wasn't ready to go home and watch TV. Nick had noticed two attractive blond haired women sitting at a table, and he walked over, offered to buy them a drink. They accepted and invited him to join them. Laurie had just divorced her husband of eight years, they had a seven year old daughter, Sara. "It's none of my business, but why did you get divorced" Nick asked. "Oh I thought I had married the perfect man, but it turns out he was an embezzler, a thief in other words a crook." Nick, chuckled, "How much did he steal? ""They are not sure, it runs from between twelve and fifty million dollars, give or take a mil. It depends on who is counting. " "Wow!"

" They sentenced him to thirty years plus, so I divorced him, and I and my little girl are on our own." There was something about the look in Laurie's eyes, That made Nick think she and her little girl would be just fine. Nick said, "I am up here alone, and single, could I ask you out sometime, maybe dinner or a movie?" "Thank You, but it is a little soon, and I do have a young child, don't forget." "Oh Laurie, said Nancy, it's not that soon. I can always watch Sara. "Nick said, "I only meant dinner. It wasn't a proposal." Laurie gave him a sharp look, than said, "Ok! Lover boy, when?

Nick and Laurie began seeing each other often. He, Laurie and Sara really hit it off. Sara was a smart little girl, not easy to fool. Her mother wasn't easy to bull shit either. Six months later, Nick received a bonus for bringing the job in early. Nick used it for a down payment on a forty foot Bayliner with a spacious cabin, a cozy sleeping cabin and a master suite, with a shower. Nick asked Laurie if she wanted to go with him when he returned home, cruising the Indian River and passing Palm Beach, Boca Raton to Pompano Beach. She agreed. Laurie and Sara came along for the three day trip. Sara loved every minute of it. Nick taught her to fish and she was already a pretty good swimmer. It was a wonderful trip. Laurie wore a small bikini. When Sara would nap, or at night when she was asleep, Nick and Sara could have private, intimate moments. As they became closer, their relationship grew more serious. By the time that they arrived at Nick's home, they were in love.

Laurie just loved living in Pompano Beach. She immediately started looking for a house nearby. As luck would have it, the place next door came on the market, and she was able to buy it. Nick and Sara and Laurie grew very close over the next six years. Than Laurie thought that Sara should have a real father and she should have a husband. Nick and her fought often over this, finally it became too much to just ignore, they broke up. Nick was devastated, he began to drink so heavily, that Laurie would not let Sara see him. Finally Nick cleaned up his act and by November, they had became friends once again. They resumed having cook outs and going fishing.

Mean while, Laurie had met Jason Sanders. Jason, dark, good looking, and muscular owned a fitness center in Boca Raton. It didn't seem like there was a big attraction, at first, but Jason and Laurie spent more and more time together. Nick hated him! Nick recalled the day he was on his boat dock. Jason, Laurie, Sara and a boyfriend were having a cookout. They were playing volleyball Jason was playing hard, showing off his muscles, He and Sara were beating the boy and Laurie badly. Jason was whopping it up, making a lot of noise, every time he scored or made a save. The boy grew irritated, than left. The three of them batted the ball around. Later, while Laurie was busy cooking the steaks, Sara had gone down to their small sail boat and was leaning over pulling the tarp tight, when Jason came over to the boat. Jason asked if she needed any help. He went over to Sara. They were leaning close together and he slid his hand up her thigh brushed it over her bottom, than placed on her breast. She giggled, letting him keep it there for a couple of minutes, when she saw Nick watching, she brushed it away.

Jason looked mighty pleased with himself. Nick was furious. *Jesus, she's only 17!*"Hey Sanders, she is pretty young to be doing that". "Mind your own business Jensen." "I'll come over there and make it my business." "It's Ok, Uncle Nick" said Sara, "He was just kidding around." Laurie hearing the argument came down to the dock. "What's the problem?" Nothing mother, it was nothing." Laurie gave Nick a hard look, turned and said, "Come on, let's eat." Nick brought his thoughts to the present, tomorrow is a work day, time for bed. After his shower, he closed the lights, locked the door and headed for bed, As Nick passed Nancy's room, she was quietly sobbing, he went in to her room, covered her with a light blanket. It was raining, and the night air was cool. Nick went into his bedroom, flipped on the TV. He couldn't watch it, he had too much on his mind. *What happened over at Laurie's house? Who did this? I could be in a tight spot*, he thought. Although he was sure, no one knew about the night with Sara, he had told Nancy about the week end trip. Surely the neighbors had seen them return, may even have heard him arguing with Laurie. He turned off the TV and lamp.

Later he awoke and saw someone in the doorway, it was dark," Who is it, he asked?" reaching for his pistol in the night stand." It's me, said Nancy. I can't sleep, can we talk," She climbed into bed beside him, "Will you hold me? Please?" "Nick. I just want to be held, can you do that?" "Yeah, sure, come over here," Nick had never, been this close to Nancy .As she moved against him, he could feel the warmth and softness of her body. He could feel her breast rubbing against his arm through her shear night gown. Nancy smelled good from her shower, she moved closer, began to gently Massage his back, she gradually moved her hand lower until she was fondling Nick. Nick rolled over, and slowly made love to her, afterwards, Nancy sighed, looked at Nick and said that was wonderful, Nick, I really needed to be held and loved tonight, thanks. Nick closed his eyes and fell into a restless sleep. When he awoke, Nancy was snuggled in his arms, asleep Nick quietly slipped out of bed.

After showering, he put on a pot of coffee, fed Rex, let him run for a while. Nick grabbed a bagel and coffee, than left for work. It was raining pretty hard, so he took the Dodge Ram leaving the trailer in the car port. Lousy weather, it's sure to upset the tourists, but it has to rain sometime. Nick drove the truck out Commercial Blvd. to Dixie Highway, turned right, went to the corner of Atlantic Boulevard. He pulled into the parking lot of Sunshine Lawn Care. Hmm! Nick chuckled, no sunshine today.

Walking into the office he greeted Sally, "Hi sweetheart." Sally was a middle age, plump woman with dyed red hair. She was their girl Friday, the one who knows everything. That was her job security, she kept everything in her head, bills ,invoices, payroll, no one could replace her. Sally had been with them since they opened the business. She was a chain smoker, and although there were no smoking signs on every wall, she had a lit cigarette hanging from her lip and one in the ash tray. Sally looked up, smiled, said "You have three messages, and John wants to see you right away." Nick pinched Sally on her bottom, as he passed. "Nick you are a rascal", she said. Nick read his messages, as he walked into John's office. Hmm, one from Kristie, did I give her my work number? One was from Mrs. Wilson, no doubt concerning her kitchen. Nick wondered if the cabinet that he needed had been shipped. Hmm, here was a message from Jake Lawson, *call me now!*

John looked up from his papers as Nick walked into the office. "Christ Nick, I am so sorry about Laurie and Sara!" "Are you Ok?" "Yeah! I'm alright," Nick answered .John looked at him, he hesitated, "Nick, are you in the clear on this? You two didn't have a fight, did you?" "God, John, she was butchered, what do you think I am?" Nick replied hotly, "Jesus Christ. I loved her, they were like my family." John said, 'I'm sorry, Nick, of course, I just did not want you to be in trouble." "Right! You're worried about Mrs. Wilson's kitchen! You aren't worried about me, money, money. It's my money too, buddy!" He stalked out of the office,

Nick went to his office, picked up the phone. He called Jake Lawson, his secretary, answered, "hold for a minute Nick. "God I am so sorry about Laurie, Nick." "Thanks," he said .Jake picked up, "Hey Nick, how is the boy?" "Not bad, considering the week end." "Nick, do you have a thousand dollars?" "What, you need a loan, come on Jake." "No, I want a retainer, buddy, you need a lawyer, a good one" ."Why? All I did was discover the bodies, I wasn't there. I didn't kill them." "Nick, you two were lovers, you have a history. Can you prove where you were all that night?" "Yes, I was with a young lady until the wee hours of the morning. A rather attractive young lady, I might add."

"Well, unless this attractive young lady will swear to that, you could be in a lot of trouble." "Jake, I did not do anything, we got along great. I loved them, you know that", said Nick. "Yeah, but you know how cops are. They want the path of least resistance, they don't really care if you are innocent or not, they want to clear the case quickly and easily." "Look, Nick send the money over by messenger or drop it off this afternoon." "The sooner we get you protected the better ""Christ, Jake, won't that make me look guilty?" "I don't think I need a lawyer at this point." "Look, Jake answered, I owe you for building the bookcases in the library .I am going to apply that to a retainer, all you have to do is sign and you are protected." "Ok. Ok, send it over, or better yet, I'll stop by."

Later that afternoon, as he left the office, Nick noticed a dark sedan idling at the curb further up the street. He got into his truck and drove out Atlantic Boulevard to Margate, where Lawson and Lawson were located. As Nick got out of his truck the sedan passed by, but he could not see who was driving. Nick thought, *What a coincidence that he and I were going to the same location.* Nick went into Jake's office, signed the retainer.

Jake Lawson said "if the cops show up at your house, call me immediately." As Nick climbed into his truck, he again saw the dark sedan, *hmm, maybe Jake is smarter than I think he is.* Nick watched to see if the sedan was following him, but the driving rain prevented Nick from seeing the car clearly. Nick picked up his cell phone and dialed Kristie's number. She answered on the second ring. "Hi, Nick, I am glad you called. We need to talk." "Yeah, talk about what?" He asked. "Yeah, but they were aggressive, they got me confused." "Confused about what, he asked? We met, had some drinks, went to my place, got laid once or twice, I think it was twice." "They kept asking me when I left, she said, I was getting confused." "You said you heard some noise from next door", he said. 'That's just it. They said, so they must have still been alive.' 'But I was still asleep," Nick shouted. "Well, I thought you were, Come on, don't get mad." "Those lousy cops," said Nick. "We are still going out tomorrow, right?" She said. "Yeah, Sure, but jeez, Kristie, you are my alibi you know." 'Oh you can count on me, don't worry she answered. See ya Tuesday.".

Nick arrived at the house, parked the truck, checked the boat lines, went into the house. He let Rex out for a run and took off the rain jacket and hung it on a hook in the hall. There was a wonderful odor coming from the kitchen. Nick looked in the kitchen, Nancy, wearing an apron, was taking something delicious looking out of the oven. Hi, she said. "Hope you are hungry, I made a pot roast." Actually he was very hungry, he had not eaten well the past couple of days. "This is a surprise, so domesticated, I would not have guessed." "I am full of surprises, same as you," she answered. "It was wonderful, Nick, the way that you held me, so tender, and made love to me. You were wonderful. Thanks that was just what I needed." "Well yeah, let's eat." Nancy and Nick cleared the supper dishes, packed the dishwasher. Meanwhile, the Weather was quickly clearing, promising a beautiful Florida sunset. "Let's take a cruise along the canal," Nick suggested. Nancy readily agreed. Nancy helped Nick cast off the lines, then Nick applied power and steered the boat into the intercoastal. The Bayliner was soon gliding through the water, the warm breeze blowing their hair. Nick cruised as far as the Hillsborough inlet, then slowing the boat turned around and leisurely headed back home. After making the lines fast and locking the cabin, Nick and Nancy went into the Florida room and each fixed a drink .Nick recalling what had happened in the room three weeks ago, quietly vowed to himself that nothing would happen between him and Nancy tonight. Nick certainly did not want to complicate matters

CHAPTER EIGHT

JONATHAN AND SARA DROVE west on Commercial Blvd. to I95. After a slight hesitation, Jonathan took the exit going North." Where are you going?" asked Sara. "I'm heading home. I have a very comfortable apartment with a guest room in Baltimore, I know that you will be safe there." answered Jonathan. "Baltimore, I have never been there, isn't pretty far North?" "Yes, but it is situated so that it misses most of the really bad weather. At least you will be safe until all of this settles down." "I'll talk to my brother and tell him where we are and what our plans are."

"What are our plans?" asked Sara. I thought that we would enroll at University of Maryland for a semester and return to Florida after all of the trouble is over." "Hmmmm, I don't know about that Let's stop at my Aunt's house in Jupiter, it's off of I95, I want to see my mother before I go anywhere."" "OK. What ever, just tell me the way." Sara thought,

I don't know what is going on, but I need to talk to Aunt Nancy and especially to Jason, after all we were supposed to get married and now I am heading North with Jonathan whom I haven't even seen in four years. What does he expect? Things are moving way too fast for me. I need to arrange my mother's funeral and find out how the cops are progressing with the investigation. Maybe I should visit Dad and ask him about the money or if he can shed some light on the killing I wonder if the killer was after both of us or just mom. All of this is really creepy.

"Jonathan, turn here on Cypress road and go to U.S.1" Jonathan who had been very quiet, followed her directions. They drove in silence for five or six miles. "Turn North at this intersection, go about five miles, than turn East onto Jupiter Drive. Within ten minutes, Nancy's house came into view. Turn into the driveway and park."

Sara went to the house and knocked on the door. The house seemed empty, she heard movement on the other side of the door. She knocked again, calling "Aunt Nancy are you there" The door swung open. Jason stood in the doorway. "Well my long lost lover, where have you been?" Sara stunned to see Jason, said "What are you doing here, where is Aunt Nancy?" "She is in Pompano because of the killing, what are you doing here? Where have you been? What happened to you Friday night? Who is your friend?"

Sara looked at Jonathan, who had gotten out of the truck. "He is Nick's brother What do you mean what happened to me Friday. What do you know about Friday?" "Just what the cops told me." Jason turned to Jonathan, "What are you looking at j.?" "I was just wondering how you came to be at this house." "You were huh, well it is none of your business, kid. You are just like your big brother, sticking your nose where it doesn't belong.. I f I were you, buster, I would leave." "I am notgoing to leave Sara by herself." "Look kid, I'll take care of Sara, she be longs with me, if you know what I mean." Jonathan looked at Sara. "It's OK, Jason and I have a lot to talk about. I'll be OK until my Aunt gets home."

Jonathan walked back to the truck. As he turned to get in he caught sight of Jason smiling and giving Sara a kiss on the cheek. Jason said, "See ya kid, turning to Sara, Come on baby let's go inside where we can talk."

Jonathan drove away, he thought, *I better tell Nick about this. That guy looks dangerous, what did he mean, she belongs to me?* He started to drive back to Pompano Beach, than stopped. *I think I had better keep an eye on Sara.* He pulled the truck into a grove of orange trees, got his camera and screwed on a 500mm telephoto lens. H e found a spot with a decent view of the house and sat down to watch. He focused on the patio door. He could see Sara clearly and a partial view of Jason. As he sharpened the focus he could see Sara and Jason hugging and kissing. *Oh no, this sucks, she digs that creep She is all over that guy. He has his hands all over her body. Now he is removing her top, oh this is awful.* As Jason stripped Sara's clothes off and started removing his, Jonathan put the camera away and went back to the truck. *I need to call Nick, he thought.*

After Jason and Sara had finished, they lay together, Sara rubbing his chest. Jason said, "You know baby after what happened to your mom, you and I should make plans." Sara said excitedly, "Really Jason, you mean we can get married?" "Whoa baby, yeah sure, but first we need to find that money of your dad's then we will be sitting pretty." "My .mom said that the money belongs to the police and that if I find it I will be a fugitive." Jason laughed, "Your mom was always a straight arrow, don't you worry, you just show me where it is, and I will handle the rest."

Sara said, "I don't really know where it is, I just have a couple of clues." "What? You don't know where it is? You've been bull shitting me all of this time? After all the trouble I went too, Christ!" Sara was scared, she could see that Jason was furious. "Jason, I think I know where it is. We will be able to find it" "you dumb broad, I knew I picked the wrong one, I'll bet Laurie knew where the money was all along." "What do you mean, you picked the wrong one, I thought we were in love." Jason laughed, "Come on Sara, you help me find the money. I'll split it 50-50, than I can live in style and so can you, but get married to a kid after I have all of that money, please."

Sara shouted, "You bastard!" She started beating her fists on his chest and smacking him. Jason smacked her hard across the face, knocking her to the floor. She looked up at him, "Don't you ever touch me again, I'm leaving, we are finished. Jason grabbed her roughly, listen little girl, you are not going anywhere. We are finished when I say we are, as far as touching you, I'll touch when and what and where that I please. Too prove that he meant what he said, he pushed her down on the bed and forced her to have sex with him. Afterward he looked at her, stop crying and fix me dinner" He underscored his remark with a hard slap across her bare buttocks. "Move, Now!"

Later, as Sara was clearing the dishes, Jason continued questioning her about the money. Sara answered, 'Jason. All I know is that there are clues that my dad sent me. I pit them in the safe in the pottery shop. Mom never noticed them.. My dad wanted me to have the money, he was very bitter with mom about the divorce. He thought that she should have stood by him." Jason said, "Well we'll just have to go to the shop and see what is in the safe." Sara answered, "You go, I'll give you the combination, you can have all of the money, I don't want any of it, my mother died because of it, just take it and go." Jason laughed, "You just don't get it do you? You'll do as I tell you too. We are going to the shop together, and we will find the money together."

Sara screamed at Jason, "Then what? You'll kill me like you did my mother?" Jason grabbed her roughly, "Careful what you say, sweetie, don't go making accusations like that." "Jason, I might be young, but I am not dumb, I know as soon as you find what you want, that is the end of me, so I really don't give a damn what you think. I surely know that there will be no 50-9 split. Just give me a truthful answer, did you kill my mother?" "No Jason shouted, I didn't!" Sara looked at him, "But you know who did and why."

"You know Sara, there is such a thing as being too smart for your own good." Sara laughed, "Jason I am safe as long as you think I can help you get your greedy hands on that money." "OK, smart ass, now tell me the combination of the safe and see how tough you are then." "Here Jason, I have it written on this card in my wallet." Sara took the card out of her wallet and handed it to him, "There!" Jason put the card in his pocket. "Sara, we can still do this together, we can still be with each other after we find the money." Sara did not answer, she knew that Jason was lying to her and would get rid of her as soon as he had no further need for her. She would have to play along and wait for a chance to escape.. She knew when he raped her this evening that he had no love for her, she had just been an easy lay for him.

What a dumb kid I was, I feel so stupid, my mother was right. He doesn't love anyone except himself Sara finished clearing the dishes, packed the garbage in the trash bag. 'Jason, I'm taking out the trash, is that OK?" "Yeah, hurry back, I want a back rub, plus some other favors you can perform for me." .Sara carried out the trash thinking , *God, I wish he would kill me, I can't stand the thought of his pawing over me every night until we find the money, she shuddered.*

Jonathan who had been waiting in the bushes behind the house .whispered, "Sara, are you all right?" "Jonathan can you help me? No, I am not all right, he is going to kill me!" 'Come on Sara, let's get in the truck and go, it's right behind those trees, hurry." Sara dropped the trash bag and ran with Jonathan towards the truck. They both climbed in, Jonathan started the engine, put the truck in gear and pulled onto the drive to the street.

Suddenly, Jason burst out of the house, screaming, Sara, come back here you bitch." He aimed his 9mm Glock at the truck and fired three or four shots. Three of the shots missed, but the fourth went through the back window, spraying glass and hit Jonathan in the shoulder. Jonathan lost control of the truck for a couple of seconds, the truck careened wildly across the road. Sara quickly grabbed the wheel, steering the truck back onto the asphalt. "Jonathan, are you OK?" "Yes, keep steering, I'll grab it in a minute. It's my shoulder, Christ does it hurt." Sara said, "Pull over, let me drive, I know the roads around here. We need to get you to a hospital." "no, I'm all right, we can't afford to stop, Jason my be after us."

Sara looked back, she saw Jason standing in the road, raising the gun, preparing to continue shooting. "Hit the gas she yelled, let's get out of here fast." "Go to the first cross road, it will take us to i95." Jonathan drove as fast as he could, when he reached I95 he turned North, and drove to the next exit, pulled off of the road and stopped at a 7-11

"Sara, get some iodine and some bandages, we need to patch this a little, it really hurts. She said, "we should go to the hospital, there is one in Port St. Lucie, we can stop there." "No Jason might think the same thing, he may check to see if he hit one of us. Trust me on this, Sara." Sara went into the store and bought whatever she could find, alcohol, bandages, tape. Sara got back into the truck. "Pull over here, let me look at that shoulder." "Not yet, let's put some miles between us and Jason." Sara said, "Fine, move over, I'm driving, meanwhile, take your shirt off, so I can pour some alcohol into the wound, you don't want it to get infected." Jonathan did as Sara instructed.

When she poured the alcohol on his shoulder, Jonathan jumped, "Hey, that hurts!" "Hold still sissy, I want to be sure it's clean, luckily it looks like it just nicked the shoulder., it doesn't look like there is a bullet in the shoulder." Sara cleaned" the wound, smeared some first aid cream on it and taped the bandage to his shoulder. "There that looks better." She gave him a pat on the back. "Put your shirt on, you're turning me on." she laughed.

Sara drove back to I95, heading North. "Maybe that wasn't a bad idea about Baltimore, how far is It." " It's about a thousand miles from here. We can make it in 14 to 15 hours. Sara asked, 'Do you have any money? We are going to have to stop, plus you are going to need fresh bandages." "Yeah, I can use Nick's ATM. When we ge t up the road a bit we can stop, get cash and maybe food. I haven't eaten since this morning." Sara drove North until she was at the exit for Vero Beach, pulling off of the interstate, she stopped at a plaza with a restaurant, motels, drug store., etc. She said, "We can get food here, and later we can patch that shoulder a little better. Maybe we should get a room, get off of the road, rest and be fresh in the morning."

Jonathan stopped first at an ATM, then to Denny's to eat. Sara parked the truck behind the building, pulling behind trees for cover. "Jason has the combination to the safe, where he thinks he'll find directions to the money. He isn't going to worry about us." "Sara. What is it with you and Jason? You guys looked pretty friendly back at the house, What happened?" Sara looked at Jonathan, "It's a long story. I thought we were in love."

She preceded to tell him the story of Jason seducing her, while he was engaged to her mother. How ashamed she was of being so stupid and how she regretted it "It was fun and exciting at the time ,I thought Jason was a wonderful man. I thought he saw me as a woman, not as an easy lay. He had me and my mother fooled." "You mean he was having sex with both of you?" "Yes, I am ashamed to admit that, but yes. All he wanted from either of us was my dad's hidden money. He thought we knew where it was hidden. My mother wouldn't have anything to do with the money, no matter how much it may be, she said it was nothing but trouble, that we did not need." "Looks like she was right" ,said Jonathan. "Yes and it cost her her life, all because of me. If I hadn't made believe that I knew where it was, to impress Jason, none of this would have happened."

"I don't know about that, said Jonathan, I think Jason knew what he was doing by hooking up with you and your mother. What was he doing at you're Aunt's house?" "I don't know, do you think he has her involved also?" Jonathan said, 'He seems like a pretty shady character to me, what do you know about him, does he have record?" "That's an interesting question. I wonder if somehow he knew my father. He seemed to know a lot about me and my mom. I just can't believe I fell for him and all of his bull shit." "We all make mistakes, Sara, don't beat yourself up over this." "Yeah, but my mother,"

Sara started to cry. Jonathan moved closer to her, putting her head on his shoulder. "Ouch!" Sara and he started to laugh. "Maybe I should use the other shoulder." "Let's pay the bill and let me fix that shoulder, we need to get a room. for the night."

While Jonathan arranged for the room, Sara bought more first aid supplies. The room had one king size bed. Sara looked and asked Jonathan, "that was all they had, not two double beds?" "Yeah, I'm sorry, I'll sleep on the floor, no big deal." "We'll worry about that later. Let me fix your shoulder, come into the bathroom. "Sara stripped Jonathan's shirt off, ran hot water into the basin, taking a wash cloth she bathed the shoulder with hot water, cleaning it carefully. She than put on a fresh dressing, taping it tightly. "Thanks Sara, that feels much better, how does it look?" "It looks pretty good, considering a doctor hasn't seen it. Good thing I'm a good nurse."

She pushed him out of the bathroom, "Now get out, I need a shower in the worst way, I need to scrub Jason off of me." Jonathan, after calling Nick and filling him in on the events of the day and evening. Nick thought it was a good idea to go to Maryland as long as Sara was in danger. "Keep me posted said Nick, I'll keep an eye out for Jason." After talking with Nick, Jonathon lay on the bed, watching television, waiting for Sara. After a half hour of hot, steaming water and a through scrubbing, Sara stepped out of the bathroom, wrapped in a towel. "Hand me my bag please, I need to put some clothes on, thanks." Shortly Sara came out of the bathroom in shorts and a t-shirt. "Wow, that felt good, nothing like a nice hot shower."

Jonathan roused himself from the bed, "Yeah, I guess it's my turn." He disappeared into the bathroom. "Try not to get you r shoulder wet." said Sara Shortly Sara heard the shower running, thought about Jonathan without his shirt and wondered what the rest of him looked like. After a minute, she thought *What the hell* she stripped off her clothing and joined Jonathan in the shower. "Move over Jonathan, I thought we might as well get this settled instead of wondering what each of us looked like naked." Jonathon was just standing, looking at her beautiful body, thinking, *Wow, is she a knock out..* Sara moved against him, soaping first his back, than the rest of his body. He grabbed her and held her tight, kissing her. They stumbled out of the shower, falling on the bed and passionately made love. Then later again, more gently. As they lay on the bed, breathing hard, Sara looked at Jonathan and said" That was beautiful and so gentle, Thanks"

Jonathon said., "Does this mean that I don't have to sleep on the floor?" Sara poked him, smiled, snuggled up to him and said, "Go to sleep dope."

Early the next morning after a brief session of sex the two had breakfast and began their drive North. Sara sat close to Jonathon, her hand resting casually on his thigh. She thought, *What a wonderful guy, he waited outside the house to see if I needed help. Then rescued me and drove with a wounded shoulder, always thinking of me, and he's pretty good in bed, not bad so far.* "How soon will we be in Baltimore?"

"Well I really live in College Park by the UM that is About twenty miles before Baltimore. Nobody lives in the city except drug dealers and gangsters. We'll be there in another five hours." Sara said, "I can't wait, I'm excited, this is going to be fun." Jonathon thought, *Yes it is!*

CHAPTER NINE

EARLY TUESDAY MORNING, NANCY fixed Nick a breakfast of orange juice, toasted bagels with scrambled eggs. She had juice, black coffee and a plain half of bagel. Nick left for work. Nancy, after clearing the dishes, showered, dressed and left the house. She was going to drive, to Laurie's pottery shop, but it was such a beautiful, warm, sunny day, she decided to walk the three blocks to Commercial Boulevard.

Nancy had a key that Laurie had given her when she had asked her to pick out some pieces for Nancy's art gallery. She approached the shop, before she could put the key into the lock, the door swung open. Nancy looked inside, there did not appear to be anyone there. Walking cautiously into the shop, she noticed smashed jars and pots littering the floor. Someone had been in here, looking for something. Had this anything to do with the murders? Maybe some vandals had broken in. She went over to Laurie's desk and immediately saw that it had been ransacked, papers were strewed across the desk. The computer was on, and some one had been copying files.

When the sisters first opened the pottery shop, Laurie had given Nancy keys to the door and the combination to the floor safe. The desk had to be moved a foot in order to see the safe and have room to open the door. Nancy pushed the desk aside, stopped down, twisted the dial a couple of turns and opened the safe. There was a small amount of cash, and a stack of papers, plus some sort of map. She counted the cash, a pack of ten hundred dollar bills still had the band around it, but two bills had been removed, there were some loose bills, tens and twenties. Nancy looked over the map, but it was just a map of the Florida Keys, the type that motels and hotels stocked in the lobby for the tourists.

Gathering the papers and cash, she stood and started to leave. She sensed a presence behind her, someone was in the shop. Nancy tried to stay calm. Suddenly an arm was thrown around her neck.

"Just give me the papers and you won't get hurt lady." said a male voice. "Take it slow, just lay it all on the desk." As she put the papers on the desk, he loosened his hold. Nancy lowered her head and out of the corner of her eye she could make out a shape. In one motion, she grabbed a piece of pottery off of the desk, and quickly turned and aimed at the shadow hitting him in the head. There was a crash, and the shadow exclaimed "God damn it!" Nancy breaking loose, scooped up the money and papers ran to the door, and outside.

Searching up and down the street she saw a tourist souvenir shop on the corner. She ran to the shop and ducked inside. Moving to the back behind a pile of T-shirts and hats, she stooped down out of sight. She picked out an extra large T-shirt with Lauderdale by the Sea written across the front. She pulled the shirt on over her blouse. Picked out a sun hat and put that on her head. She slipped her skirt off, letting the shirt cover her bottom. Then she picked up a pair of sandals and sunglasses. Stuffing her shoes and skirt into her tote bag, Nancy went to the counter and paid the clerk Nancy asked the girl to snip off the tags, saying she was headed to the beach.

She went outside and sat on a bench in the square, just another tourist taking in the sights and sun. She looked for anyone, who appeared suspicious or looked as if he had just been smacked in the head. There was a man observing the crowd of tourists, he wasn't dressed for the beach or even the warm weather. He certainly did not look like a tourist, he appeared to look more like a gangster. The man wore the kind of dark suit, favored by the gangsters that you saw in the movies. He looked very evil, his face gave her the creeps. Nancy bought an ice cream cone at a shop along the street, eating it, while she watched the ocean. The man after looking around the area, finally left. Nancy then casually walked back to Matt's house, making sure no one was following.

As Nancy entered the house, she was greeted warmly by Rex. He wanted her to take him out for a run. Wait Rex, let me change my clothes. Nancy went into the bedroom, hid the money and papers as far back as she could reach in the closet. She then put on her shorts and a different colored blouse, collected Rex's leash, and they went walking. Nancy couldn't get the map out of her mind. What could it be? Was it some week end trip Laurie and Sara had taken? Could it be directions to Jason's place? Had Laurie ever stayed there? Not that she had mentioned. She and Laurie shared everything, especially about the men in their lives. Well she hadn't told her about the weekend trip that she had taken with Nick Oh, I have more things to worry about than that, she thought.

The police said they would release the body soon, and she had a funeral to plan .Nancy knew that she would have to visit Laurie's ex-husband, in prison and give him the terrible news, of Laurie's murder and Sara's disappearance. Reggie was very sick, the bad news could kill him. Reggie loved Sara so much, her visits were all that he had to look forward to. That was the only reason that he had to go on living. Well, I'll deal with that, tomorrow, thought Nancy. I have a lot work to do and a lot of people to notify. Than there is the problem of Laurie's house. I'll have to hire a cleaning service to get the house back in shape, when the police finish their investigation.

She took Rex back to the house, and fed him. Rex is another problem, maybe Nick will take him, He and the dog were close, they got along with each other. Nancy exhausted, went into the bedroom, she lay on the bed and thought about the man at the shop. What are they after, they killed Laurie, broke into and searched the pottery shop, and strong armed her after she opened the safe. Did they think the money Reggie Richards had stolen was hidden nearby or in the house?

She would have to study the papers and map that she removed from the safe. Nancy wondered if she was in any danger, after all they killed her sister and her niece was missing, *I wonder where Sara could be, is she safe, is alive, is she is still alive, where is she?* Nancy fell into a troubled sleep, thinking about her problems.

Four thirty that afternoon, Nancy awoke from her nap she got up, cleaned up in the bathroom, packed her things, retrieved the money and the papers from the closet. Nancy carefully put them into the tote bag, wrote Nick a thank you note and left in her car. She drove to her home in Jupiter, about an hour drive up I95. except at this time of day. It took her almost two hours to get home through horrendous traffic. Nancy thought about Nick as she drove. She had made love to him the other night. He was sweet, by just holding her, but she wanted more than that and after all, he is just a man. Most men could not resist her charms. Even Jason had taken a chance and had seen her on the side. Nancy kept things quiet at the time, because she did not want to hurt her sister Laurie. Jason was a good lover, but Nancy always wondered about Nick. Now she knew why her sister, Laurie didn't seem to be head over heels in love with Jason. Nancy thought Laurie still had a thing for Nick, no wonder, Nick was prime. Nancy would make sure that she would see a lot more of Nick.

When she arrived home, Nancy carried her things into her home. Nancy loved her house. It was a one story four bedroom, stucco home with two and half baths, living area, that they called a great room, a dinette and a beautifully equipped kitchen, Florida room with a double carport. There was also an outdoor pool with a cabana area. Nancy stripped off her clothes, took a long hot shower. Toweling off after her shower, she thought about the papers and money. She also wondered about the man in the pottery shop. *What was he looking for, was it connected with the murders? Maybe he was just a thief.* Putting on a bikini, she picked up the tote bag, and relaxed at the pool. She dumped everything out of the bag. There was eight hundred and fifty-five dollars in bills. The bills were clean and crisp. *Where did the money come from? Was it money Laurie took in for a sale?* Nancy looked over the other papers. Most were invoices for shop supplies. The maps were of Florida Keys, one section had writing on it, maybe directions. Nancy was very tired from the trip and her ordeal at the pottery shop. Stuffing the papers back into the tote bag, she thought, *I'll look at them tomorrow.* She carried the bag into the house, leaving it on a chair. Nancy went into the bedroom, peeled off her bikini, slipped into bed and fell asleep.

CHAPTER TEN

WHEN HE ARRIVED HOME, Tuesday evening, Nick read Nancy's note. He showered, getting ready for his date with Kristie. Nick was not anxious to go out, the past few days had been rough. It was a warm, pleasant evening, Nick decided to drive the BMW with the top down. As he drove up Commercial Boulevard to Bay View Drive on the way to Pompano, he thought about what Kristie had said to him about the cops. He would have to have a talk with her tonight. He crossed over Federal Highway to Cypress to Katie's apartment building.

The lovely red head, whom he had met Friday evening answered the door. She was wearing a tiny crop top and short shorts, she didn't appear to have anything on underneath. Nick said "Hi, Kristie home? You are her sister, right?" "Sure come on in, I'm Katie, her big sister." Nick entered the room and said "Hi, remember me? I'm Nick we met Friday night." "Oh yea, you're the guy that her in all of that trouble with the cops." She said, "Sit down, Kristie will only be a minute." Katie walked over to Nick, leaned over him and said, "You look even better in the day light." She was standing with the sunshine behind her, making her top transparent. Nick was having hard time keeping his eyes off of Katie.

The apartment was nicely furnished with a white couch, matching love seat, and black marble topped tables, and a flat screen TV A white carpet over a hardwood floor, covered the conversation area. There were a couple of tastful prints on the wall. It appeared that the girls had a comfortable income between the two of them. Kristie entered the room wearing one of those tiny black dresses, that accented her lovely body. "Wow! You look really great." said Nick. "Thanks, do you think it is too short?" "Not at all, besides, you have very attractive legs, you should show them off."

"Thanks, hey Nick, those cops have been bugging me to death. Can't you ask them to stops, they act like you ae an ax murder." "I'm really sorry, that you got mixed up in all of this, Kristie, but I didn't know that one of my dearest friends was going to be murdered. that night." "You mean, you knew her?" asked Kristie. "Yes, I dated her for six years." "Christ! No wonder the cops are so hot on you". "What is that supposed to mean? Nick asked, because I knew her, I ran over to the house and murdered her?" "Well, I don't know, maybe it was jealously thing. Stuff like that happens every day". "Yeah, well it doesn't happen to me, Nick almost shouted.

"Hey, hey, keep it down" said Katie, coming into the room. She was still wet from her shower and had a towel wrapped around her, that just barely covered her. "Oh Katie, quit showing off, go put on some clothes. Katie has a thing about clothing, she hates to wear any." Katie answered, "It's from those cold Michigan winters, I had to wear a ton of clothes to keep warm. You are out with a guy and it took forever to get naked. Here in Florida, I can just wear the essentials. Katie sometimes you are impossible, stop flirting with Nick" "Well, he's really cute and he has a nice. butt."

Kristie said, "Come on Nick, let's get out of here." As Nick and Kristie walked to the car, Kristie said "I'm sorry Nick, it just that cop, Davis, he will not let up on the questions." "OK, just forget about it, let's go have a nice dinner and relax."

Nick took her to the Sea Watch Restaurant on A1A IN Fort Lauderdale. The Sea Watch, a very good beach front restaurant, the tourists and locals alike know that it serves good food at reasonable prices, along with a very romantic atmosphere. It is particularly inviting on the nights when the moon hangs low over the ocean. Drinks are served at a dark and romantic outside deck, where patrons wait to be seated for dinner.

"Oh Nick, this is wonderful, so romantic" said Kristie. After Nick and Kristie had a lovely dinner, they went upstairs to the lounge, to top off the evening with a drink. They each had the house specialty, double margaritas, by then their earlier disagreement had been forgotten. "It sure is a beautiful night, said Kristie, I love the moonlight shinning over the water and the breeze coming off of the ocean" "You think this is beautiful, how would you like a moonlight boat ride?" "Sure, where is the boat?" "At my place, how about it? Asked Nick. "Aye, aye, captain, take me to it."

They left the restaurant and Nick had them at the boat in ten minutes. As the engines warmed, he checked the liquor supply. Than he cast off the lines and pulled slowly from the dock. As they cruised up the canal heading to the intercoastal waterway, Kristie leaned back on the lounge.chair Nick fixed them both a drink and sat on the edge of the lounge. "Cheers to you Kristie, a beautiful girl." Nick toasted her, Kristie took a big swig of the drink, leaned forward and kissed him. "Cheers yourself." The short skirt of the dress had ridden up on her thigh and Nick placed his hand high up on her thigh. She kissed again, this time with a little more passion. Kristie asked. "Can you park this thing, Nick? I want your undivided attention." "Give me a couple of minutes, but hold that thought."

Nick pulled the boat into a cove on Lake Santa Barbara, stopped the engines and let out the anchor. When he returned to the deck, Kristie had slipped out of her dress and was only wearing her bikini panties. Nick took her in his arms and kissed her, running his hands over her body, caressing her breasts. They kissed again. As Kristie began removing his clothing, he guided her to the master suite. Nick lay her back on the bed, removed her panties and they made love. Kristie proved that the skill of the other night was no fluke. They both worked hard to please each other.

Later as they lay together on the chaise lounge, sipping a drink, Kristie was bathed in the light of the moon. Nick thought that she was absolutely beautiful, what a lovely body. They started to kiss and grope their naked bodies, than they made love again.

Later Nick dressed, started the engines, pulled up the anchor. He slowly made his way back to his dock, with Kristie standing in front of him, steering. While Nick was tying the lines, Kristie slipped into her black dress. "What a wonderful night. Nick, thanks/" Nick asked Kristie if she wanted to spend the night. "No, I have a couple of early appointments tomorrow, she answered. Kristie sat very close to Nick as he drove her home. She kissed him good night, than kissed again. He ran his hands over her body. "Maybe I can come in and spend the night." said Nick. "Umm, that would be great, but I won't get any sleep, and I do have to get up early tomorrow morning." "Thank you for a lovely evening, Nick. Dinner was wonderful and dessert was absolutely great, both courses. She gave him one last kiss, and ran into the house."

CHAPTER ELEVEN

NANCY AWOKE WEDNESDAY MORNING and immediately began notifying friends and the few relatives that she had of the Memorial service for Laurie. There were not many relatives, their parents had passed and outside of an elderly Aunt, there were no others, just Sara. Nancy thought *I'm all alone, I am twenty--eight and there is no one else, just me.* I am going to miss Laurie, she wondered what had happened to Sara. Nick said she was save with his brother, how did Nick's brother get mixed up in this? How did Sara get caught up with the killer? Nancy would talk to Reggie at the prison, he might have an idea who could be responsible. Nancy had too many things to accomplish that day and very little time. The day was another warm, balmy day. Nancy originally was going to wear a T-shirt and shorts, than remembered that she would be in Gainesville, the weather would not be as warm in the north. Also, she would be visiting the prison, she had better dress more conservative. She put on a black turtleneck and jeans and a pair of running shoes. It still emphasized her body, but what are you going to do she mused, if you got it, you got it. And it sure doesn't hurt to have it.

Nancy packed her overnight bag, she did not plan to arrive until evening and would spend to night in a motel. Gathering the papers that she had taken from Laurie's safe she left the house. Nancy drove out of the driveway and headed for the Florida turnpike. Nancy planned to follow the Turnpike for 225 miles to I75, exiting in Gainesville, where she planned to spend the night. Nancy wanted to be fresh in the morning for her visit with Reggie. Nancy left home one in the afternoon, and after a brief stop for a sandwich and to freshen up, she arrived about six in the evening. She found an EconoLodge off of I75, checked in using her credit card, and settled in for the night.

After a light dinner, Nancy leafed through the papers that she had gotten from Laurie's safe. Unfolding the map, she started to read what she thought were directions. They did not make any sense to her, but she continued to study the wording. it read: **9o60G7060T8EE8HTSYEEK9 7ASH9UR41EEDB8 7TAIL4EEM68** The letters and numbers were in three lines. Than underneath the wording read. ***Find the red beacon at sea w180 degrees plus 50-feet than S. a kennedy foot down a fathom and a half.*** The paper appeared to have been folded with another as if were part of a letter. Sara wondered if Sara's father had sent it to her. *Could this be where the money was hidden all along? Was the thousand dollars in the safe part of the loot?*

Nancy studied the papers but could not make any sense of the wording. She read the directions and studied the map, but it was just a map of the Keys, the type that motels have for tourists. Nancy, tired from her drive, fell asleep while studying the message it was a riddle to her.

The ringing phone brought her out of a deep sleep. Nancy was disoriented, than she realized that it must be the 7 a.m. wake up call. Shaking the sleep out of her head, she got up, fixed the little pot of coffee on the counter. She than took a long hot shower, the fatigue that had accumulated over the past few days seemed to slowly ease. Nancy had not realized how tired she had been. Stepping out of the shower, and toweling briskly, she felt much better.. Putting on a pink scoop neck top, fresh jeans and running shoes, she was ready for the day.

Nancy admired herself while putting on the little make-up that she used. Nice body, face is well, pretty, nice skin and nothing beats natural blonde hair. *Maybe I should look for a guy to settle down with, I am all alone, it would be great to have a family. Oh well, time to think about that later ,now I have to break the terrible news to Reggie.*

After having a light breakfast, Nancy arrived at the stat prison around 9:30 a.m. She got into the visitor's line, signed the log stating whom she wanted to see, The guard gave her a number and she sat in the waiting room until her name was called. The guard said, "Miss, Reggie Richards is a very sick man, you will have to visit him in the infirmary upstairs. Reggie is too weak to come down." Nancy and the guard took the elevator to the third floor. It was not quite as dismal up there. The inmates were behind bars, but there was a sitting area where you could sit and talk to the inmate. In the main prison, they did allow any physical contact of any kind. The attendant wheeled Reggie out to her. Nancy was stunned when she saw Reggie's condition. He looked as if he had lost sixty pounds, his hair was white and his face was so pale' it almost matched his hair.

Reggie did not recognize her at first, then he said, "Nancy, what brings you here?" Where is Sara,didn't she come with you? His breathing became heavy, his hand was shaking." No, Reggie, she did not, try to keep calm. I am afraid I have terrible news for you." Reggie, alarmed, looked at Nancy, "What is it?" She put her hand on his shoulder, there is only one way to this and that is to say it." "Laurie was murdered Friday night and Sara is missing, although we know that she is in safe hands." "What! Reggie screamed. "Where, how? Oh God!" They were at home, someone must have broken into the house and stabbed Laurie" Reggie roke down sobbing and crying,

"My beautiful baby, Sara, where is she?" She is safe, out of the area for now." Reggie composed himself, "Do they know who did this?" "They have a suspect, the cops are questioning Nick Jensen." Reggie answered, "Nick Jensen didn't do this, I can tell you that." 'It will be unsettling for me, but tell me what happened, and the condition of the body."

Nancy told him about the morgue and the conversation with the medical examiner Reggie was shaking, "Damn, I knew that rat bastard had something to do with this." "Who, what bastard?" asked Nancy. "That greedy smooth talking, slimy Jason." "Jason! Jason Sanders, how do you know him?" asked Nancy. "Jason spent five years as my cell mate. He paid a lot of attention to Laurie and Sara would come to visit.Ididnn't like the way he looked at them ,especially as Sara became older and more mature." Reggie was crying, coughing and shaking. "Miss you will have to keep him calm, he can't be upset like this." said the attendant. "OK" siad Nancy. "Reggie we are having a service for her. Do you think they will let you attend?"

Reggie answered, "I doubt it, but I will make a request." "Reggie do you want me to say anything to the police about your suspicion of Jason?" "No, he is too slick not to have an alibi. Anyway, he doesn't have the balls to do it himself, he would have paid some one to do it." Nancy asked Reggie about the paper she had found in the safe. Reggie looked at her, suspiciously, "Where was it? That belongs to Sara." "Yes it was in Laurie's safe at the pottery shop, I haven't shown them to Sara."

"Nancy you must get rid of those papers, at once." Reggie told her. "As long as you have them, you and Sara are in danger. That is why Laurie was killed. if they think you or Sara have those papers, they will torture you until you tell them what you know." "Who are they?" asked Nancy. 'Jason and his partners. He is connected to the Miami mobsters. Jason thinks he is an important man in the mob, but they are just using him, because he brags about the money. If they ever find it, or he does, they will kill him. The whole time he was in jail, he pestered me about the money. He offered to splt it with Laurie and Sara, if I would tell him where it is. Jason said I was going to die in here anyway, but I did not want that bastard anywhere near those two. I told him that the money was gone, but he did not believe me.." Reggie continued, "When he got out of jail and I found out that he had not only found Laurie and Sara, but he had used his oily charm to seduce Laurie, I almost died right than.

I could say nothing negative about him to Laurie, so I tried to send the message to Sara. I told Sara where I had hidden the money. I wanted it to be hers. I never told Laurie, as far as she knew, the money was gone." "Wow!" said Nancy, "I had no idea, Jason is a nice man, he likes to chase women, but other than that he seems harmless." "I am telling you, Nancy, be very careful.Get rid of that paper, it is not worth dying for." "Does it tell where the money is hidden?" asked Nancy. "You will not find it without breaking the code. Only Sara has the code and if you have that paper, she didn't tell them where the money is hidden. Remember, Nancy, your life is in danger, be careful. Nancy said goodbye to Reggie, "I am so sorry, Reg."

Nancy left to prison with Reggie's warning ringing in her ears. She drove to her home in Jupiter, arriving around six that evening. Once she settled in at home, she thought about the map and the paper. Reggie had refused to reveal the contents. Nancy would have to decipher it herself. Laurie had told Nancy that Jason had been in jail for passing worthless checks. Laurie said, "Just my luck. Every time that I think I found the right man, he is either a felon or afraid to commit to marriage. When Laurie had asked Reggie about Jason, he warned her to stay away from him. Laurie just thought that Reggie was being jea;ous.Jason deemed like a very nice man, she couldn't imagine him harming her or Sara. After

Nancy arrived home, she busied herself with the arrangements for Laurie's memorial service.She called some close friends of hers and a couple of clients from the gallery. Nick Jensen was home when she called. "Hi Nick, it's Nancy. I just wanted to tell you that the service for Laurie is in Boca Raton tomorrow at 2 p.m. The chapel is off of Yamato Road on S.W.. 86TH Street." Nick said, "I know where that is. How are you holding up.?" "Oh, it is OK, I just got back from seeing Reggie." "How did that go?" "It was pretty bad, he is not well at all, the shock of this could finish him." "That's too bad, I know that he loved Laurie very much." "It will be nice to see you again, Nancy ,Is there anything I can do to help?""Right now, everything is under control, I can handle it." said Nancy."I'll see you tomorrow, maybe we can have dinner sometime, after all of this is over."said Nick."That my friend is a date." Nancy said as she hung up the phone .

She then placed a call to Jason Sanders. "Hi. Jason. It's Nancy "Well this is a pleasant surprise,What can I do for you? Something sexy I hope." "Jason. I'm calling about the service, it's tomorrow art 2 p.m. in Boca. It's at Yamato Road and 86th Street.. That pretty little chapel there." "Oh yeah the service, I'll be there. Hey! How about you and I have a drink afterwards and talk about old times." "Well Jason. She answered, "Don't you think it is a bit too early for anything like that, Laurie was my sister.""Heck, that didn't stop you when Laurie and I were seeing each other. We were pretty hot and heavy for a while. Have you forgotten that trip to Naples?" Nancy sighed, "You never change do you?" "Why change, most women like me the way I am." he laughed. "Give it a little time Jason, than we'll see."

The morning of the memorial service dawned bright and clear. A typical warm, breezy day in South Florida. The crowd was small, just friends, a couple of clients and Nancy. Although Reggie wanted Nancy to bring him to the ceremony, his doctor's refused. They did not think he would survive the ordeal. They were not worried about an escape, he was too weak.Detectives Davis and Gabriel also attended the service. As the mourners filed in to pay their last respects, the two cops looked them over. They were looking for someone suspicious. Although Davis was positive that Nick Jensen was the killer, Gabriel on the other hand, was not so sure .So far, according to the evidence, or could be any of the persons under investigation.George Gabriel had been a cop long enough to know that everything is not as it appears.. As far as Gabriel was concerned, he did not have a prime suspect. The two detectives paid their respects to Nancy expressing their sorrow. They promised to do whatever was necessary to find the culprits.

At the funeral director's suggestion, Nancy had the body cremated. He said he would never be able to make her appear as she had and it would be better if everyone remembered her as she were in their hearts. Nick Jensen was there with his business partner, John Daly and John's wife Rita.Nick, John and Rita spoke to Nancy, offering sympathy and any help that she might need. Nick offered to help with anything concerning Laurie's house or boat. He promised to keep an eye on it while it was vacant. "Thank you Nick" replied Nancy, "But I think I am going to move down there until everything is settled. Jason has offered to help, also."

Sanders was sitting in the same row as Nick and his party, neither of the men acknowledge each other. This did not go unnoticed by the detectives. "It doesn't appear that they care for each other." observed Davis to Gabriel. The detectives noticed Sara and Nick's brother standing in the back of the chapel. They did not mingle with the other guests, and left immediately after the service. Nancy kept the service short and simple. It took less than an hour. As Nick was giving his condolences to Nancy and saying goodbye,Jason arrogantly interrupted. "As Laurie;s fiancee, I think that you should be offering you sympathy to me." "I have nothing to say to you Sanders, if you will excuse me, I was talking to Nancy." Nick turned to leave,Jason grabbed his arm and said., You think you're somebody special, but everyone knows you were jealous of me." "Jason, let go of my arm, you are way out of line. This is not the place for this conversation. Laurie was very special, show a little respect."

"Who the hell are you to lecture me?" growled Jason. People had stopped to watch the confrontation. Nancy stepped between them. "Jason, please don't ruin this ceremony." As Nick walked away, Jason called after him. "I'm not finished with you Jensen "Yeah, well maybe I'm not finished with you Jason, after all, you were the last person to see her alive." Nick turned on his heel and left. Jason turned a deeper color and hissed at Nick. "You are making a powerful enemy, Jensen." Nick, ignoring him, kept walking, catching with John and Rita.

"What was that all about?" asked John. "Some guys just can't help being assholes." said Nick. "Wasn't that Laurie's fiancee?" asked Rita. "Yeah, that's hard to believe." Nick answered. "You know, I think that Laurie was just trying to get to you." said John. "I think she still cared for you. She was just trying to get your attention, hoping that you would come to your senses. Laurie would never had married that guy". "Well last weekend, we spent three days on the boat in the Keys, it got pretty romantic. I brought the subject up with her on the trip home. She did not want to discuss it. She said that I didn't want the same things that she did." John said, "I still think that is was a matter of time, before you two got back together." "Well we will never know." answered Nick. "Let's get out of here John." Rita, Nick and John went to their car. As they were driving away, they saw Jason having an animated conversation with Nancy.

Jason was asking Nancy to have lunch with him that afternoon. At first, she declined, but remembering her conversation with Reggie, thougt that there was a chance of getting information concerning the money.Nancy finally agreed to meet him at Barney's on A1A in Pompano Beach. They found a quiet booth in the back with a view of the ocean and the beach. Jason irritated her by watching the girls on the beach. Nancy said, "Jason if you want to look at the girls go sit on the beach." "What? Oh sorry, I was just looking." "Yeah, with your tongue hanging out," snapped Nancy.

"What do you want? You wanted to have lunch. Thee must be something on your mind." "You what's on my mind, baby." Jason smiled. "Let's order, Jason. "Waiter, bring us two gin and tonics, make mine a double." Nancy said, "I meant lunch. See here Jason, you are not going to get me tipsy in the middle of the afternoon. I have too much to do this afternoon." "Aww, come on, just one drink, then we'll order lunch." "OK, one drink." The waiter brought their drinks and left.   Jason picked up his drink, "Here's to happier times." Nancy said, "Well, I'll drink to that." When the dinks were half finished, they ordered baked grouper and a salad for lunch. Jason ordered another round of drinks."Jason. I mean it, you're not getting me tipsy." "Oh Nancy, relax." The waiter served lunch, asked if they needed anything else, than left them alone.

Jason looked at Nancy, "You know, I always thought that you were the more beautiful of the two sisters" "Jason, stop, poor Laurie was a beautiful. woman." What a horrible thing to happen to her." "Yeah, of course." said Jason. "I just mean if you hadn't left us alone that evening. I probably would have beeen with you." Nancy sipped her drink, "You were giving her a lot of play that night. That's why I left." "You kind of pushed the issue, said Jason.

"Anyway that is in the past, what about the future? Our future." "What do you mean, our future? You have a plan?" "When it comes to beautiful women, I always have a plan." "Oh yeah, how to get them out of their panties" she answered. "Nancy, why are you being so mean to me?" "I know you, Jason. You are either trying to get me into bed tonight, or you have something cooking in that brain." Jason answeed, "Actually both, I want to get you into bed tonight, and I have an idea, that you might want to hear ."OK Jason, I'll bite, what is the idea?"

Jason, taking her hands in his, answered. "I think Laurie knew where her ex-husband hid the money.""You do, what makes you think that?" "Sara mentioned something about her father wanted her to have the money. I'll bet that he told her or Laurie where it was. Nancy said, "Well they lived pretty comfortable in that house in Pompano Beach, I and I know Laurie was going to buy a car for Sara's birthday." "Exactly, answered Jason. "Where would she get that kind of money?" "She did very well, selling her pottery, especially during tourist season. When I showed her pieces in the gallery, they brought a good price." "Guess that you are right, still I think either Sara or Laurie knew where the money was." Nancy said, OK, so what is you're plan? Does it involve me?" "Of course, it would include you. Tell me, did Laurie have a safe deposit box or a safe in the house? I don't remember seeing one in the house." "You checked that out, did you?" smiled Nancy. "Well, I poked around a little." "What makes you think that she had the money, Jason?" "I sort of knew Reggie, said Jason. "Really, you did? How?" said a surprised Nancy, or she hoped that she sounded surprised. "Well, I went to jail for passing a bad check when times were tough. I met Reggie in jail. Didn't Laurie tell you?" "She told me that you had been in jail, she didn't mention that you knew Reggie." "Reggie and I would bull shit in the recreation room" said Jason.

"All right, so what about you're plan? I t is illegal, of course." "Not if they don't catch you." he laughed. The waiter brought the check, Jason fumbled with his wallet. "Honestly, Jason, you ask me to lunch and make me pick up The check. Ohhh" Jason said, "Come on baby, just think how jealous all of the girls in here are." "Oh brother, are you full of yourself." "Seriously Nancy, let's go down to Laurie's house and check it out. Let's see if we can find some sort of paper or a diary of Laurie's or Sara .I'll bet they had some hot things to write about me.'"Jason, stop, you're wearing me out."Jason said,

"Laurie might have had a safe in the pottery shop." Nancy looked at him. *Did he know about the safe? Was he setting her up?"*Ok she said, "Why not? Let's go down and check it out. Want to meet me there around ten?" Jason answered, "Do you want me to spend the night with you, so that we can get an early start?" "No!" Nancy said, "This is business." "Ok he siad, thanks for lunch, I'll meet you there at ten" He leaned forward to kiss her goodbye. Nancy drove slowly home thinking.*Reggie was right! Jason is after the money. She'd better be careful. I f he found out about the papers, it could be trouble for Nancy. Well she will make sure, Jason does not find the papers. Now, how I get him to help and not steal the money? Nancy eould have to use all of feminine wiles. Since Jascon fancied himself a ladies man, that should be easy.It might involve climbing into bed with him, but trhey had done that before.It wasn't terrible. Now, how do I figure out that writing that did not make any sense to her? I know an old boyfriend who is with the FBI. I'll ask him to look at the papers, maybe he can figure it out.* If she convinced her friend to look at the papers, she and Jason could search the house and the pottery shop. She would need to hide the fact that she had already opened the safe. Nancy would have to caeful, Jason might get suspicious, but Nancy thougt that she could handle Jason. Nancy climbed into bed, tomorrow is another day.

CHAPTER TWELVE

WHERE WAS THE MONEY? Reginald Richards had been a successful broker for Anderson and Greene of Palm Beach, Florida. He had built his fortune over the years as a legitimate broker. Reggie rose quickly in the firm. He had the talent, the charm and the pizzaz. Reggie was the man they sent to handle the widows, a very handsome, charming gentleman, Tall, trim, blue eyes, hair graying at the temples, perfect to separate the old widows from their money.

Reggie met Laurie O'Brien at the pool of the Four Seasons Hotel in Palm Beach. She was in town on assignment for the Sports Illustrated swim suit edition. Reggie was immediately taken by her beauty. He used every bit of his charm sweeping her off of her feet in a whirlwind courtship. Three months later they were married in a lavish ceremony on the beach.

Reggie and Laurie were a stunning couple. Not many could resist the combination of Laurie's beauty and Reggie's charm. They entered Palm Beach society, participating in the many balls and affairs. It was at one of these affairs that Reggie developed the idea of marketing his ponzi scheme to the numerous Palm Beach widows. Reggie would charm the widows while he outlined the investment plans. If he had to take them to dinner, dancing or even to bed, nothing could stop him from closing the deal. Reggie did not consider this as cheating on Laurie, it was business. Reggie adored his wife, soon Laurie was pregnant.

Reggie was thrilled when his daughter was born. He doted on his little girl. When Reggie came home at night his daughter, Sara would run to him and throw her arms around his neck, smothering him with kisses. Reggie thought that there was no greater love than that of a daughter for her father As Reggie's success and wealth grew, he spent money lavishly. He liked to keep up with his wealthy neighbors Meanwhile, Laurie was worried, it seemed that Reggie spent more, and worked harder than ever. He was seldom home. Little did she know that Reggie was in effect running in place. The harder he worked, the closer he was coming to the crash.

He had devised an investment scam that promised huge returns with small risk. As with all Ponzi schemes, it worked well at first. When the promises faded along with the returns on the investments, the investors started asking questions, than went to the police, than asked for their money back. Reggie had to leave town.

One beautiful Florida morning, Reggie kissed his pretty little girl Sara goodbye. Leaving a half million dollars for Sara and Laurie he gathered the cash from the safety deposit box along with an assortment of bearer bonds and left for Key West. He had worked out a plan to establish a new identity and would later send for Laurie and Sara. Reggie had failed to calculate the fury of a scorned and embezzled widow. When he seduced and scammed the widow Van Horn, he faced the wrath of a formidable woman. When John Anderson, president of Anderson and Greene found Mrs. Van Horn waiting for him to open his office his worst nightmare was about to begin. John Anderson was astounded at the enormity of the problem. My God, this could ruin the firm. How could this have gotten so out of his control. Anderson and Greene faced bankruptcy. He had trusted Reggie Richards, but then so had every one.

A private detective finally found Reggie, working as a bartender at a club in Key West on Duvall Street. Although Reggie had dyed his hair, and grown a mustache, the detective, hired by Mrs. Van Horn found him. Reggie tried to buy him off, with cash, and promises of wealth, but the detective notified the police, collected his fee plus a handsome reward offered by Anderson and Greene and Mrs. Van Horn. Reggie was prosecuted and convicted of felony grand theft. He was sentenced to thirty years in the Florida State prison at Gainesville. The police claimed that he swindled his victims out of a total of fifteen to twenty million dollars. The police had recovered about a half of cash that he had left with Laurie. They did not find any bonds or certificates. When he was arrested, Reggie Richards had thirty dollars and twenty eight cents in his pockets. The question is where was the money? Jason Sanders had met Reginald Richards in Florida state prison. They were cell mates for two years until Richards got so sick that they put him in the infirmary.

Jason thought it was cute that Reggie would write and e-mail his little girl in code. Reggie said "This is between my daughter and me, she did not abandon me because I went to prison. She still loves me. I am going to set her up for life." "She will be the only one who will benefit by me going to prison. "Jason always looked over Reggie's shoulder when he sent e-mails or was writing a letter to Sara, Jason had never been able to figure out the code. When the girl was young, Reggie used to write her simple riddles. Sara would return her own little riddles. Over time, Reggie and the girl devised a pretty sophisticated code. Jason was sure that Reggie had hidden the money, but he could never get Richards to admit it .Reggie maintained that the cops had stolen most of it, and the rest was recovered.

The insurers sold all of Reggie's possessions, and his wife divorced him. He would die in prison, penniless and alone. The only bright spot in his life was SaraWhen she came to visit him, he was a different man. He would light up with the love that he felt for his child. Every one could see how much the girl loved her daddy. Jason had managed to get Sara's e-mail address, writing to her, posing as a high school student from New York. By now, she was fifteen or sixteen years old. The last time Sara came to see Reggie, her mother was with her. Both of the women were attractive. The mother was a beautiful blond with a shapely body and the daughter possessed the same qualities. Jason than formulated the plan in his brain. He would find a way to get to know Laurie.

Jason was a good looking dark haired man. He toned his body everyday in the prison gym, and he had always had a way with women. Women always found his dark good looks appealing. Jason gathered all of the information that he could manage about the women by talking and bull shitting with Reggie. Reggie was very proud of his beautiful ex-wife and daughter. He would act like he hated his ex, but Jason could see he was proud that he had been married to such a beautiful woman. By the time Jason had served his five years, he had gathered all of the information he needed. He didn't know where the money was, but was pretty sure the kid knew where it was. He thought by getting to know Laurie and Sara, he would find it. After all, he did have a way with women, especially young girls. That's part of the reason he had served five years behind bars. Jason planned on somehow getting the information from those two women. I'll just use my charm, it has never failed.

When Jason was released, he moved to Boca Raton, Florida, only about 20 miles north of Pompano Beach, where Laurie and Sara lived. He opened a fitness spa with money from his gangster friends. They advanced $100,000, with the promise of a substantial return on the investment. They also knew Jason would be able to con the women. The partners thought Jason had a good chance of finding the money. Reggie had told him that Laurie's sister had a gallery in Jupiter and sold some of her pottery. An art gallery is an excellent way to meet women. It is so legitimate, so sophisticated, it does most of the work for you. Jason first made contact with Nancy, who also shared the beauty of her sister.

Jason smooshed Nancy at the gallery, inviting her out for a drink. They discussed body toning and fitness, while enjoying their drinks Jason gave Nancy free work out lessons at his spa. Jason chatted with Nancy, telling her of his interest in pottery. Nancy mentioned that her sister, Laurie created some fine pottery pieces. He arranged to meet with Nancy and Laurie at dinner. Laurie had a shop on Commercial Boulevard in Lauderdale by the Sea, Laurie showed Jason some of her pottery Afterward, Jason and the women went to dinner at the Aruba café across from Laurie's shop. They sat at a table overlooking the beach, on a beautiful Sunday afternoon. Laurie had brought her daughter Sara. Jason had a wonderful time impressing and flirting with the ladies. By the end of the meal, he had their undivided attention, just where he wanted them.

Nancy could see how attracted Laurie was to Jason. Actually all three of the women present at the dinner were under his spell. His dark, good looks, beautiful, charming smile, and his, toned and muscular body. Nancy thought if you looked up hard bodies in the dictionary, there would be a picture of Jason. "Well, as much as I hate to leave, said Nancy, I do have some shopping to do. Sara, why don't you come with me? She asked. I want your opinion, I am buying a present for Jane's daughter." Nancy nudged Sara. "Oh, sure, said Sara" Finally catching on that the idea was to leave her mother alone with Jason. He rose from the table, excused himself and escorted the two women to the door. Jason shook hands with both and bestowed a kiss on each of their hands." It was a pleasure, ladies, till we meet again," he than returned to Laurie, at the table.

" Oh my, isn't he charming asked Nancy?" "Yeah and is he a hunk!" Sara exclaimed "Why, Sara," laughed Nancy. "Well, he is!" Sara said. After leaving the Aruba, Laurie and Jason continued the evening, stopping at Stan's on the water. Stan's was a dark romantic lounge. While sipping their drinks, Jason asked Laurie to dance. It was the kind of place where people actually danced with each other. Instead of standing in front of each other and shaking. Jason then took Laurie for a drive up A1A. Once they drove through Pompano and were almost to Boca, the noise and lights disappeared. It was a romantic drive with the car top down, and the balmy Florida breeze, adding to the atmosphere. As they talked, Jason discovered that Laurie had recently ended a long relationship with a Matt Jensen, a neighbor. When they finally arrived back at Laurie's, she willingly agreed to another date. Jason did not press to be invited inside. He gallantly bade her a good night. He did not want to rush things, he wanted Laurie's trust. Driving home Jason found himself thinking about. Sara. What a little fox! She's only sixteen, but wow, what a cute body.

That long blond hair, with that Florida tan, wow! Calm down, he told himself, you need to take things, slowly. Jason needed to get close to Laurie and act like a father, or at least a big brother to Sara. There would be time to seduce Sara later. As far as Laurie went, he didn't think it was going to be easy to get her to drop her panties. It would take every bit of his charm. Meanwhile, Laurie found herself humming as she prepared for bed. It had been a wonderful night. Jason had been a perfect gentleman. Laurie did still love Matt Jensen, but that was over and Jason really was a handsome and charming man. We'll see, she thought, before drifting off to sleep.

CHAPTER THIRTEEN

KRISTIE HAD A HOME to show early Wednesday morning. She drove over to Atlantic Boulevard and headed west. When she reached University road she turned south for six blocks to N.E. 41st Street. As Kristie pulled up to the vacant house, there was a dark Mercedes sedan waiting at the curb. Kristie, had an uneasy felling, there is something familiar about that car. Where had she seen it before? Kristie got out of her car, just as the man emerged from his.

"Hi," she greeted him, extending her hand, "I am Kristie Ryan." The man responded, "Hello, Del Bono, here," accepting Kristie's outstretched hand. "Well, Mr. Bono, let's get started. Will your wife be joining us?" "Oh, No. he answered. She will be busy this morning, but she trusts my judgment." Kristie now became very uneasy. *How many wives allow their husband to pick out a house without seeing the kitchen?* Excuse me one minute," "I have to report in." She took out her cell phone and dialed Katie.

"Hey, can you come over to the house, I am showing, No. No, I just want you to interrupt me. I need an excuse to get out of here," said Kristie. "I am at University and 41st, try to hurry." She closed the phone. "All right, Ok, Mr. Bono, let's view the house, shall we? "

They walked up to the sprawling, Florida style house. The walls were earth tone on fake adobe, with a red tiled roof. It had the Spanish style that was so prevalent in South Florida. Kristie searched for the key on the ring, found it, she opened the front door and stepped inside.

"Mr. Bono this is the foyer, and as you can see, off to the right is the living area with the connecting dinning room." "Please Ms Ryan, call me Del," he asked. "Thank you and I'm Kristie, no need to be so formal." "Yes, he said. I hope to know you much better.' Kristie looked at him. He smiled back. "Umm, well this leads back into the kitchen. You're sure your wife doesn't want to see the kitchen?' Kristie asked. "No, No, she trusts me," he smiled again. "Ok, connecting to the kitchen is a Florida room, overlooking the pool and cabana area." "Very nice,' he said. "Can we get a look at the bedrooms?" "I would like to compare their size?" "Certainly, follow me back here."

Kristie led the way down the hall to the sleeping area. "Notice that they are in the back, very private," she said. "Yes, he answered. I was counting on that. "Kristie showed him the three bedrooms, stating the size of each one. The master bedroom has French doors leading to the patio and pool, it's very tasteful. "Well, what do you think Mr. Bono, uhh, Del?"

"It's very nice, do you know, the yearly cost of the pool maintenance?" He asked. "Let me look at the sheet. Kristie answered It's about $2500.""Yes, Mmmm. How much are the taxes? "Consulting her papers, Kristie answered. "$9500.""What is the asking price?" Bono asked her. "The house is priced at $950,000.""That's a little more than I planned on spending". "Well, Sir, do you have a specific number in mind? Would you like to make an offer?" "Hmm, wait, let me get my case out of the car."

When he left, Kristie took the opportunity to call Katie. "Where are you?" She whispered. "This guy gives me the creeps." "I am almost there, said Katie, traffic sucks." As Kristie closed, the phone, she thought, I'd better get to the front of the house. She hurried out of the bedroom into the hall, bumping right into Bono. "Opps, pardon me," she said.

"What's your hurry? Where are you going he asked? You look nervous" "Here now, calm down", he took her hand than quickly twisted her arm behind her, while putting his other hand over her mouth. "Now, just be quiet, and stay calm" he said .Kristie tried to pull away but he held her tight. "Now, easy, if you don't struggle, you won't get hurt". He flipped open his case and took out a pair of metal handcuffs.

Kristie started to struggle with the man, scratching and kicking. During the struggle, her blouse was ripped off. He punched her hard in the stomach, Kristie collapsed on the floor. He quickly snapped on the hand cuffs. "Wha-What do you want," she whimpered. "Just you, dear, just you. He answered.

Now! He said, as he turned her toward him, "Let me see more of you. Very nice," he said. "Oh, please stop, please." Kristie pleaded. "Oh my dear, once I start, it is very hard for me to stop." Kristie said "Some one is meeting me here very soon." "Nice try, I don't think that is true. Come, he said let's go back into the bedroom. You'll be comfortable on that thick, soft carpet." He pushed her into the bed room. . Kristie turned away from him.

"You have a beautiful body, Kristie, don't try to hide it from me. Turn around dear so that I can see all of you." Kristie, with tears running down her face, shook her head. "Do it! He screamed at her, Now!" Kristie slowly turned towards him. "Turn around please," he asked. Kristie hesitated. "This will go much easier if you cooperate," he said. Kristie turned... "Turn all the way?" she stammered. "Yes, that's fine, beautiful, my just beautiful." "Please, Kristie said, just rape me. Get it over with. Please, please don't hurt me. I won't fight you. I'll do what you say." "Yes, I know that you will," he smirked

"Well you see, Kristie, I am not interested in sex. I am more fascinated with how different parts of the body react to stress, particularly the kind of stress that I inflict. ""Oh no," moaned Kristie. "Please, please don't" "You see," said the man. "This is the part I enjoy the most. The more you beg me, the more pleasure. But keep begging me, you just might convince me." "Remember, I told you, once I start it's very hard to stop. I just get so caught up in the pleasure." He opened the snaps on his black case. Kristie's heart sank she knew she would not survive whatever terrible things were about to happen to her.

Katie hung up the phone. *I wonder what that is about? Well Kristie sounded a little nervous, I'd better get going and see what she wants.* She hopped into her car and sped up the street. She sped all the way to next traffic light and stopped .The morning traffic on Atlantic was worse than usual. Probably an accident up where you merge on to I 95. Oh damn, come on, Katie started worrying. Katie tried to maneuver through the traffic .She resorted to her tricks, catching a guy's eye, giving a big smile, while asking him to let her go in front of him. It worked sometimes. But the worse the traffic, the less effective it became. She finally saw an open lane and sped up the outside lane past the jam. Now Katie turned on the speed. Maybe, she should call the cops. Naww, Kristie would be pissed if the cops pulled up and spooked a client. It sounded like she just wanted Katie to help her get rid of the guy gracefully. At last Katie turned onto University, Now to find 41st and the house. Oh, shit! Katie suddenly realized that she had gone the wrong direction on University. She would have to turn around in the heavy traffic and go back. Damn it! She shouted. Get out of the way, Damn it. Her cell phone chimed. "Yeah? Kristie, are you all right?" "I am almost there, this traffic sucks. I'll hurry" Katie was finally going in the right direction, would she be in time? Katie speeding up the street approached the house, she noticed Kristie's car and a large sedan parked at the curb. As she jumped out of her car, she spotted a gardener trimming the grass at the next house.

"Did you see a young woman go into that house?" pointing at the next house. He shook his head, bewildered.. "Oh, never mind, come with me," said Katie. He hesitated. "Come on I'll give you twenty bucks." They ran to the house." Kristie! Kristie! Where are you," yelled Katie? "I brought the cops with me." Katie heard Kristie scream inside the house, "Help! Help!" Before the man could stop her, Kristie ran out of the room and down the hall. Katie was standing at the end of the hall with the gardener. The gardener stared at Kristie. Katie grabbed her, and they ran to the pool area.

As Katie dialed 911, they heard the engine of the large sedan, than heard the car pulling away from the curb and going down the street.. Katie, looked at the gardener, "For Christ's sake, stop starring at her and give the lady your shirt." "Men, Jesus!" "Kristie, where are your clothes?" Katie asked as the gardener handed her his shirt. "I… I think they are in the back bedroom, she said. I'm… I'm not sure." Kristie was shaking and shivering. "Where the hell are the cops? I think she is going into shock."

Katie turned to the gardener, 'stay with her, I am going to find her clothes." Taking a pair of scissors out of her purse, Katie fearfully went down the hall, looking in each of the rooms. Katie picked up Kristie's torn blouse from a corner of the room. Gathering the clothing, Katie hurried back down the hallway. Kristie was sitting on one of the pool lounges. Her shoulders were shaking as she sobbed. Katie said to her,

"Here Kristie let me slid your skirt up until they can get the handcuffs off." Looking at the gardener, she said sternly. "You turn around. Wait, here is your twenty bucks, thanks, for your help but you had better get back to work." The gardener left, looking back over his shoulder. Katie sat next to Kristie, and put her arm around her. "Thanks, Katie, I am sure you saved my life, or the very least from a terrible ordeal." "Why did the man attack you, did he?" "No, he didn't get that far, you saved me. I think I am going to find a new job." F ive minutes later, two cops in a patrol car pulled up to the house, one was a female. The female officer took one look at the two women and took charge. "What the hell happened?" she asked. "My God! Turn around honey, let me take those handcuffs off of you." After she undid the cuffs, she said to Kristie,

"Come on inside where we can get you dressed without anyone gawking at you." She turned to the male cop. "Go out to the cruiser and bring in one of those uniform shirts of mine and a coffee for this lady." Just then the ambulance pulled up, as the medics hopped out the female cop pointed to Kristie, "looks like she might be in shock." The medics sat Kristie in a chair and started to attend to her. After a while, Kristie was strong enough to walk to the ambulance.

The were getting ready to leave for the hospital when Detectives Gabriel and Davis arrived in an un marked police car. Detectives Davis and Gabriel got out of the car, approached the two officers. "We heard the call and just happened to be in the area, what happened?" "It appears this woman was being molested by someone posing as a buyer for the house," answered the female officer. They looked over at the women, Gabriel recognized Kristie." What happened Ms. Ryan, are you all right? ""I am a little shaken up, detective. It was a terrible experience" Kristie answered. Then she started to cry.

"Give her a break will you?" snapped Katie. "Let's get her to the hospital." Damn cops always there when you don't need them." "I would like to get a statement from you, miss. I'll see you at the hospital" said Gabriel. As the ambulance sped away to the hospital, the attendant gave a sedative to Kristie. "You have one of those for me?" asked Katie. The attendant, a young man, obviously overwhelmed by the beauty of his two passengers, shook his head, "Sorry, no."

Gabriel, before he left, for the hospital, instructed the officers. "I am calling for the crime lab to investigate here. Don't let anyone in the house. Don't touch anything .Make sure that they to report to me." The detectives left for the hospital .The two detectives found Katie and Kristie in the emergency room. Kristie was being admitted over night for observation. Gabriel turned to Katie, "That was a very brave of you" he said.. "Katie, how can I ever thank you?" said Kristie." You would have done the same for me. I am glad we stopped the bastard. Men are such creeps." "Could you identify this man," asked Gabriel. "Yes! I'll never forget that evil face". Kristie answered. "One other thing, It seemed like I had seen that car somewhere before. But I can't remember where right now."

CHAPTER FOURTEEN

GABRIEL AND DAVIS WERE in their office. "George, it's been almost a week, we need to get something going on these murders." "Well Clarence, we got some of the ME reports back. Let's see what they found." Gabriel looked at the report. According to the ME they had come up with a bunch of hairs, and fibers from the murder scene. The ME had managed to get DNA samples from Nick Jensen and Jason Sanders. They both had volunteered, the samples, claiming that they were innocent and had nothing to hide. Clarence said. "I think Nick Jensen has a great deal to hide." "Come on, Clarence. Why are you so hot on this guy?" "I'll tell you why. He lives next door, he could have easily slipped across that lawn, what 50 feet? He has a motive and opportunity." Gabriel said. "What about his alibi, Kristie Ryan? Don't you think the attack on Kristie had something to do with the murders?" "No answered Davis. I think the guy just took advantage of being in an empty house with a good looking woman."

Gabriel said. "Well, what she described, sounded like it was more than just being infatuated with a pretty woman. Kristie had been in the area of the murder scene, Friday night, than she was attacked on Wednesday. Did she see something, Friday? Maybe she doesn't know what it was. Did she see the killer? Did he see her?" "You know how I hate coincidence," said Gabriel. "Well we have not really questioned her forcefully, yet," said Davis. "What do you mean, forcefully" asked George? "Well you know, push her on the facts. How late was she really there? What did she notice when she left. Were there any lights in the victim's house? Did she hear anything strange?" Davis answered.

"Ok said George. If she is not an alibi, what was his motive?" "He was very close with the victims." Davis snorted "Jealously, that old thing, jealously. The woman broke up with him after six years, They lived next door to each other, she flaunts the new guy at him every week end. It had to piss him off. Don't forget the young girl, said Clarence They were pretty close, according to him. Now he sees her spending her time with this new guy. This guy isn't bad looking by the way. A young girl could easily develop a crush on him. I'll bet he was as jealous of the kid, as he was the mother said Clarence, slapping the table. Who discovered the body? Who walked through the house?" "Who waits three hours before calling the police?" "Nick Jensen answered Davis, that's who." "

Boy! You sure have it for him" said Gabriel. "Listen George, you get used to a sweet young thing hanging around you all the time, and then suddenly she stops. Well, think about it." Gabriel said, "you think he was doing anything with the girl?" "I donno," said Clarence. "She sure wasn't bad looking. She did have sex with someone she knew according to the ME. They could have had something going." "Let's look at the evidence, we have" said Gabriel.

" Ok, we talked to Kristie Ryan. Kristie said she left Jensen's house around 4 am. She heard moans coming from the Richard's house. She thought they were having a sex party. It wasn't Jensen, she just left him." Davis said, "Yeah, but she doesn't really give him an alibi." Gabriel asked. "You think he ran next door, after she left, had sex with the girl, than killed the mother?" "I don't know, how he did it, but he has a motive. He had the opportunity. The neighbors said the three of them had gone away for week end."

"Ok, said Gabriel. Doesn't that give Jason Sanders the same motive, jealously?" "We saw there were bad feelings between those two guys. After all, the women and Jensen went away for, what, two or three days to the Keys? Where did they spend the night?" "Was it a motel on one of the Keys? Is that why Sanders went to the Keys? Friday night. Was he searching for evidence? Did he really go to the Keys, Friday night? Maybe after that trip with Nick Jensen, Ms Richards wanted to break it off with Jason Sanders. I want to know where Jason Sanders was in that house last Friday night. We know he was in there, but where, when? Did he have another reason for being there other than to have dinner? He could have been the one that had sex with Sara. Did the mother catch them in the act? I want to know exactly what Jason Sanders did in that house, Friday. I want to know if he went to the Keys Friday night and why. Did he really have a meeting Saturday morning or did he just need an alibi?" This time it was Gabriel who pounded on the table.

"Ok, Ok, you have made your point" said Davis. "I'll tell what, you concentrate on Sanders and I will investigate Jensen. One of them is probably guilty, let's see where we stand on the evidence collected at the murder scene." The detectives called the ME into the office. "Tell us what you have, so far.". "We have a match of hair samples found in Sara Richard's bed" stated the ME. Both of the detectives looked at him. "Ok! What's the match?" Asked Davis The ME said. "We have a scalp hair that matches Nick Jensen." "From her bed," Davis, smiled? "Well from the area, maybe the bedroom floor" answered the ME. "We also have a pubic hair brushed from the bed that matches Jason Sanders, also he is a match of the sperm sample found on the sheets." This time Gabriel smiled. "That's who she had sex with, before the mother was killed?" Davis asked. "Are you sure?"

The ME looked at him, nodded his head. "We also found hair in the bed that matched Nick Jensen." "My God! Shouted Gabriel, She was screwing everybody." Clarence said. "That is your motive." George said. "My God Clarence we have motive for both Jensen and Sanders and anyone else she might have been screwing, what a horny little bitch. ""I say we get a warrant for Jensen's house, we sure have enough evidence for a search of his house, car and boat," said Davis.. "Ok said Gabriel. You see the judge."

CHAPTER FIFTEEN

NICK HAD ATTENDED THE Memorial service for Laurie. During the service, Nick was overwhelmed by the events of the past few days. He realized how much he had loved Laurie and Sara, he had always considered them his family. How could he had been so stupid? Why didn't he marry Laurie as she had wanted him to do? After the service Nick had gone drinking, trying in vain to ease his pain. Early Friday morning, Detective Davis, forensic technicians and six patrolmen descended on Nick's house. The police banged on the door, than just pushed their way inside. Nick having just gotten out of bed, said, "Whoa, wait, what are you doing ?"

Detective Davis handed him the search warrant. "Stand aside we have a warrant to search your home, boat and vehicles." "We will be at least two or three hours, you may want to wait outside. "Nick, while reading the warrant, went outside and phoned Jake Lawson. "What's up Nick?" "They are searching the house, Jake. Can they do that?" "Do they have a search warrant?" "Yes." "Hold on, I'll be right over, don't say anything to any one. Got it?" "No one!" "But Jake, I have not done any thing, I am not guilty of anything." "Don't talk to any one, even to say you are innocent. See you in about 15 minutes."

The cops proceeded to carefully vacuum every area. It wasn't long before one of the cops in the Florida room, said "It looks like a stain on this couch." Take a sample and be careful. Later other one held up a pair of white lace panties. "I found these down in the cushions of the couch," he said. The

ME chief looked over at him, "Give them to me, I'll bag those." They were vacuuming Nick's boat, It appears there was quite a bit of action in this bed.

Than the technicians called the Davis out to the garage. One of them directed his attention to the knife taped under the trailer." Is that your knife, Mr. Jensen?" "No." "Can you tell me what it is doing there?" "I have nothing to say on the advice of my lawyer," he answered. "I bet, you don't, that does it" said Davis. "Turn around, Mr. Jensen, you are under arrest for the murder of Laurie Richards, anything you say can be used against you in a court of law." Nick said. "Aww, come on, this doesn't make sense, why would I keep the murder weapon there? I could have easily taken it out on the boat, and dumped it in the canal."

Jake Lawson, driving into Nick's driveway, heard the last exchange of words between Davis and Jensen. "Nick, do not say another word. "Closing the car door, Lawson turned to Davis, asked "What are the charges?" "Murder 1, " answered Davis. Jake looked at Nick, "Don't worry, I'll have you out by the end of the day. They don't have enough evidence for that kind of charge." Davis said, "Jensen had sexual relations with the victim, and possibly the daughter." "It is not against the law to have sex." Said Jake. Davis spoke to the police,

"Keep looking for evidence, there is probably more." A couple of the detectives seemed uncomfortable with the directive. It seemed as if they were trying to incriminate Nick regardless of the evidence. A gun was found in Nick's bedroom and more evidence in the master's suite on the boat. The technicians gathered their equipment and left for the office, thinking that they would be analyzing the evidence all week end. Davis put Nick into a patrol car and drove away.

Later, when Davis brought Nick into the interrogation room, Jake Lawson was waiting. Davis said, "Sit over in that chair, Jensen," giving him a slight shove. Lawson said to "Nick, don't speak unless I tell you too." Detective Davis flipped on the tape recorder, stated his name, the date and identified every one present. There was a mirror on one wall of the drab, green room, presumably a reflective window. They sat on mismatched folding chairs around a gray metal table

Davis started the questioning. "Mr. Jensen we have evidence that you were at the scene of the murders. "Lawson answered, "My client discovered the bodies, of course he was there, so?" "There was also evidence that you had had sex with both of the victims, in your home and also on your boat." "Again, Detective, It is not against the law to have sex," said Lawson. "With a seventeen year old girl?" "I never had sex with the girl" said Nick. "Be quiet, Nick, I'll do the talking" said Lawson. "Why don't you let him explain consular?" "He doesn't have to explain anything at this time." "Well, if he is innocent, maybe he could help clear up some details." Detective you arrested my client on a charge of Murder 1, I want to hear the evidence, beside the fact that he was present at the murder scene and he had sex with the victims." "During the search of his home, we found a gun in his bedroom drawer." So what? The victim was not shot, he has a permit for the gun. Come on detective, Surely you have more evidence that this." Davis stood and shouted, "Good, what about the knife found in the garage, *that* was the murder weapon."

"Anyone could have planted the knife in the garage, it is never locked, furthermore, you haven't proved it is the murder weapon, there are not any prints on the knife. You have a few pieces of flimsy evidence, nothing more." "Yeah, well people have been convicted on just this kind of evidence." Lawson said "My sources tell me that there is evidence of the girl having sex with Jason Sanders. He was engaged to the mother, therefore he had sex with both victims. Why don't you arrest him?" "What sources? Where did you hear that?" shouted Davis. "It's true, isn't it detective? I want to see the District Attorney, now, I don't think you have enough evidence to charge Mr. Jensen."

Detective Davis, after glancing at the mirror, left the room. After a brief time Davis returned to the interrogation room." Your client is free to go" he said to Lawson. "I must warn you that your client is still a suspect and should not leave the area." "If my client leaves the area and we think you need to know about it, we will notify you. Let's go, Nick," Lawson and Jensen left the room. They walked out of the interrogation room. Nick turned to Jake and said. "Jake you were terrific. Thanks! ""That was just round one", he answered. "They will be back." Out on the street, it was starting to drizzle. Nick walked with Jake over to his car. Jake said

" Look Nick, I mean it they won't quit. Especially Davis he has it in for you. ""They have the same evidence on Jason Sanders." "Nick, you should brush off your investigative skills. Try to find out who is behind these killings, why they are trying to frame you." Jake said. "That knife did not get there by accident." "We have to find out what is behind those killings. The police just want somebody to stick it on. Their job will be done, right or wrong." "Yeah," said Nick "I see what you mean,. I am going to have to clear myself." Jake shook hands with Nick. "You can use any of the firm's employees or facilities, whatever you need." "Thanks Jake." "Oh it will cost you" he laughed .Jake got into his BMW started the engine, pulled into the traffic.

Nick walked over to his car, deep in thought .*Who could be behind this? Who planted the knife in my garage? Who attacked Kristie at the house? Kristie! I had better get over there and see if she needs anything.* Nick started the car, opened his cell phone, Punched in Kristie's number. Katie answered on the first ring. "Katie, how is Kristie? Are you two all right?" She said. "No, I think you had better come over, Nick." "I am on my way." Nick drove down Sunrise boulevard to Dixie highway, turned north onto Dixie and sped up to Cypress road. The traffic was light, but man, those traffic lights. Outside of New York city, he could not think of any other place with so many traffic lights.

Nick arrived at Kristie's apartment in ten minutes. Katie answered the door, and as usual she had on very little clothing. "Come on in Nick, she said. Then she hollered, "Kristie! Nick's here." Kristie came hurrying into the room. "Nick! I am so glad you are here," she started sobbing. "Hey, what's wrong? Get hold of yourself." "Nick, I'm I'm scared. That incident with that terrible man has gotten me really upset. I don't know what to do. Maybe he knows where I live, maybe he will come back." "Kristie, I think you and Katie should stay at my house until you girls feel safe." "You girls pack some things. I have plenty of room. "The two women went off to pack.

Katie hollered, "You are close to the beach, right Nick?" "Yes, you can walk there in about five minutes." he answered. "Sweet," said Katie. When the girls were both packed, they put their things in the car. "Should we take our cars?" asked Kristie. "Sure," said Nick. "There is plenty of room, you guys are going to want your freedom, with out depending on me to drive you every where." They drove in a caravan of three cars, east on Cypress to Bay view drive to Commercial boulevard. When they arrived at Nick's house,

Rex ran to meet them. Katie greeted him, "Hey boy, hi, Oh you are a pretty boy." Rex could hardly contain himself, with all of the attention he was receiving from Katie. The girls took their suitcases into the bed rooms. Katie said, "Aren't you two sleeping together? Why do you need you own room, Kristie?" Kristie looked at Nick, "Katie we are not that close yet." "Sure, right" grumbled Katie. "Nick, can I sleep on the boat, use it as my room?" "Sure, Katie, there is a king size bed in the master's suite' "How comfortable is *that* Kristie" asked Katie? "I just assumed you have already slept in it." "Oh, just put your clothes in there and shut up, Sorry Nick." "There's no problem. You girls can sleep wherever you want. Eat whatever, do whatever, make your selves at home."

After the girls had settled in, they gathered in the Florida room to have a drink and to discuss the events of the last couple of days. Katie was wearing one of Nick's shirts and a bikini bottom. Kristie said, "Katie, you are not home, wear some clothes. Isn't that Nick's shirt, boy you sure do make yourself at home" Nick laughed. "That's all right, I want you girls to be comfortable." Katie poured herself a drink and sat on the couch. "Thanks Nick. I hate to dress around the house. If I bother you, just say something. Sometimes I just don't realize the effect it can have on a man." "Relax, he said. I am fine."

Nick addressed Kristie "Ok! Kristie, you are afraid that this man will come back and attack you again? Why?" "He just gave me the creeps, he was evil. I don't know what he would have done to me if Katie had not stopped him. He probably was the one that did those things to that poor girl next door. Why did he come after me? ""I think he saw you leave my house that morning. He probably figured that if something happened to you. that would be one more connection to me."

Nick looked at both of the girls and said. "I am going to do some investigating on my own. I don't like the idea that someone is trying to frame me." "Why? Why me?" Katie spoke up. "Can we help you, Nick?" "We could be like detectives, do you have a gun?" Nick said, "Yes I do. It is a 45 semi-automatic. But that's not what we need right now. We have to figure out why Laurie was killed and why does someone wants me to take the fall?" "Kristie, I want you to study those e-mails, see if you can figure if they were from high school kids or was it someone trying to get information from Sara." "Katie, since you are living on the boat, I want you to look through my office. I want you to bring any thing that you find to my attention. You might see something that I could have overlooked." "Oh goodie, Katie Ryan, girl sleuth," she said.

"Well, Ok, but this could get dangerous. After all if the attack on your sister is related to the murders, they may try again, they could include you this time." "We have to be very careful." Nick lectured .Kristie went into the kitchen, fixed some crackers with cheese and pretzels .She brought them out and sat them on the table she said to Nick." I am afraid to go home. I don't think I am going back to work for a while. He knows where I work. I have some money saved, so that won't be a problem." Nick said, "I still have a key to Laurie's pottery shop, maybe we should go there and look around, there may be a couple of clues at the shop." Katie said. "Good I am going out to the boat and get started. It such a beautiful day, I'll put on my swim suit, while I work." Kristie rolled her eyes. "If she wasn't my sister, I could bat her one. But I know she is just being Katie, she is a free spirit."

Since the pottery shop was located in the tourist district and parking could be a problem, Nick and Kristie, decided to walk to the pottery shop. They walked over to A1A, then to Commercial Blvd. a distance of about six blocks. Nick opened the door of the pottery shop, as they stepped inside, he switched to sign on the door to read closed. "We don't want any tourists wandering in," he said. "Kristie look around in the desk, see if there is any thing of interest, such as a letter. "I don't know what we are looking for, but maybe when I see it, I'll know." Kristie asked. "How long did you and Laurie date each other."

Nick related the story of how they met and got together. "This Sara, seems like a beautiful, young girl," Kristie said. "She is" Nick answered. "A lot like Katie, a free spirit." "Oh look, here is a letter from a Reggie." "Reggie was her husband, let me see it" Nick read over the letter. *It was addressed to Laurie, it was telling her to be careful of Jason. That he had been in jail with him, and*

Reggie considered him to be someone to prey on woman. He particularly warned her about him with Sara. Jason likes young girls. Nick said. "Maybe we have something here." They poked around the shop some more, Kristie said, "It looks as if someone has been here before us."

Nick turned on the computer, began reading the e-mails. Most of them were orders for pottery. He saw some to Sara that caught his eye. They all seemed to be from a chat room, and other high school students. A few of the messages were very personal, pretty descriptive in a sexual way. Knowing what he knew about Sara, he wasn't surprised. Sara obviously was experienced sexually, she had proven that to him. Nick printed the e-mails to take along with him. Kristie and Nick gathered any papers that they wanted to study in more detail and left the shop. After locking the door, they walked home, enjoying the warm, pleasant weather.

When they reached Nick's house, Kristie said "I'll make lunch for all of us." Just then Katie came out of the bathroom, stark naked, toweling her hair. "Katie!" exclaimed Kristie! "Opps, sorry I didn't think you would be back so soon." she continued to dry her hair. Nick could not help staring. What a body! "Katie at least cover up," shouted Kristie! Katie put the towel around her and smiled at Nick.. Nick thought Oh boy, this could be trouble. Katie seems to be doing anything to agitate Kristie. "Come on Katie said Kristie, don't screw up a good thing. Nick has been wonderful letting us stay with him. Don't mess it up with your shenanigans."

"Oh, relax Kristie, he has seen a naked woman before. Haven't you Nick?" She asked coyly. "Yeah, don't worry about it Kristie. Its ok, I want you two to feel at home." "Katie, you know what I mean" said Kristie. "Yeah, I know, but Nick isn't like that, he wouldn't try to do anything behind your back." "Ok, Katie, but try to be a little more modest." "Right back at ya, big sis, Will do." After Katie had put on a blouse tied at the waist and a pair of shorts, they sat down to a lunch that Kristie had prepared. She had fixed a salad of greens, sliced tomatoes, cucumbers with a light dressing. And a few small ham and turkey sandwiches Kristie served this with glasses of iced tea.

Kristie was very quiet, while they were eating. Meanwhile, Katie talked away about their life back in Michigan. Kristie had met the man that would become her husband, while vacationing in Miami Beach. After Kristie was married and moved to Florida, Katie had followed. "That was a big mistake on my part" said Katie. "I was very young, and I got into drugs, actually just for the thrill of it. But of course, I got hooked. I did some very stupid things, that got me into even more trouble. Soon Kristie intervened, she saved me from myself." I moved in with her and her husband, while trying to get clean and back on my feet. "Unfortunately, it caused problems in their marriage and they eventually split. He husband continually made advances towards me, I really did not do anything to encourage him. Thank goodness my sister did not blame me for the break up of her marriage. After the divorce, we bought the house together and here we are."

As they were talking two cars pulled up to Laurie's house, next door. Nancy and Jason got out of their cars and walked up to the house. *This looks interesting*, thought Matt, *I wonder what they are up to*. That evening, after dinner, Nick and the girls were out in the Florida room having a few glasses of wine. Kristie was drinking quite a bit and was getting a little smashed. Katie, drinking her share was also a little high. Both of the girls were laughing and feeling pretty happy. Nick was tired, he had a long day, he stood and said. "Well, good night ladies, sleep well." Kristie went over and whispered to her sister. Katie laughed. "Kristie you had better be sure about that." When Nick got to his room, Kristie had followed him. "I have a surprise for you. I want you to get in bed and turn off the lights and wait for me." Nick smiled, "Sure, he said," he undressed, lay in bed, than turned out the light. Shortly she came into his room, slipped into bed beside him, she snuggled her naked body against him. Nick reached for her and kissed her. He ran his hands over her soft, warm body in the darkness, he began to kiss with increasing passion, than she helped him slip inside of her and they made intensely reckless love. Nick was overwhelmed by the tenderness and intensity of their lovemaking. This was different than what they had experienced before. Afterward as Nick lay thinking, he turned towards Kristie, only to discover Katie lying next to him. 'surprise Nick, I hope you are not mad at us. No, Katie, I am not mad, surprised, but not mad. 'Goodie, can we do it again?" 'We sure can" said Nick as Katie moved into his arms. Nick awoke late the next morning to the smell of fresh coffee .Kristie and Katie were in the kitchen and had prepared a breakfast of orange juice, eggs, ham, hot cakes and fresh brewed coffee. Nick entering the kitchen sheepishly said "Good morning ladies." "Hi Nick" they chorused. "Did you sleep well?

CHAPTER SIXTEEN

JASON AND NANCY PARKED their cars in Laurie's driveway. As Nancy was getting out of her car, she glanced over at Nick's house, noticing the two extra cars in the driveway. "It looks like Nick is entertaining." she said. Jason looked over at the house. "I thought Jensen had been arrested.' "Oh Jason, you don't think Nick killed Laurie, he loved her and he adores Sara." "Exactly" said Jason, "He was jealous of me, that's why he did it." Nancy looked at Jason, "Really now, let's take our luggage inside and get settled, we have a lot of work to do" They carried the bags inside the house.

Nancy had called a cleaning service that specialized in crime scenes to clean the house and garage. Everything smelled of disinfectant and deodorizer. The carpets and furniture were spotless, there were no signs to remind her of what had taken place in the house. Nancy settled into Laurie's old room, the largest of the rooms. "Jason, you can have either of the other two bedrooms" "Why don't I just bunk with you, it will be cozier?" Nancy sighed, "Come on Jason, let's try to be serious" Jason walked down the hall to the other room and threw his bag on the bed. Nancy could see that she would either have to move to a hotel, or eventually give in to Jason, he was relentless with one thought on his mind.

Nancy sat at the desk in Laurie's bedroom, and read through Laurie's papers There was a notebook where she had kept important papers and notes pertaining to the pottery shop. Nancy opened it to a page dated December 20, the heading read: Jason and Sara? Nancy continued to read, *Is Jason trying to seduce Sara? Should I marry Jason? I need to talk to Sara. Trip with Nick, what did it mean? It was pleasant being with him again. Sleeping with Nick, wasn't in my plans, but it was very nice. Did Sara try to seduce Nick that morning or was she just showing off? After all, I was in the same bed, although half asleep. Nick was gracious enough to get out of bed without causing any trouble .Later, I saw Sara remove her top, teasing Nick, we really need to talk. Very disturbing, I hope that she doesn't tease Jason that way, he would not hesitate to respond. Laurie had written in her book that Jason was coming to dinner Friday, I think that we will talk about postponing any engagement. I need to find out how Sara feels about this.* Nancy turned the pages, looking for more information.

Obviously her sister wasn't sure of a marriage to Jason. She wondered could this have angered Jason? After thumbing through the notebook and not seeing anything further of interest. Nancy found a letter in Sara's dresser. It was addressed to her mother. Sara revealed her love for Jason and described his seduction of her. She told of her plan to find the money and share it with Jason. He will never have to work. Nancy put the letter away, Jason really was a scum bag, he seduced a young innocent girl and betrayed Laurie.

For the first time, Nancy realized that Jason was a dangerous person. She feared that if Jason didn't kill Laurie, he probably knew who did. She would have to be very careful when dealing with him. Nancy went out to the kitchen. She said to Jason, "I'll think I'll go to the Publix and get groceries." "Yeah, sure, I have to go to plantation to see someone anyway."

Before Jason could leave the house, there was a knock at the door. Jason opened the door, "Well hi…umm detective." "Hello, Mr. Sanders" Detective Gabriel said, showing his badge. "I have a couple of questions, if you don't mind." "Well. I am in kind of a hurry, can't it wait?" "Oh, it won't take long, can I come inside? ""Yeah, come on in, let's get it over with." Gabriel came into the house, nodded to Nancy, "Afternoon Ms Johnson." "Hi detective, I just came down to clear out some of the things, Jason offered to help." "Right, well I have some questions for Mr. Sanders, can we go into the living room?" Jason led the way, than turned and said,

"What is all of this about detective? I answered your questions the other day. "Gabriel took a seat on the couch, pilled out his notepad "I have information that you were in prison the same time as Reggie Richards." Gabriel began. "Yeah, so?" said Jason. "I also found evidence that you and Sara had sex in her bed, the night her mother was murdered." Nancy said, "Jason, how could you, you betrayed Laurie right in her own home, with her daughter, that beautiful young girl." Jason snarled, "Mind your own business, yeah I had sex with her, she started it. But they were both OK when I left." "Did her mother happen to walk in and catch you and Sara? Was there an argument?" Nancy said, "Jason, I can't believe that you would do that. Betray Laurie by having sex with her daughter!" "Why? She liked it, she even started it most of the time, I wasn't going to say no." said Jason. "So you were here last Friday night, you had dinner and managed to have sex with the daughter with her mother in the house. You accomplished all of this and still managed to leave at seven, correct?" "Well maybe it was closer to eight." said Jason. "Mr. Sanders, I want to inform you, that in light of these facts along with your previous criminal record, you are a prime suspect in this murder." "Big deal, are you going to arrest me?" "Not at this time." said Gabriel. "Good, then let me tell you something detective. You do not have enough evidence, and you are not going to scare me by making accusations. So bug off, I have an appointment to keep, and I intend to keep it. I'll see ya," said Jason. Jason left, Nancy noticed him looking over at Nick's. She then saw the reason for his attention. A stunning red head in a small bikini was washing Nick Jensen's boat. I wonder who she is thought Nancy. Detective Gabriel turned to Nancy, "Ms Johnson, I think that Jason is a very dangerous man. I would be very careful around him. He is looking for something, At this time, I don't what it is, but be careful." "Yes detective, I will, I still can't believe that he seduced that innocent young girl, she was so sweet." "Well, he has a record of doing just that." answered Gabriel. The detective left, warning Nancy once again to be careful. "I will detective, good bye." Nancy went to the grocery store across AA1A from the Sea Colony condos. She filled the cart with cereal, vegetables, steak and chicken. Nancy sure did not feel like being a cook for Jason, but she knew he was too cheap to spring for dinner. Nancy could order take-out when she didn't want to cook. She drove back to the house, as she was pulling the car into the driveway, she saw Nick and beeped the horn. He waved hello. "What brings you down here?" he asked. "Oh just trying to move some, pack some clothes snd household things. "Maybe Sara will want to sell and move to Jupiter with me. "Jason come along to pack?" asked Nick. "He had some clothing here and he wanted to pick up his work out equipment., Jason isn't so bad." said Nancy. "He isn't so good either." answered Nick. "Who is your new shipmate?" Nancy asked, nodding at Katie. "Oh she is staying here with her sister. They need a place to stay and I have the room, so why not? We became friends last Friday." Nick, you sure work fast." Nancy laughed. "Maybe one of them will cuddle up to you in her night gown" "Oh, it's nothing like that. They just need a place to stay." Nancy laughed again. "Sure, see you around Nick, you be a good boy now." Meanwhile Jason was driving out Commercial Boulevard to I95. Once on 95 he headed south to Miami. He took out his cell phone and punched in a pre-programmed number. It was answered on the second ring. "Yeah!" Jason said "Carter, it's Jason, I'm on my way over, we need to talk." "You should not be coming here, we shouldn't be seen together." he said. "I'll be there in ten minutes." Jason was so engrossed in his conversation that he failed to notic that Gabriel was following him. The detective followed

Jason's car, leaving enough distance between vehicles so that Jason did not suspect that he was being followed. Jason got off of I95, heading west on Oakland Park Boulevard. He continued west past Invinerry, past the golf course, crossed over the Turnpike , then turned south on Route 441. He turned into a side road about a half a mile further. Jason stopped the car in front of a single wide trailer, the third one down the dirt road. The knock on the door was answered immediately, the man pulling Jason quickly inside, and slamming the door. "Carter, aren't you glad to see me? I have some money for you. Of course, you did mess things up. I didn't want you to kill her. I wanted the information but I wanted her to stay alive." "Yeah, sure, after you screwed with the daughter, how were you going to let her live? If I could have found the kid, I would have killed her too, after I extracted the information from her." "Carter, you underestimate my charm. I could have talked my way out of it." Carter said, "Boy, are you full of it. I did you a favor getting rid of her. Did you find the paper?" "No, said Jason. "That's why I am here. What safe did she say they were in?" "She didn't, but the sister was in the pottery shop, looking around. She opened the safe and took some money and papers." "Why didn't you stop her?" asked Jason. "She mist have heard me behind her, she smacked me with a piece of pottery, just as I was about to grab her." "So that's where you got that welt on your head." laughed Jason. "Very funny. But if I had not gone to the pottery shop, you would still be wondering where the safe is. You were supposed to have them wrapped around your finger. I think that little girl was the one that had you tied up" Jason snarled, "Oh yeah? I'll find the money. If that broad took it out of the safe I'll get it from her. We are staying in the house, looking for something that will give us a clue about the location of the money. If she got something out of the safe, that means she is stringing me along. I'll teach that bitch to mess with me." Carter said, "Hey, I am not doing anything until I get more money. You said five thousand for the kill, although I will say the work has been enjoyable." "Yeah, Carter, what happened with the girl you were going to do to frame Jensen." "I got interrupted, boy she had a body that I would have enjoyed working on." Jason said, "You really are a sick puppy. Instead of screwing a woman like that, you want to mess them up." "Every man to his own vices, Jason." "Here is three thousand, that should hold you for a while." "Wait Jason, you told me five thousand. Come on, you are holding out on me. The partners are not going to like that. They agreed to the kill for five thousand. You my friend are looking for trouble, screwing with them" "Shut up Carter, now drive down to your house in Marathon. I'm sure the money is somewhere in the Keys, I am just not sure exactly where. But my friend, I assure you I will find out .I'll be in contact with you, after I put some pressure on Nancy." As Jason drove back to the house he thought. *The backers think that Reggie hid the money on one of the keys. They also think that Reggie told either the kid or the mother where it was hidden. Noe Nancy might have something that gives a clue to where it is hidden. If Jason could find the money, he would do whatever he had to to get himself out of the country. We'll see what Nancy knows, she will tell me, even if I have to beat it out of her.*

CHAPTER SEVENTEEN

NANCY WAS FIXING DINNER when her cell phone rang. "Hi, are you coming home? I have dinner cooking. It should be finished by the time you get here." "I really would like to sample your cooking, but it not possible to do that at the moment." "Oh it's you, Sam. I didn't expect to hear from you so soon. What's up? Do you have answers already? What is it?" Sam answered, "Maybe I could receive a small payment for my information." Nancy answered, "I'll make it worth your time if it is the information that I need."

"OK, can you come up to Vero Beach? I can show what I have and we can arrange payment accordingly." "I don't know Sam, that is a two hour drive. Can't we do this tomorrow?" "Why don't you come up this evening? I'll meet you at the Holiday Inn in Vero Beach and we can discuss payment over a couple of drinks. Than you can spend the night with me. I have a very nice room with a king size bed." "Well, I don't know." she answered "It's that way or no way, honey." said Sam. "All right, I'll see you tonight, give me a couple of hours to get there."

Damn, I sure don't want to go to Vero Beach tonight. Thought Nancy. Sam sounded like as if the payment was going to be a night in bed with him. I'd better leave before Jason returns, I don't want him tagging along or following hme to Vero Beach. Nancy hurriedly put the half cooked food in dish, placing it in the refrigerator. She put the utensils in the sink to soak.

Nancy left the house and drove north towards Vero Beach. She planned to make a quick stop at her home in Jupiter. Nancy was forming a plan of action that she would use, once she had reached Vero Beach .She stopped at her home long enough to grab a prescription bottle of pain killers. After a quick change into something sexy, she was on her way. After two hours driving I95 she pulled into the parking area at the Holiday Inn. She walked into the bar,

Sam was sitting at a table. He rose to greet her. "Wow, you look lovely, Nancy, this is going to be a fun night." Nancy gave a kiss on the cheek. "Hi, Sam, it's good yo see you again." "I already ordered, would you like a drink?" "Yes Sam, a vodka martini please. So how have you been. You've become a special agent since I last saw you." "Yeah, Nancy I am so sorry to hear about Laurie, how is Sara." "Sara is safe, she is in Maryland for the next couple of months." The waiter brought their drinks. "Sam raised his glass here is to a fun night. It will be like old times. I still remember that night in Boca Raton, and the night after that." They chatted as they ate their steaks. Nancy had a small Filet and a salad. While they were eating,

Nancy asked Sam to show her the papers. "They are in my briefcase, can it wait until after dinner?" "Sure Sam, be a sweetheart and get my sweater out of my car. Here are the keys, it's the gray Audi, thanks." While Sam went to get the sweater, a second round of drinks arrived. Nancy quickly reached in her purse, and dropped two pain killers, and a sleeping pill into his drink, than stirred it briskly. Sam returned, took a big swallow, than turned to Nancy. "Let's go up to my room, I'll give you the papers, than we can have some fun." "That sounds delightful, Sam." she kissed him on the cheek as the walked to the elevator.

While riding the elevator Sam kissed Nancy and began running his hands along her body. "I can't wait to get you in bed." "Business first, Sam, then we'll play." Sam opened the door to the room, they went inside. Sam took another swallow from his drink, that they had brought to the room.

Sam pulled out his briefcase, showed Nancy the codes that had been deciphered. "It looks like what ever it is you are looking for is buried on one of the keys." "Nancy looked over the papers, stuffed the in her handbag. "Thanks, Sam she said. Sam took her In his arms, kissed her, than began unbuttoning her blouse. "Time to pay the piper." Nancy slipped out of her blouse and bra, went over to the bed. She beckened to Sam. Sam finished his drink, started unbuttoning his shirt, and walked towards Nancy. H e stumbled into the chair. "Guess I drank that too fast." he said. He took one more step, reaching for Nancy, than fell face first on the bed. Nancy rolled him over, quickly undressed him, pulled the spread over him. She left a note thanking him for a wonderful night. Nancy quickly gathered her bra and slipped into her blouse, grabbed her purse and quietly closed the door. She hurried to her car, and headed home.

CHAPTER EIGHTEEN

WHILE JASON HAD BEEN inside of Carter's trailer, Detective Gabriel called his office and had his assistant run a check of the address. Then he noticed the big dark sedan parked on the other side of the trailer. Gabriel noted the license tag, called the office again. "Hi, it's Gabriel again, I might be on to something regarding the murders. Check out the owner of a black Mercedes sedan. License no. MM2241DG. Call me on my cell. No, the car I am driving doesn't have a radio. Yeah, yeah, big deal." He walked around the property, back near a wooded area he noticed a dumpster. Gabriel went over to investigate. Carefully looking inside he gently lifted a rumpled rain coat and gloves, with traces of blood. While he was stowing the package in the car, his cell phone rang.

"Gabriel here." "Hey George, the car is registered to Carter Melman, resides at 1508 S. fifteenth street in Marathon, Florida. We have a work up on him if you would like it." "Great! Shoot!" "Mr. Melman has a record for assault, a second degree sexual offense. The assault charge was dropped. He was convicted of the sexual offense. He was sentenced to eight years in the Florida State Prison, paroled on July 15, 2004.""Great work," said Gabriel. He called the state prison. "Hi, this is George Gabriel." "I have another favor to ask. Fax me information on Carter Melman. He was there from 1997 to July of 2004. Send me whatever you have. Also let me know of any connections with Reggie Richards or Jason Sanders. The fax is 305-656-5554 Thanks."

As Gabriel closed the phone, Jason came out of the door, got into his car and drove away. Gabriel started to follow him, but than he decided that Jason was probably returning to the house in Pompano. Furthermore, he had to get the car back and trade it for a department car, "Damn. Those dug dealers know how to live." Of course, the one that had owned the car was in jail for about ten to twenty years. George wanted to get back to the office and read the fax from Gainesville, returning to the police garage, he gave the keys to the attendant, mentioning to him that it was a nice ride, and went upstairs to the office.

Davis was at his desk. "Where the hell have you been?" "I, my friend, was detecting. I, my friend, have practically solved your case." "Oh, now it's my case. Ok big shot, just what did you detect." Gabriel filled him in on his discoveries, finishing his report to Davis, he said "I left the rain coat and gloves with medical examiner." "Wow! You have been detecting," said Davis. "Let's check the fax machine. See if they have sent any information." One of the other detectives said

"Hey Gabriel, someone left a pile of papers on your desk, while you were out." "Thanks," Gabriel answered. He and Davis spread the papers over the desk. As he read the information, Gabriel experienced that feeling that comes over you when everything falls into place. "Damn!" said Davis. "This is it." "Well, not quite, but we sure are on the right track." The fax read: Carter Melman, age 42, height five foot, ten inches, approximately 190 pounds. Male, caucason, brown hair, brown eyes, incarcerated at Florida state prison March 1997 through July 2004. Has suspected ties to Miami mobsters. Melman was friendly with Jason Sanders and Reggie Richards during incarceration. Played weekly ping pong games, and they were on the same team for the tournaments played between cell blocks. "

What we have here is a full blown conspiracy" said Davis. "After we get the raincoat back from the ME maybe we can find out where it was purchased, and whom is the owner." "Ok," said Gabriel. "Let's go to the captain. We are going to need to put Melman under surveillance and Jason Sanders and maybe Nancy Johnson as well." They went into the captain's office. After they made their case, the captain said.

"I don't know, all of that could all be a coincidence. Just because they were in jail together, doesn't mean there is a conspiracy there. I can't authorize personnel to go to the Keys. We will have to observe them in this immediate area." "If this leads down to the Keys, we are going to have to call the state police." When Gabriel left the office, he was greatly depressed. What a shitty job, he thought. Well Gabriel, thought, I'll keep tabs on him, while he is in the area. If he leaves, I'll deal with that when it happens.

Gabriel decided to go home early. "George, I am overwhelmed, home two nights in a row," said his wife. After playing with his daughter for an hour, he read her a story and tucked her into bed. George sat with his wife watching

TV , than after they had gone to bed. George wanted to make love. His wife said "can't we just talk?" "Talk about what? Come on I finally get a chance to be home and you want to talk. "His wife looked at him and said, 'I don't think I want to be a cop's wife any longer." They lay together, George answered, "maybe it's time for me to quit. I could get used to this kind of home life." His wife said "well George, I don't know if I want to do this, any longer. I think it is too late for us, or at least me." George laughed, "Wonderful, I make an effort to come home and now it's too late."

The following morning Detective Gabriel drove to Laurie's old house neither Jason's or Nancy's cars were in the driveway. He sat in his car, deciding what to do. While he was thinking, he caught sight of that gorgeous redhead on Jensen's boat. She just had on a blouse tied at the waist and the bottom of a bikini, she was playing with the dog. Man, Gabriel thought, that girl is a knockout.

As he sat there she approached his car. Well, she sure isn't shy, walking up the road in a bikini. "Hey detective, how are you doing? Are you spying on us?" "Hi Katie, No, just checking some things out." Katie smiled "you mean like my outfit?" Gabriel could feel the color rising in his face. Katie laughed. "You should come over and help Nick out, I think we are wearing out the poor guy." "I don't think I could be much help in that department," he stammered. 'Oh, Detective, we could teach you. I am a very good teacher." "Well, I am a married man" he said. "Some of my best students were married men" Katie answered. " Any way I came up here to ask you a question, detective." "What is that?" He asked.

"Well, if a girl wanted to buy a gun for protection, what would you recommend?" "Katie, guns are dangerous things. Have you ever fired one?" "No, but I bet you could teach me all about it. Guns I mean."" So what should I buy?" She asked. "Well, for you, I think a Smith & Wesson, '"Horton Special"It's a 44 caliber, 6 shot. It has a 3 inch barrel, so it isn't too big for a girl like you." "Oh detective, I have never seen one too big for me", smiled Katie. Gabriel blushed again. Katie asked. "Can we go get one, now? I'll put on a pair of shorts." "Tell you what. If you wait until tomorrow, I'll take you to buy one, and teach you how to use it. We'll go to the department range" said Gabriel. "Why detective, how sweet!" Katie squealed. giving him a big hug through the window. "I'll be waiting. What time?" "Somewhere around nine or ten," said Gabriel. "Good, come down to the boat and knock. That's where I stay." 'OK, I'll see you tomorrow." Gabriel admired her body as she walked away. Wow! What a girl. Gabriel thought, I'd better move the car, if she saw me, Sanders can also see me. He moved the car up to a side street and waited there. Soon, Jason came by in his car, pulled the car into the drive way and went into the house. Jason stayed in the house.

Gabriel growing tired of the wait, decided to go back to the office. Nick watched Katie walk out to the street and speak to someone parked in a car he then realized it was detective Gabriel. As she returned to the boat, he wondered what they had been talking about. He was on the phone with a friend connected to the Miami FBI trying to get some help deciphering the code." Sure Nick, fax it down to me. I'll get someone to run it through the computers. How have you been? I haven't seen you since we worked that missing person case together, what five, six years?" "Oh, ok." Nick answered. He gave him a quick run down on the week's past events. "Christ, Nick. I thought Pompano was a quiet little city."

His friend was special agent James Biker. They had been friends growing up when they both lived in Melbourne. Now James was a mid level agent working out of the FBI Miami office. "You know, Nick, that money is federal property" he said. "Yeah, big deal! I am not after the money. Some one killed a person very dear to me and they are trying to pin the murders on me." "I want to find out who it is, and I think the money is the key to everything." "You are probably right" James answered. "It is either money or love or in these times, dope. I'll try to have an answer by tomorrow. Meantime keep your head down, buddy." Nick answered "I intend to do just that."

CHAPTER NINETEEN

THE FOLLOWING MORNING, DETECTIVE Gabriel decided to take the day off. George drove over to pick up Katie. He was wearing a light blue golf shirt and tan shorts, topped off by a Marlins hat. Gabriel walked down the dock, stepped onto the boat and knocked on the door." Is that you, detective? Come on in, I'll be just a minute. Katie called to him. "Sit down and have a coffee." George went into the cabin, Katie was pouring coffee into a mug," Good morning detective, cream or sugar? "No thank you, it's fine black." "You look very nice, this morning detective, why I think you're blushing .Hey, can I call you something besides detective." "My name is George." 'Great, I'll call you Georgie, OK?"

"Sure, fine are we ready?" "Yeah, do I look OK Georgie?" Katie was wearing a pair of pink short shorts and a pink halter top." You look wonderful, he said. Katie gave him a big smile. As they walked across the lawn, Katie took his hand. Katie said, "Let's take my car. It's very warm and we can put the top down. It's the kind of day that I could drive around stark naked, letting the warm air rush over my body." George let that image pass through his mind. "You drive , Georgie." said Katie. He adjusted the seat for his height, drove out of the driveway as Katie settled herself in the seat close beside him.

"You look nice, Georgie, you have really nice legs" said Katie.. Said Katie. "They could use some sun, you'll have to come to the beach with me." George asked Katie, "Do you sunbath topless?" "Sure, don't you? answered Katie. George couldn't help but laugh. He pulled into a strip mall on Federal

Highway, they walked into a gun shop arm in arm. The proprietor greeted them.

"Good morning detective Gabriel" he said, looking at Katie. "Good morning young lady. What can I do for you.?" "H I Bart." said Gabriel. "This young lady is Katie, she would like to purchase a gun." Well, we certainly can help you do that What do you have in mind" I have a small .22 Derringer that you might like. Katie turned to George. "You pick it out Georgie, I really don't have any idea." Bart raised an eyebrow when he heard her call him Georgie. Gabriel looked un comfortable. "Bart, lets look at a snub nosed .38 Smith & Wesson." "Perfect, said Bart. He went over to the glass topped casee in the rear of the shop, they followed him over. He picked up the blue metal pistol. "Here , hold it , see how it feels." Katie held the gun, "Not bad, I thought it would be heavy" George took the piece from her and looked it over, He worked the mechanism, six shots. The he spotted a .9mm Ruger P95. "How about this one?" "Katie hold it, is it too heavy?" asked Gabriel. Bart said, "That might have a strong kick." Gabriel answered, "Not much more than a .38 and it's more accurate with ten shots." Katie said, "It's not any heavier than the other one." George said, "We'll take this and two boxes of ammo, plus a cleaning kit and how about something to carry it in while we are traveling in the car."

Bart produced the ammo and kit. He went into the back and brought out a black leather case "This might do. I don't think a guy would carry a piece in this, but it would do just fine for a lovely lady." Katie gave Bart a dazzling smile.. Bart cleared his throat, "Is that all right?" "It's perfect." said Katie. Bart rang up the sale. "Normally you would have to wait seven days, but with the detective vouching for you we can waive that." "You'll vouch for me, won't you Georgie?" Katie asked. Katie paid with a credit card and filled out the necessary forms. George took the package. "Let's go, thanks Bart." "Bart answered, "It's been my pleasure, detective." Katie took George's hand and they left the store. They got into Katie's car. George drove west towards the everglades .Along the way, he stopped at a sporting goods store. He purchased ear protectors and three or four targets. When George came out of the store, Katie was sitting in the car with her head back and eyes closed. Her red hair was shinning in the sunlight. *What a beautiful girl thought George.*

He got into the car started the engine and pulled onto the road. After passing two strip malls, and an apartment building, the landscape gave way to scrub pines, a few cabbage palms and high grass. George pulled onto a dirt road and drove into a clearing under some mangrove tees. "We will practice out here, it is more private." "Where are we Georgie?" "Almost to the everglades, but the ground is not swampy and we can shoot without disturbing anyone." Katie got out of the car stretching her arms and legs. "OK teach, let's do it." "First, let me show how to load the gun. Make sure there is not a bullet in the firing chamber. Then push the magazine in from the bottom. Release the safety and you are ready to fire. Let me set up some targets .said Gabriel. He set one at fifteen, twenty five and then forty yards.

"OK, now when you aim hold the gun steady. Aim for the center of the target, than squeeze the trigger gently. Want to try?" Katie said, "Show me first." George shot off a couple of rounds at the forty yard target. "Oooo Georgie, you're good. Now let me try." Katie aimed the gun, George corrected her stance a little as he did this, Katie moved closer to him. He could smell her hair. "Try it" he said. She shot the first shot and jumped back. "Wow that kicks." "Just hold it steady" he said, reaching out to straighten her arms. Katie leaned closer to him pushing her body against his. George said "Shoot!" Katie squeezed off a couple of rounds. "Hey, that was pretty good. Try it again." She fired ten shots, emptying the magazine. "How was that Georgie"

"You are doing really well." said George. He took a magazine and showed her how to reload. She leaned closer to him so that she could see better. Gabriel handed her the gun turned her around and raised her arms into the firing position. He was standing close behind her. Katie took aim, wiggling her bottom up against him. George felt himself becoming aroused, he was breathing heavy. "Oh detective, is that another gun that I feel." George moved his hand up, cupping her breasts. Katie, without flinching, fired off another ten rounds. Turning to George, she tilted her head up and kissed him. She said, "I think I got it, you know the form and all." George pulled her closer and kissed her again. He was becoming more aroused. Katie put her hand on his crouch and squeezed. "We may have to do something about this detective." "Katie, I'm sorry, I did not." Katie stopped him. "So that's the kind of guy you are, teasing a girl like that. It's a good thing I am out of bullets." Katie, I'm married, I shouldn't be doing this." *'You're married?'* Katie squeeled, than burst out laughing at the look on his face. Katie led George over to the car, They kissed some more, George removed Katie's top caressing her breasts. Katie got a blanket from the car, pulling George down beside her. She unzipped his trousers, fondling him. Removing her shorts, she slid him into her.

Afterwards, as Katie and Gabriel were laying together on the blanket, a shot rang out., spraying up dirt as it hit the ground nearby. George said, "Katie, get down, behind the car." Another shot kicked up dirt, only closer. George said to Katie, stay here behind the car." He scrambled and rolled over the ground to get his gun. Another shot rang out. George answered fire with three shots. The next shot pinged off of Katie's car. "Damn you, that's my car!" Katie shouted and stood. "Take this you lousy bastard." She fired ten rapid shots, spreading in a wide arc .The culprit yelled and started to run toward the everglades. George fired another round of ten shots after the fleeing figure. The detective took off running after the shooter.

The man ram up an embankment into the mangrove trees, with George close behind. The shooter turned and fired three or four shots at George. One caught George in the shoulder, and he fell dropping his gun. George was hit in the left shoulder. "Shit, that hurts!" yelled George as he scrambled for his gun. The gunman saw George fall and was approaching him for a kill. Katie came running up, firing as she ran. The gunman fled into the trees. "Ws that you're wife, Georgie? Wow." George looked at Katie standing next to him, stark naked. He started laughing. "Well, I'll bet that form will make the magazines.

You screw ball, I don't know who that was, but he either wanted to kill us, or he was pissed that I was getting laid." Katie said, "I think I got him, he was limping." George looked over at Katie. 'Are you OK?" "No, I'm pissed off. Here I was all mellow and feeling great. Than that bastard started shooting. Hold me a little while Georgie, I'm scared." George held Katie close beside him in the car, calming her down

Katie said, "Georgie, you're hurt, you're bleeding. Oh Georgie, are you OK? We have to get you to a doctor, quick." 'it's OK, It's a flesh wound, it's just bloody. It's not serious. We'll patch it up. If we go to a doctor it will have to be reported and we will have to explain what we were doing this afternoon." "We'll have to get you home and fix that. I'm an excellent nurse. I've had first aid training. Who do you think that was Georgie? Do you think that he meant to kill us?" George answered, "Maybe he was just trying to scare us." "Well he sure in hell did that." answered Katie.

"Let's get you bandaged and get some food. George backed the car out of the clearing and with Katie snuggled up beside him. It wasn't until George was driving back to the city that he thought about his wife. My God, she would be devestated, not to mention furious .She didn't seem to want to be married to him any longer. Who knows, maybe, Naww, Katie was ready for a good time, nothing more. Katie moved closer to George. "Georgie are you alright?" George said, "I feel lousy, should I tell my wife?" "Relax Georgie, we don't have to get married or anything. We just had some hanky, panky. don't beat yourself up." As Katie talked she was cleaning George's wound.

She finished and bandaged the shoulder. "There good as new almost. Who do you think was shooting at us Georgie?" "I don't know, it could have been someone who happed by and saw us naked and screwing and wanted to have some fun. They missed pretty close, maybe intentional." Katie laughed, "I'll bet they were surprised when we started shooting back." George joined her laughter, "I don't think it had anything to with the case." Katie said, "That's good, I wouldn't want to think someone was stalking us." George drove them back to Nick's

CHAPTER TWENTY

NANCY AWOKE THE NEXT morning from a deep sleep, she checked the clock, it was ten, later than she had wanted to sleep. tired, She got out of bed, walked into the bathroom and turned on the shower. Nancy let the hot water cascade around her, it felt so invigorating running down her body. After a half an hour, Nancy was starting to feel revived; she turned off the shower, than as she reached for a towel, she felt it being pushed in her hand. Nancy wiped the water from her eyes.

"Jason! What are you doing here?" "I thought I might dry you off. I got here too late to wash your back, unless you want to get back in the shower." "Never mind, you just keep your hands to your self. What do you want? Why are you here? Stop gawking at me!" "Why baby, I missed you last night. You left me without a note or anything. I thought we would be making wild love last night.' 'Jason, remember, its business." "Oh I remember, we are partners, except now you seem to be doing a solo. What's up baby?" "Nothing, I just had to take care of some business at the gallery and decided to stay here last night. No big deal." Jason looked over at the night stand and the papers sitting there. "Is that your gallery business?" "Yes, Why?" "Well, while you had that lovely body in the shower, I kind of looked around. And here were these papers and a map and cash." Nancy said. "I told you, I had some business to take care of for the gallery. The money is a deposit for a sale on a painting."

"Yeah?" "Then what is this paper on an Orlando FBI letterhead? "'Oh that. A friend of mine did some research for me .He is an agent up in Orlando". "Bull shit! You got this out of the safe at the pottery shop." Nancy felt a chill, suddenly she was scared. "How did you know I went to the pottery shop?" 'It's in my interest to know what you do, I watched you." "You did not said Nancy. I picked these up Sunday." "Were you the person that tried to strangle me? What's going on Jason?" "That's what I want to know. Where did those papers come from?"

"All right, Jason. I found the papers Sunday in Laurie's safe." "I didn't know Laurie had a safe," said Jason. "I guess she didn't trust you very much" answered Nancy "Look, said Nancy. I just got in late last night. I had a friend look them over. I don't know what the result was, I was going to call you and go over the papers together." "Good," said Jason. "Let's go over them." "Do you want some breakfast first?" "No!" "I have to put on some coffee. Let me dress, wait for me in the kitchen." Nancy put on a shirt, tied at the waist and a pair of shorts .She went down to the kitchen and put on the coffee. Jason was drinking orange juice direct from the carton. "Ugh! Use a glass, Jason. ""Oh I don't have any disease." "Well, you are not home. Use a glass" Jason closed the refrigerator. He poured a cup of coffee. Nancy poured one for herself. "Ok! Let's look at the documents," said Jason.

Nancy pulled out the papers and spread them on the table. One paper contained Sam's hand writing. It said. *We ran this little puzzle through the computer. It will run every conceivable combination of the words until they make some kind of sense. Here is the result. The Money is buried in the Keys at Mile There are numerous combinations of mile markers.98, 89, 99, 77, 78, 76, 68, it depends on the significance of the numerals. If they count left to right, front to back or together .As far as the other puzzle. The meaning of that puzzle will depend on which mile marker the riddle is referring too.* Jason said. "They did know where the money was! I was right!" "What do you mean? You were right?" "Uhh it was just a hunch I had." "How did you know about any money" asked Nancy? "Laurie would not have told you about that. Is that what the killer was after?" "Jason, what did you have to do with all of this?"

Jason said "Don't ask questions. You may not like the answers." "You have been holding out on me", said Jason. "If I hadn't surprised you this morning, you would have split." "Jason, "You know that I can't do this by myself. The feds said that it was at one of those markers, but they didn't specify which one." "Let's try to find the marker, if we find the mile marker we will find the money." "I don't think my partners are going to like that" said Jason. "What? I thought I was your partner. Who are the others?" "Don't get excited baby, I owe some money to some friends for financing my business." "Yeah, well that comes out of your half, not mine." "Sure, sure baby, there is plenty to go around." "Jason, how much do you think there is?" "I don't know, the estimate is around ten million dollars give or take a million. There is plenty for everybody.

He asked, who did you talk to about this, can you trust him?" "Oh just a guy I know." "He is a federal agent, right?" "Yes." "What did you tell him?" "Nothing, in fact, I drugged him at dinner, took him to his room, stripped him and put him into bed. When he wakes up, he'll think that he got laid. I even left him a thank you note." "Well, I don't like cops, they are too nosy, especially federal agents" said Jason. "He just might come after you. I think we have to get to the Keys as soon as possible." "Jason, I know you were in jail with Reggie, he told me all about it. You set up the whole deal to meet with me, and Laurie, just to get the money."

Jason laughed. "That's what charm is for, now I am going to get the money plus I got to have sex with the two sisters and the young daughter." "Jason! You bastard! You did seduce that girl, how could you?" Jason just laughed." It's too bad she left. She was a great lay, almost as good as her mother." Nancy slapped him hard across the face. "If I had a gun I would shoot you right on this spot," she said.. He walked over and put his arms around Nancy. "Aww come on. We are going to be rich. We can have a great time." He held her tight, lifted her chin and kissed her. "You bastard," she cried.

Jason looked into her eyes, while putting his hands around her neck. He saw the fear grow, then the panic. Nancy kneed him in the groin, scratching and clawing at him, than struggled free. She ran from the room, through the house to her bedroom. Nancy slammed and locked the door. As she picked up the phone to call the police, Jason was banging at the bedroom door. The door splintered under his pressure, Jason grabbed the phone out of Nancy's hand. She beat at him with her fists, she kicked and scratched. Jason swung a fist and connected with her head. Nancy went down, Jason sprang on top of her, pinning her to the floor. He grabbed a pillow off of the bed. While Nancy struggled, Jason pressed the pillow over her face. Keeping her pinned with his body her exerted pressure on her mouth until she stopped resisting Jason removed the pillow and looked into her lifeless eyes.

Damn I didn't want to go that far. She pissed me off. Now! Damn. Well I would have had to get rid of her eventually. Ok, Think, Jason. What would Carter do? Hmm, should I mess her up with a knife? No, I can't stomach that. I'll just get rid of her body. Jason pulled a spread off of the bed, wrapped it around Nancy's body. Jason lifted the body over his shoulder and carried it downstairs. After backing the car into the carport, he hoisted her body into the trunk of his car. Before Jason left, he pulled her car into the back of the carport, then after locking the house drove out of the driveway. Jason went south on U.S. 1 until reaching Indiantown Road. He turned west towards Lake Okeechobee, there were numerous drainage canals back there. He planned to dump her body in one of the canals. The alligators would take care of most of the body. Jason was close to Port Mayaca, when he saw a swampy area with a deep ditch running into it.

He pulled over into the trees. Opening the trunk, he pulled the body out and removing the spread dumped Nancy's body in the swamp. He pushed the body further out into the canal. Jason went back to the car he carefully pulled out of the muck. Being as careful as possible pulled onto the firm ground. There were some tire tracks, but he didn't disturb the area too much. Nobody would see anything out of the ordinary. Fishermen and trappers pulled into these spots everyday. No one would think anything out of the ordinary took place. If he was lucky, they would not find her body for days, possibly weeks. Than she would be hard to identify and really there was no one left to even report her missing. Jason stopped at service station off of the turnpike. He used the rest room, washed his hands and face. He ran the car through the car wash to clean the mud off of the tires and fender, filled the gas tank. Then Jason drove home.

CHAPTER TWENTY ONE

LATER IN THE AFTERNOON, George Gabriel dropped Katie off at her house. He was not ready to go home, he wanted to think about the days events and what it might mean to him. He decided to check on Nancy Johnson, he had not seen her for a couple of days. He drove to Jupiter on I95, than east towards the ocean, then north on U.S. 1 to just past the inlet. When he found her house, he pulled the car into the driveway. She had a beautiful home, two floors along a quiet shady street. Everything looked very calm and peaceful, there were royal palms and tropical plants bordering the walkway to the front door.

Detective Gabriel rang the bell, it echoed through the house, there was no answer. He walked around the house to the pool area, there were no signs of anyone. Gabriel walked back to the carport and checked out the car. Nancy could be out with friends. Still it seemed strange for the car to be parked so out of the way. As if someone was trying to shield it from the street. George had a growing suspicion that something was not quite right. He decided to call the local police. Gabriel identified himself, and explained the situation to the chief The chief of police said to Gabriel," well I don't know, detective, you have no proof of any wrongdoing. "Yeah, but I have a gut feeling, we already have one of her relatives in the morgue." "Ok," said the chief, "I'll send a car over and we can look around. What is the address?"

The patrol car arrived about five minutes later. Two patrolmen got out the older of the two approached Gabriel. George showed his badge. "I would like to look around inside, think we can manage that? Sure" said the cop, he turned to his partner, "Get the lock picks out of the car. The chief said it was ok, because of the circumstances, but I am not comfortable breaking into a citizens house." "Well, you never know, we could be saving a life said George. "Give me the picks, I'll do it." He shortly had the door open. That was easy. George and the two cops entered the house.

Gabriel walked into the tastefully decorated living room, stopping to admire the paintings on the walls. They were Nancy's, she is a pretty good artist thought George. The older cop called from the kitchen, "Detective, you might want to look at this." He turned to his young partner. "Do not touch anything." Gabriel walked into the kitchen. He noted a pot of coffee on the counter, the warming light was on. There was an orange juice container on the table. It looks as though someone left in a hurry. "Let's check the rest of the house. Be careful, someone could still be in the house."

The younger policeman checked the downstairs bedrooms, they were empty. The upstairs contained the master bedroom, a dressing area and the master bath. George and the other policemen looked in the bedroom. The bed was unmade, a pillow was lying on the floor. There was a damp towel on the bathroom floor. "We better get the crime inspectors over here, don't touch anything. Either Nancy Johnson left in a big hurry or she was forced to leave. Her car is still in the carport." The patrolman called the chief, explained what they had found. "I'll be right over, I'll bring some help."

Detective Gabriel asked the chief, "Can I get an APB on Nancy Johnson? She is an attractive blond, about five foot three, maybe twenty eight." "Yeah I'll get it on the air right now. Say, Gabriel, do you think we can get some help from Broward county?" "Although I should call the state police." "Whatever you need, if you want Fort Lauderdale to help, just mention my name." "You said she had a relative in the morgue, who is it?" "Her sister , she was tortured and murdered." When the crime lab truck arrived, George asked for a copy of any evidence they might find. "Check that car also, it looks suspicious where it is parked." George thanked the chief and the patrolmen for their help. Gabriel headed home on I95. His gut instinct told him that Nancy was dead. The last time he had seen her she was with Jason Sanders. I am going to drive to the Keys, and check Jason's alibi for that Friday night. Somehow he knew that Sanders was involved in all of this mess.

Katie came into the house, as Nick and Kristie were getting ready to have dinner. "Hey Katie, you hungry?" 'I'm famished," said Katie. She sat at the table with the two of them. Kristie had made a salad of fresh greens, vegetables and some slices of fruit. Nick had roasted a chicken on the grill. "Mmmm good stuff," said Katie. Kristie asked "Where have you been all day? How did you work up such an appetite?" "I was out shooting with Georgie, Uhh detective Gabriel." Nick started to laugh. "You call him Georgie?" "Sure, that's his name." "I'll bet his wife doesn't even dare call him Georgie," said Nick. "There are probably a lot of things his wife doesn't dare do" Katie answered .Kristie looked over at Nick. "Oh boy!"

"What?" asked Katie, "Don't be so nosy." "Nothing," said Kristie, ""But I know that look, and I don't think Georgie had a chance today." "Well, maybe not, but he sure enjoyed it, little sister." "Katie," said Nick. "If you were dressed like that he did not have a ghost of a chance." 'Hey!' said Kristie. "What is that supposed to mean, Nick?"

The phone interrupted the conversation. Nick picked it up. "Jensen here. Hey Hi Jim. You have an answer already?" "What the hell is going on Nick? Are you having a scavenger hunt up there?" Biker practically shouted. "What? What are you talking about, Jim?" "The computer guy that I sent the code to, said he just did one of those for an agent in Orlando. The exact same words, the exact same code!" "Oh Oh," said Nick. "Do you know who he did it for?" "Yeah!" "One of the agents in Orlando. The guy was real pissed off, seems the woman slipped him a mickey and left him in the hotel room." "Who was the woman, do you know?" Asked Nick" I'm not sure, the agent in Orlando was a guy named Sam Smith." "Do you think he would tell me, if I asked?" "I don't know, he was really pissed" said Jim. "Thanks Jim, thanks a lot." "Yeah, well this sounds like it could be something important," "Don't leave me with egg on my face. You keep me informed, especially if you find the money. I don't want to arrest you and your client." "Ok thanks, Jim. I'll keep you posted. If anything pops, by the way. What did you come up with?" "I sent it to you overnight, you should have it tomorrow." "Thanks again, buddy."

Nick hung up. Nick said. "I think we have trouble." "What happened?" Both girls asked. "Someone else has the same code and got someone at the FBI Orlando office to decipher for them. Than they drugged his drink and left him in a hotel room." "Who?" asked Kristie. "He said it was a woman, she slipped the guy a mickey and took off with the answer." "It had to be Nancy." "You mean the sister that stayed here with you for a couple of days. Do you think she saw it in the diary" asked Katie. "No, she would have taken it with her. I'll bet she found something down at Laurie's pottery shop," said Nick. Kristie said," If she has it, then Jason would know about it. I have not seen him since yesterday or Nancy for two or three days." "The answer will be here tomorrow," said Nick "We can worry about it then."

Kristie, smiled. "So big sister, how was your day?" "I bought a gun and Georgie taught me how to shoot." "What? Let me see the gun" said Nick. Katie showed him the gun." That is a formidable weapon. Be careful" said Nick.. Kristie said "You know how to shoot, you used to hunt with that gun nut boyfriend you had when you lived in Michigan." "I never shot a pistol, they are different, Georgie showed me every thing." "I bet that he did" answered Kristie "Why do you want a gun, Katie?" asked Nick. "Well I think it is time I moved back to the house and I thought I could use the protection." "When are you moving back home" asked Nick? "Oh maybe tomorrow, I am going to take Rex with me OK?" "Sure, he just mopped around all day because you did not take him with you." " I did not want him to get hurt"

Katie said. "Well maybe I'll go pack. What about you Kristie?"" I'll stay as long as Nick wants me." "Kristie you can stay as long as you want." "Ok, I'll see you guys in the morning."" Do you need any help packing" asked Nick. Kristie said "Looking for one for the road, Nick?" "See," said Katie. "It is time for me to go. Christ, Kristie, I don't screw him every time I see him" She stormed out of the room, "Come on Rex." Nick said, "What was that all about, Kristie?" "Yeez, I'm sorry, that was a stupid thing to say. I'll go talk to her," she headed down to the boat.

Nick thought, it might be better if both girls left. It was getting too domesticated around the house. Next thing they would be shopping together at Publix. He had to admit to himself that he had grown very fond of Katie the past few days. Nick tried to be careful around Kristie, he thought that she might be suspicious about his feelings for Katie. He could hear the girls laughing and giggling. Well, I guess everything is Ok between them. They came into the house. Katie grabbed Nick." We decided to give you a going away party," she said. They dragged him towards the bedroom There they did a sexy threesome.

Nick awoke the next morning with the two women lying beside him. He eased himself out of the bed so he wouldn't disturb them. Went out to the kitchen and put on the coffee. He fixed a breakfast of fruit, juice, hot oatmeal and bagels with cream cheese and strawberry jelly. He let the smell of fresh brewed coffee wake the girls. They each struggled into the kitchen, looked at the breakfast and then at Nick. Katie said. "We must not be doing it right, he is supposed to be exhausted, not us." Kristie said. "Well, *he* definitely is doing it right." "My God I think it rejuvenates him." They sat down to breakfast. Nick poured each a cup of coffee and gave each one a kiss.

"That was some going away present," he said. "I only wish you could be here for my birthday or Christmas." Katie said "I'll be here. Ok, Kristie?"" We can do this every once in a while, huh?" "Sure Katie, as soon as I can gather my strength back." While they were having breakfast, Gabriel drove into the driveway. Katie looked guilty. Kristie said," For god sake Katie you two didn't get married yesterday did you?" "Why don't you care about how I feel, about you doing Nick." "That's different, we're sisters, we share." Gabriel tapped on the door. "Georgie!" said Katie running to the door. She opened it and gave him a sweet kiss. Gabriel came in looking a little embarrassed.

"Hi George," said Nick "Sit down, have some breakfast." George looked at Katie. "Do they know?" "We are all friends here, Georgie. I share everything with my sister. I mean everything." Gabriel looked even more uncomfortable. "You get used to it," said Nick. "Have some breakfast." George took a bagel and some strawberry jelly. Katie poured him a cup of coffee. "Just like wifey," she said. They all laughed. "I am moving back home, Georgie., George said "Well not to put a damper on the mood, but Nancy Johnson is missing. I went to her home yesterday, and she wasn't at home. The local police and I went inside and it looked as though she left in a hurry or someone had forced her to leave. The coffee warmer was still on and she had not cleaned up the breakfast area or bedroom." "Maybe she is just a slob" said Katie. "No, this looked like she was interrupted at breakfast.

I drove to the Keys late last night and checked Jason's alibi for that Friday night. He had stayed there but did not arrive until three in the morning." "So, he doesn't have an alibi" said Nick. "No, he doesn't." "Good, maybe Davis will get off of my case." "Well, we haven't found Nancy or Jason for that matter, Nick. I think this is all about Richard's money or the money he was supposed to have hidden." Just then a Federal Express truck stopped out front. The driver brought a package to the door. Nick signed for the package, took it over to the table. "Detective, this might prove interesting. This is the code we found in Sara's diary." "What?" "What diary?" Nick explained "Sara had a diary that Katie found in my office on the boat. Sara had hidden it in the back of the drawer, under some old papers. It had a code of some kind, It looked as if her father had sent it to her. Anyhow I got a friend at the FBI Miami to get a computer guy to break it. When he sent it to him, the guy blew his mind. It seems as if an agent in the Orlando office got him to do the exact same code about two days ago.

We think Nancy got this guy to break it for her. Then she slipped him a mickey and left him in a hotel room." Gabriel laughed. "Let me see it" the detective said. "Wait a minute, said Nick, we found it, we are not going to be left out of this. I don't want any of the stolen money. I just want to know who is behind this thing, who is trying to frame me." George said, "Relax. This isn't going to be police business yet. My lieutenant doesn't want me to pursue this outside of Fort Lauderdale, and it already leads to the Keys. It involves the circumstances in Jupiter, however that turns out. So I decided to take some vacation time and work on my own. Not to mention, what a great time I had being off yesterday." Everyone burst out laughing.

"Hey," said Katie. "Maybe Georgie and I can go to the Keys for a couple of days, you know and investigate things." They laughed again. "Well, I am going back to the Sea Breeze, either today or tomorrow. I want to verify some facts, and see if I find Jason. I am hoping that Nancy and Jason are together, searching for the money." Nick opened the package and spread the contents on the table in the Florida room. Nick unfolded the paper. It read: *Nick here is the computer result. It runs the message numerous times until it has wording that is readable. We deciphered the message to read as follows: The Money is buried in the Keys at MileNow the part we can't figure is the numerals. They could be: 98, 89, 99, 77, 78, 76, 68It depends of the significance of the numerals in the code.* Gabriel said, "I knew it was in the Keys somewhere." Nick was sitting there, thinking. Wait a minute. He raced out of the room and picked up a sheath of papers. "These are e-mails from Sara's father. I am sure I saw something in there about either numerals or mile markers." They each took sheets of paper, and studied them. After about twenty minutes, Katie said. "Look, this piece says the numerals mean nothing unless they are consecutive." They all reached to read the original code. "It is mile marker 68" said Kristie.

Nick looked at the map, "I think that is on Indian Key." "There is not a whole lot on that Key it is pretty deserted, just a few mobile homes, a couple of restaurants and two or three small motels, a nice stretch of beach, but that's it." Katie said. "There may be a whole lot more on that Key than you think." "We need a plan," said Nick. "Let's put our heads together." Katie said. "Well I need a break". She stood up and taking Gabriel's hand she led out the door toward the boat, looking back she said. "We are going to put our heads together. We'll be back." They and Rex disappeared onto the boat.

"How does *she* do it?" asked Nick. "I would think you would know by now", said Kristie. Watching Katie and George walk to the boat, Matt had an odd feeling, *could it be jealously? Am I falling for Katie,* he thought? Nick and Kristie started planning to go to the Keys. You and I could take the boat. We need to look for a beacon and that will be on the water. We will need to stock the galley, and I am going to have to fill those tanks. I haven't done that since our date that night. Well we did not do too much boating that night, at least not moving. Nick thought about that dress "Bring that black dress with you, "We might get to go dancing." "Sure," laughed Kristie. "You want to know how *she* does it" Just then George and Katie came back from the boat into the Florida room. Kristie said, how did you make out with you heads together? "Well, we made out," said Katie. "Katie, pretty soon, you and I will have to share," said Kristie. Gabriel blushed. Katie said. "Sure, little sis, we can help you out."

Nick, exasperated said. "Ok let's get to work." Gabriel said. "Ok, just be aware, these are dangerous people. I think the killer is an ex-con, a professional. I think he was just supposed to get information, but he went too far." "Well how about Jason having sex with Sara, wouldn't that have caused trouble with Laurie?" asked Nick. "I don't know, Nick, maybe they shared too" answered George. Now it was Nick's turn to blush. "I don't think Laurie was the kind of woman to share, especially with her daughter." "Maybe it did cause some trouble, but at this point we don't know what happened." "Ok, we can assume that they also know that the money is buried in the Keys, but they do not know the exact location, unless they had information regarding the numerals. W e seem to have the only information As far as the mile markers are concerned."" We think that we know the location. I think that Nick and Kristie should go down on the boat to Indian Key for starters, check for a beacon somewhere." "Katie will go down in her car, I'll follow along. I don't want them to see us traveling together. They know me. But I don't think they know her, and it would be best if she is not known."

"That will leave Katie alone," said Nick. "I'll be Ok, I'll have my gun and Rex." George, said. "I'll keep a close eye on her." Katie said. "I hope you can get more than your eye close. After all the Keys are very romantic and I don't want to be there all alone." Gabriel just shook his head. They all laughed. "Ok, let's get ready for the trip tomorrow." Katie said goodnight and she and Rex went to the boat. Katie settled into bed with Rex by her side. She wanted to be fresh for her drive and her adventure tomorrow. She climbed into bed naked and was soon fast asleep.

Later that night, Katie was awakened by Rex. He was growling, looking out towards the cabin. She lay still, "Hush Rex" she whispered. Katie could hear someone moving things around in the cabin. She felt the boat move as the person moved over to the side. Someone was on the boat. Katie was scared, *Oh Shit!* Than she remembered the gun. She quietly reached over to the table by the bed, and got the Ruger. She slipped out of bed, and silently moved to the doorway. Katie stepped through the doorway, it was pitch dark and Katie could not see anything.

Suddenly an arm grabbed her around the neck. Katie was paralyzed with fear. "Drop the gun sweetheart." Than the intruder chuckled. Well this is a treat" the intruder said, "Naked as a jaybird." "What do you want?" asked Katie "Just be quiet, and do as you are told." Katie started to struggle and yelled "Let me go!" At the sound of her voice, Rex charged at the man. Growling and snarling, Rex leaped on him. The intruder started to run and jumped over the side into the water. Katie picked up her gun and fired five or six rapid shots into the water. She shined a light on the water, but she did not see anyone. Katie stood on the deck of the boat, tears running down her face. "Good boy Rex, you saved me, good boy," she caressed his large head.. Nick came running onto the dock. "Katie are you OK!" He shouted, panic creeping into his voice. "Katie! Where are you Katie!" "I'm ok Nick, Rex scared him away." "Rex? When did Rex learn how to shoot a gun?" "No, before. The guy had his arm around my neck and Rex went after him. He was great, my hero." Katie was sobbing, "Oh Nick, hold me, please." Nick held her in his arms.

"It's Ok Katie, it's over. Do you think you hit him?" "I don't know," Katie said she started to shiver. Come inside the house, Katie," Nick wrapped a blanket around her. Kristie arrived out of breath. "What happened? Is Katie all right?" "Yes, she is fine, she was just scared." "What was all of the shooting about?" "It seems there was an intruder on the boat. Katie and Rex chased him, he jumped overboard." Kristie took her sister in her arms. "Come on Katie you and I are going to sleep together tonight." Katie said 'Bring Rex too, he saved my life." The two women and the dog went into the house to bed. Nick looked around with the flashlight, but did not see anyone. He locked the boat and went into the house.

CHAPTER TWENTY TWO

THE MORNING DAWNED SUNNY, warm and breezy. It was mid way through January and the impatiens had blossoms of bright red and yellow. Katie having packed her clothing, stopped in the house for breakfast, was anxious to leave. Nick was not happy about her going alone. "I think she should go on the boat with us. It's not safe for Katie to travel to the Keys alone .Someone out there thinks that we know where the money is and they are not going to stop until they find it." " Oh, I'll get Georgie to follow me until I am on the overseas highway. He can make sure no one is watching me".

They agreed last night that Katie would stay at the Sea Breeze on Islamorada, a short distance north of Indian Key. Islamorada is a tourist area for Floridians. This is the Jersey shore for people that live in Florida. There are a string of motels, bars, clubs and marinas along both sides of the Island. The warm Atlantic on the east, and Florida bay, mixing with the waters of the Gulf of Mexico on the west. The Keys are a necklace of islands running south from Miami, then curving west. Key West is actually 80 miles south Naples on the Florida's west coast. Islamorada is about 20 miles south of the central edge of the everglades. Floridians call the Keys below Key Largo "down island."

Katie would have a two hour drive, depending on the traffic. It was a Wednesday, so she would be ahead of the weekend crowd. As Katie loaded the car, Rex was settled in the right front seat, and had already curled up in a ball and was snoozing. Katie as usual was wearing a limited mount of clothing. Nick wondered aloud how she had ever survived a Michigan winter. Katie said "She drank a lot to stay warm." Katie wore a pair of pale yellow short shorts and shirt, knotted just below her breasts. It showed off her, tan flat stomach and every thing else above it. She had her red hair tied back and the top down on the convertible. George was there to see her off. He looked as if he wanted to jump in Rex's spot and go with Katie. He checked to make sure she knew where she was heading. "Yes, I know I am going to the Sea Breeze on Islamorada. Yes, I have everything, including my protection, meaning my pistol, and Rex. I'll see you there, some time. Now you just make sure none of the bad guys are following me. I'll call you guys when I am settled in my room. Georgie, try to sneak in my room once in a while. Wear a disguise, like Groucho "Marx, or Harpo. See ya."

Katie waved as she drove off. George said to Nick. "Well I am going to get on the road myself. I have your cell number, so you and I can keep in touch. I hope our plan works, but I don't want to expose these girls to any danger, unless we have to." Nick answered, "I am with you George. I think we should grab the money and let them find us. But you are the boss." George drove off, in the borrowed Audi, while Kristie and Nick finished preparing the boat for the trip. Nick had already gone to the marina and filled each of the tanks with 100 gallons of diesel fuel. He packed the food, and the clothing. Before leaving he unfastened the dingy from the boat at Laurie's dock and tied it behind his Bay Liner. After making sure that everything was secure in the house and garage. Kristie and Nick untied the lines and slowly pulled away from the dock.

Heading south on the Interrcoastal, they passed under the Commercial Boulevard bridge, then the Oakland Park bridge, past Sunrise Boulevard, on under the 16th street Bridge. On this trip, they would cruise past some of the most expensive homes in North America. Past Fisher Island, Key Biscayne, into the Biscayne bay to the first of the Keys, named Elliott key, just north of Key Largo. Key Largo is the largest of the Keys and the first stop for tourists on the road. It is a beautiful trip by auto, but a sensational trip by boat. The true beauty of the keys can only be appreciated from a boat. The sea is calm and blue green. The little islands are lush with vegetation. Nick could only try to imagine how they must have looked to the first people to see them. They took their time. It was about a sixty mile trip to Islamorada. Nick's estimated time of arrival was about six hours. It was a warm, beautiful day, the water was about 75 degrees. Since they were not in any hurry, once they moved past the heavy boat traffic of Miami, they pulled in a small, quiet cove.

Kristie anchored the boat and both of them went skinny dipping. There was a wonderful feeling of freedom, swimming in the warm waters, free of clothing. Kristie and Nick swam for awhile and after sunning themselves on the deck, they went in the cabin. After getting under way once more they cruised down the Atlantic side of the Keys. The water was deeper on the

Atlantic side, there were not as many reefs as on the western side. They pulled into the Islamorada marina about seven that evening. It was just getting dark. Night comes late in the tropics, even in January. Nick made the boat fast, and hooked up to the water and electric. Kristie fixed dinner, while Nick served drinks for the two of them. Kristie said, "Oh, Nick, this is like a honeymoon. This is so romantic." Even Nick had to admit it was pretty romantic. Ah, the magic of the Keys. After they had finished dinner, and cleared and washed the dishes, they went ashore. Nick and Kristie headed to the Holiday club. There was music and dancing. It was a pretty good crowd for the middle of the week.

While they were dancing, Kristie said. "Nick! That man at the bar, don't look. He is the man that molested me at the house. Let's get out of here!" Nick danced Kristie over to their table, left some money for the drinks, and. they returned to the boat. Nick called George on his cell phone.

George Gabriel had a lot on his mind. *What was he doing? This is crazy, I am supposed to be on vacation. Why am I going to the Keys? To follow Jason? To follow Katie? For a little vacation? If it's for a vacation, why am I not bringing my wife and child. He seemed to have forgotten he had a wife and child these past couple of days. That sure isn't the George Gabriel we all know and love.* His cell phone interrupted his thoughts. Gabriel opened the phone, "Gabriel," he answered. " Kristie just saw the man that attacked her at the house, he was at the bar in the Holiday club," Nick sounded excited and a little nervous. Gabriel asked, "Is Jason there? Where is Katie?" "No I haven't seen Jason. I haven't seen Katie either. She should be here by now. What the hell is going on George? Did you follow her to the highway?" "Yeah, nobody was behind her, she is probably taking her time. She has the dog, maybe she had to stop. I'll call her "said Gabriel.

Before Gabriel could call Katie, his cell phone rang." It was Lieutenant Shaw. The lieutenant was talking fast, "George, I know you asked for some time off, but you have to get up to Port Mayaca, right away. That's somewhere around Lake Okeechobee. I think it's near Indiantown road. The police in Martin County found a body in a drainage canal near the swamp. The sheriff gave us a preliminary description of the body" We think it might be Nancy Johnson. Also we got the analysis of the blood on the raincoat and gloves. It was Laurie Richard's. We sent a search team with Davis to the trailer park.

I need you to go to Okeechobee and check out that body. Then Martin County is sending a team to the Johnson house in Jupiter. I need you to get over there ASAP." The captain hung up.Damn! George dialed Katie's cell number. There was no answer as Gabriel headed for the Turnpike, turning North, he had the blue light flashing, forty five minutes later he turned west on Indiantown road. A short time later, Gabriel saw the gathering of patrol cruisers, the crime lab wagon and ME truck. The detective parked along the side of the road. He walked over to the group of cops and investigators, flashed his badge, he asked "Who is in charge?" A county sheriff answered. "For the time being, me." "I am, Sheriff McKenzie, Larry McKenzie," extending his hand. "Detective George Gabriel, Broward County police." "Sheriff, we think this murder is connected to the woman killed in Pompano Beach." "That so?" "Yeah, can I look at the body?" "Sure, detective, they are about finished with it." "It's not in real bad condition. It doesn't look as if she has been here very long. Luckily, two fishermen snagged it sometime this morning." "The body was sunk in the mud, looks as if an animal or two had nibbled a bit, but if they hadn't found her, when they did, the body may never had been found in this swamp." "If a gator had dragged it back to its den; well."

George, went over to the body, he said to the ME, "Can I have a look?" The ME pointed over to the corpse. They had turned the body on her back. George stared down at the mud splattered body of Nancy Johnson. She had on a pair of shorts. The body had been slightly mutilated, probably by animals. The ME said. "She was a pretty woman, what a shame." "Yeah!" said George. "There is a lot of that going around." "Sheriff, that is Nancy Johnson, her sister was murdered in Pompano Beach a week ago this past Friday." "Dang," said the sheriff, "Guess I'd better call the state police." "What was the cause of death?" The ME answered. "She was strangled, and maybe smothered no sign of rape or sexual molestation, but we can't be sure until we do the autopsy." Gabriel got back into the Audi. "Nice ride detective," said the sheriff, "Things must be going well in Broward County." Right! George waved.

As he drove off, he called Katie on her cell phone. No answer. *Damn it. Why doesn't she answer, Where was she? I hope nothing has happened to her. I'll never be able to forgive myself.* While George drove, he thought about Katie. *Was she just screwing around with him? Yeah, probably. Why was he getting himself so involved? Enjoy it while it lasts. You have already cheated. So you either keep playing around as long as Katie wants to, or you straighten out and be a good husband. Right now, it is too easy, screwing around. Yeah, but no one knows better, than he, that eventually you usually pay for your sins. One way or another, you pay. Someone had killed Nancy. Why?*

Gabriel opened his cell, called Orlando information. Five minutes later he had special agent Sam Smith on the phone. "Look, detective, I don't want to discuss it. It is FBI business." "Sam, Nancy was killed either yesterday or the day before." "What! Who killed her? What happened? Damn it. Shit!" "I don't know, but I have my suspicions. I think she was killed for the code." Smith said "Somebody is after that money. We got the same deal from Miami. This has become serious, I'd better inform the chief," said Smith.

Gabriel arrived at Nancy's home, the Martin County detectives and Medical Examiners were busy searching the house for evidence. George introduced himself, than spotted the two policemen he had spoken to at the house a couple of days ago. The older of the two addressed Gabriel. "We haven't found anything new. They are checking to see if any of the fibers and collected hair match anything on the computers." Gabriel said, "Check with Fort Lauderdale. Check to see if anything matches what they found at the murder scene in Pompano." "We'll do that detective." Gabriel looked around the house, but did not see anything that he had not observed the other day.

George went outside and called the lieutenant on the cell, after giving him a report, he got in the Audi and drove back to headquarters. He drove the Audi into the garage, hung up the keys, walked into the building and went to his desk. Davis, busy typing, looked over at him. "Where the hell have you been?" "I was up in Jupiter. They found Nancy Johnson's body in a swamp." "What? Jesus." Davis said. "Well they linked the coat with the blood to a Carter Melman. That's the guy who was staying in the trailer?" "Right," said George. "That's who was driving the Mercedes, that's who attacked Kristie Ryan at the house." "Where is he? Don't know, he left town," said Davis. George pulled out the report they had ran, when he checked on the car. "Melman is connected. He was in prison with Jason Sanders and Reggie Richards Christ, it's the Miami mob, it's the money. They are after the money,"

CHAPTER TWENTY THREE

GABRIEL THOUGHT ABOUT KATIE. *Damn! Carter had a home address in Marathon on the keys. That wasn't very far from Islamorada. Christ he better warn Katie to get out of there. He opened the cell phone, called her number, no answer. Shit! Where the hell is Katie.* Gabriel called Nick Jensen, no answer! Damn it!

Katie and Rex were moving right along, flying down the Palmetto Expressway, going past the airport. She went over to the Turnpike on the Don Shula expressway, and would soon connect to U.S.1. That would take her past Florida City, Homestead, and finally the road through the Keys. She was thinking about the look on Georgie's face as she pulled out of the drive. *If ever there was a look of longing on a man's face, that was it. Katie kind of laughed. She had not planned to seduce him, but when she saw him dressed down, he had a pretty good body. Actually he wasn't bad, all over. But hey, he's married. I never have broken up a home. There are too many single men out there, well not a great many, but if they didn't have to be too young, there were plenty of guys. Here in Florida, you could usually find one with money. They were the guys on their second time around. They had divorced their wife, and were looking for a new model. For the women, it was different, if you were divorced, had a couple of kids, the pickings were few. The guys wanted girls like her. Single, kept their bodies in shape, didn't mind screwing around with the right guy. She had her pick. except for Nick, she really had a thing for Nick. Too bad Kristie saw him first. Well, she really didn't. Katie pointed him out to Kristie while sitting in Mulligans. If she had not had a date with that yo yo, she would have moved in on Nick that night. She was glad that Kristie let her share Nick sometimes. Man, he was good in bed, even with the two of them, he did ok. She wished she was on that boat with Nick, cruising down to the Keys. Boy, I'll bet that is romantic.* Katie thought, *I'd better stop thinking like this, I'll be so horny when I see him, I might attack. Well maybe, George would stop in and ease my desire for a bit. She would have to be careful with George I sure don't want to screw up a nice guy. He really is not my type.*

Rex was making uneasy motions, so she pulled to the side of the road, so that he could do his doggy business. They came into Islamorada about noon. Katie parked the car, checked in to the Sea Breeze, went up stairs to her room. She fed Rex and than he settled in a sunny spot to nap Katie put on one of her tiny bikinis, a sun hat, sun glasses, smeared sunscreen on her body, picked up a cover up and headed for the beach. As she was waiting for the elevator, she noticed an older man looking at her, of course men always looked at her. This one looked kind of different. The elevator came and she stepped inside, pushed the lobby button.

She made her way to the beach, rented a chair and a cushion. As a tip she gave the guy a big smile, and some eyes. He was a blond beachie guy with very white teeth and a tight spandex swim suit. Katie thought maybe she might check out that spandex, or rather what was in it. But for now she settled in to get some sun. She sat in the lounge, removed her top and lay back. The sun felt good on her body, Katie thought, she had better put some sunscreen on the parts she had just uncovered. She sat up and started applying the lotion to her breasts. Katie saw the blond guy watching her and smiled at him, than she lay back to enjoy the sun.

Katie felt a shadow fall over her, and she opened her eyes. There was a handsome, dark haired, muscular guy looking down at her. He gave her a beautiful smile. "I couldn't help noticing you are alone, would you care for some company?" Katie smiled, "Sure, pull up a chair." "Can I buy you something cold to drink," he asked. "Sure, How about a Cosmo?" He looked at the blond guy, "Get us a Cosmo and a Heineken and bring that lounge over here," he ordered. when they were settled, and their drinks were brought to them, He said, "Well here's to?" "Katie Ryan," she answered. "Jason Sanders," he said. What a pleasure to meet you." Katie almost choked. *Jason?* "How nice to meet you." She felt him starring at her and pulled the wrap around her. "That's probably enough sun for today." Jason thought, *now I know where I saw her, she is the girl that's been on Jensen's boat this week. What a coincidence, or is it? Where the hell is Jensen?*

Katie and Jason talked for a while, then Katie said, "Well I have to go upstairs and shower and wash this stuff off of me." Jason, asked "Can I buy you dinner tonight?" "No, how about a drink later, I'll meet you at the bar about nine or so, ok?" "Sure, I'll see you then" said Jason. Katie waved and walked away. She thought there is something familiar about him. Jason watched her go. *I am going to be inside that bikini tonight, or my name isn't Jason Sanders.*

Katie got on the elevator, rode up to her floor, and returned to her room. It was a pleasant room that overlooked the west side. She couldn't see the marina from there, but on her side there were a couple of dive boats docked and a fishing pier. As Katie entered her room, Rex jumped up and ran to greet her. "Ok. Ok. Let's go out." She put his leash on him and took him for a walk around the grounds. While they were walking, she saw that man watching her, Rex was doing a low, warning growl. Katie pulled Rex on the leash and led him back up stairs. Back in the room, she opened the doors to the patio and let Rex lay out there in the air. Meanwhile, she went to shower off the sun screen and salt air. Katie turned on the water, stepped out of her bikini, and stood under the shower, enjoying the hot water. As she was coming out of the shower, toweling the moisture off of her body, there was a wrap at the door. She looked through the peephole, it looked like a bellman. Wrapping the towel around her, Katie opened the door, about an inch, "Yes?" "Miss, these are for you," he was holding a basket of flowers. "Why, who could have sent these? Wait." She went over to her bag, got out a five dollar bill. Turning to the bellman, she handed him the bill, and took the flowers, as she did, she accidentally dropped the towel. "Thank you," she said, gathering the towel from the floor. "No ma'am, thank you!" said the bell man starring at her body. "Opps, Sorry," said Katie" No apology necessary, miss." She shut the door, laughing. I could have saved five bucks. The flowers had a card.

See you tonight, Jason. Hmm that's nice. How did he know my room number? Katie tried to call George on his cell, no answer. Then she tried Nick and Kristie, there was no answer. Katie started to feel a little uneasy. Checking her bag, she saw the black case with the 9mm Ruger. Nick and Kristie should be in the Marina in a couple of hours. Katie would stop by to see them, she would feel safer than. Meanwhile, she got herself ready for dinner, and her drink with Jason. Katie was wearing little black dress similar to Kristie's. It looked as good on her as it did on Kristie. She wore a pair of low heel sandals. She took a light shawl in case the evening air was cool. After a light dinner of a salad and an iced tea, she strolled around the grounds. It was full of tropical flowers and green bushes. There were a lot of Coconut Palm trees swaying in the soft breeze. She took a walk over to the marina, but did not see Nick's boat.

Around 9 p.m. she walked into the bar, as she walked, heads turned. She liked that feeling, she knew she looked stunning in that short, black dress. It emphasized her trim body and her shapely legs. Jason was waiting, saw her coming and escorted her to a table. "You look lovely," he said. He actually meant it. This girl was a knock out. She smiled, thanked him, sat and ordered a drink. "That dress looks sensational with you wearing it," said Jason. "Thank You," answered Katie "And also for the lovely flowers." This guy is smooth, most men say you look good in that dress. giving the dress the credit. He gives the woman the credit for looking good. Katie sipped her drink. She thought, keep you're wits about you tonight, Katie girl. This guy is dangerous. They ordered another drink, Jason moved closer to Katie, their heads were almost touching.

Nick closed the phone, "Kristie come on we got to get moving.George is planning on arriving here in three hours. Jason and his friend are very dangerous. You need a disguise, we have to get you a wig, a pair of sunglasses and a couple of tops. We have to find Katie, now! She could be in real danger." "Nick, what is it? What happened?" "What did George say?"

"They found Nancy Johnson's body in a swamp. Jason is not anywhere around, they think he is down here looking for the money. Nancy had the same code unscrambled by a friend at the FBI two days before we had. Now she is dead." "The man who killed the Laurie is the same man that molested you at the house." "Oh my," said Kristie. "It gets worse. We know he is here in Islamorada." "Nick! If he sees Katie, he might think it is me." "Worse than that" said Nick, "They may think Katie knows where the money is." "They may try to make her tell them where it is." Kristie said, "Let's get moving Nick. What do we do first?" "First, we get a disguise. Then we look for Katie." "Let's get going. Hurry!"

They left the boat and went ashore to search for a souvenir shop. Nick found a shop that sold T-shirts, hats, sun tan lotion, etc. Kristie bought a couple of baggy tops, a pair of sunglasses and a sun hat Then they went into one of the better shops looking for women's clothing. Kristie was looking through the clothing, when she spotted what she was searching for. In the hat department, was a selection of fashion wigs. She picked out a blond wig, not a very expensive one, something women used to cover their hair after being in the surf all day. Kristie tried the on the wig, was satisfied with the look, than paid the clerk.

Putting on a pair of tortoise shell sunglasses, Kristie approached Nick, and asked "Sir, do you have a light?" Nick, surprised, asked, "Is that you, Kristie?" "No, it is somebody else." "Well we should be able to get by with that put on that baggy top to hide your figure." Kristie put on the top, the glasses, the wig and the hat. "Perfect" said Nick, "You look like any other tourist. Let's look for Katie."

They went over to the Sea Breeze motel. Matt stopped at the desk, described Katie to the bellman. The bellman got a big smile on his face, said "Yes sir, she is in room 224. She may be at dinner, at the moment, I saw her

pass by in a short black dress. It looked like she was going out for the evening."
Nick said to Kristie, "She is here all right." They went up to 224 and knocked.
There was no answer, but they could hear Rex barking. Nick tried the door.
It was locked. He looked for a house maid, found one around the corner,
turning down the beds. Pardon me, miss. My wife and I are locked out of our
room, could you let us in, we need to get a wrap for her?" The maid looked
critically at Kristie, then Nick. "Yeah, sure." She opened the door. "Thanks,"
said Kristie, her and Nick, stepping inside.

Rex ran over to greet them, tail wagging. Where is Katie, boy?" Rex's tail
kept wagging. Kristie said "Everything looks ok, nothing is disturbed. Leave
a note for her, let her know her what slip the boat is in." "Tell her we took Rex
with us. She can come get him tomorrow morning." Nick put Rex's leash on
him and they left the room. They went down in the elevator, stepped out and
took Rex walking around the grounds. Kristie sad, "Nick! There is that man,
look." Just then Rex started to growl and snarl. "Easy boy" Nick said. "He
must remember him from the night of the murders." "Nick you should call
George." "He said he was coming down some time this evening." Kristie said,
"I hope he arrives soon." They took Rex for a long walk along the beach, than
walked him back to the boat. Katie was sitting on the chaise lounge waiting
for them. Katie!" "Screamed Kristie you are Ok! Thank God." "Of course I
am ok," said Katie. "Why did you take my dog?" "Very funny, Katie, he was
lonesome, and hungry and whining." Katie answered, "That dog is always
hungry. He is just like a man, wants to sleep with me, always wants to be
fed, than takes a nap." " Look what I bought," Katie held up a lilac colored
case. "Isn't it pretty? It's for my intimate things." She opened it, inside was the
Ruger 9mm."Clever," said Nick.

"All right girls, I think it is time that I gave you a lesson how to get a boat
underway." Nick walked them around the boat, explaining how each control
functioned and how to operate it. He took them below and showed them the
engines, the bilge pump. Now we are going over to get gas, I want to show you
the safest way to take on fuel. "Nick why are you showing us all of this" asked
Kristie? "I have a feeling that things are going to get dangerous. If anything
happens to me, I want you two to be able to operate the boat, we may need a
quick get away." Kristie asked "What could happen to you?"

Nick asked, "Katie what did you think of Jason?" "He is a dangerous
man," she said. "He is used to getting his way. I left him at the bar, I told
him I was going to the ladies room. I came over here looking for you. I didn't
want him to take me back to my room. I did not trust him." "Right, Good
idea" said Nick.. Kristie asked, "You mean, he is still waiting for you?" "Yeah!
Let him wait," giggled Katie. Nick said "Ok ladies let's get underway, Kristie
start the engines. Katie untie the lines and pull up the fenders." The girls did

as they were instructed and with Nick's directions were soon moving away from the slip and across the marina. "Kristie, steer for the Gulf gasoline pier, slowly." Nick helped her glide to the dock, Katie jumped onto the pier ready with the line. An attendant ran over to help. "Allow me, miss, I'll be glad to do that." Kristie said "Katie take off that dress." "Now, right now? Aren't we paying cash for the gas." "Very funny, put on something more appropriate." Katie answered. "All of my things are at the hotel." "I'll find you something of mine to wear" said Kristie.

While they were fueling, Katie put on a pair of shorts and a bikini top, "Is that better?" The attendant pumping the gas, said "It looks good from here." Nick just laughed. These two were a handful. But what a pleasant handful. They cruised south towards Indian key. The girls were running the boat. Just off of the key, they found a quiet, sheltered cove and dropped anchor. They all settled in for the night. Katie asked, "Can I sleep with you guys, that bed is a lot softer than the one in the other cabin." Kristie answered, "If you promise to be good." Katie smiled, "That's a promise. I'll be really good." "I meant behave yourself" said Kristie. The three of them settled in the master suite for the night. Nick was in the middle of the two girls, well it don't get much better than this.

Sometime in the middle of the night, Katie quietly woke Nick. "Shhh, follow me," she led him out side and up on the top deck, she had spread a blanket on the deck. "Lie down here, Nick, just look at all of those stars, it must be a billion of them." "Isn't it beautiful? You can't see the stars in the city because of the lights, but out here it is overwhelming." "Yeah it sure is" answered Nick. Katie lay beside him, "This is so romantic, Nick." Katie snuggled closer to him, she kissed him, Nick kissed her, back, than later they made love. Katie whispered "I love you Nick, I don't know how to tell Kristie, but I am sure I love you." Nick answered, "I love you too Katie. I guess Kristie will be pissed, but I do." They lay together for a while, than drifted off to sleeping in each others arms. The next morning, along with the smell of fresh brewed coffee, Rex awakened them with his warm, wet nose. Oh, Oh thought Nick. I had better get down to the stern deck. Kristie had set out the dishes for breakfast, she poured him some orange juice, gave him a kiss. "Sleep well, Nick?" "Yeah I did, you aren't mad are you?" "No, I don't mind sharing, with Katie, and besides, I think Katie is in love." Kristie brushed off Nick's protests, "Anyway, I needed a good night's sleep after our exhausting trip from Pompano." Katie appeared on deck wearing absolutely nothing. She stretched. "Good morning sis, you're not mad are you?" "She said she could use the sleep after the trip down" said Nick. "Wow! That must have been some trip, maybe you can wear me out on this one." Kristie said, "Katie put some clothes on and have some breakfast." "Rex and I are going for a swim first".

She turned to Rex, said "Come on boy" She dived into the water with Rex right behind her. "Oh this is great! Come on in you guys, it is so warm, Ohhh" Nick looked at Kristie, she shrugged, took off her clothes and Nick and her dove in. The three of them were splashing around, the girls squeeling and playing. Rex doggy paddled around. When they were all tired, they climbed back aboard the boat, Rex got on the boarding platform, shook a big shake, then jumped on board. They lay down on the deck to dry. Nick thought, it's like a porno dream, and I am the star. I am sure I am going to wake up soon.

Nick got up, pulled on a pair of shorts and a T-shirt. He climbed in to the dingy and after un tieing the line, started the engine. "Where are you going?" asked Kristie. "I want to explore a little, see where we are." Nick headed out of the cove into more open water, He was looking for the red beacon that he saw last night. The beacon was on the horizon, probably warning of a reef or sand bar. A flashing red beacon, he timed it, the flash was every thirty seconds. One flash that held for about three seconds. Nick aligned the little boat with the light and slowly headed for the shore. The sea was very calm, as so often it is in the keys. He ran the boat up on the shore, pulled it onto the beach, a little out of the water. Then he walked up the beach, towards the dunes, measuring his steps. As he crested the dune, he could see that the highway was not far away. Nick kept walking toward the road, as he approached the blacktop of U.S. 1, he saw the marker. Mile marker 68. These markers, while used on every highway become addresses in the Keys. A motel will identify its location, such as at mile marker etc. Nick turned and walked back to the skiff, pushed it into the water, started the motor and went back to the boat. He looked for the girls, but did not see them. They were below deck below, studying the charts of the keys, making notes. "Good idea," he said. "You might have to know how to use those." Kristie had some questions about the numerals and notes on the charts. Nick explained that most of the numerals were the depth of the water. Some of the notes would give you compass readings. The easiest way to find your way on the water was by following compass readings. "Let me see the rest of that puzzle, about the beacon."

They all sat together and studied the puzzle. Nick said. "I found the beacon. So if I went 180 degrees, that would take me to shore. If I keep walking, I end up at the road and the marker 68." The girls were excited. "What about the rest of it?" "I don't know yet, we'll have to figure it out as we go." They decided to cruise back to Islamorada, to get some equipment to help in the search. Nick let the girl's skipper the boat. He helped them get the feel of steering and following the charts and markers. Along the way Nick explained the different kinds of markers and bouys, and what they meant. An hour later they pulled into the slip at the marina and made fast perfectly. "Good job ladies, you learn quickly. You will make excellent sailors."

Nick and Kristie went to search for a store selling lamps and shovels. Katie went back to her room to get her things. Rex took another snooze. Kristie found some heave duty lamps, Nick bought some shovels and a used metal detector at the ship's chandler. He also bought a hand held compass Nick went to the gun shop and purchased a long range, scoped rifle. "Do you think we need that?" asked Kristie. "Yes, I expect that there will be trouble and a hand gun will not quite do the job." Nick's cell phone buzzed.

"Yeah this is Nick," he answered. "It's Gabriel, what is happening there?" "Not much, we might have an idea of the location of the money." "I am about an hour away," said Gabriel. "Don't do anything about the money until I arrive. Where is Katie staying?" "She is at the Sea Breeze motel on U.S. 1" answered Nick. "See you soon," said Gabriel. "What doe he mean, don't do anything about the money until he arrives?" asked Kristie. "I did not hear him say anything about the money. It must be the reception down here" "Right" Kristie laughed. Nick said, "Everybody wants to be the hero and find the money. I just want to clear myself, and the money is the key. Find the money and the killers will find us, than we can deal with them."

CHAPTER TWENTY FOUR

GABRIEL ISN'T GOING TO see *me* soon, thought Nick. "Kristie, let's get the boat underway, we need to be back at that cove before dark." "What about Katie?" "She can keep Gabriel busy while we see if we can find out what all the fuss is about." Kristie called Katie. She told her the plan. "See you soon, bye sis."

"Yeah! Bye is right." Katie answered. Katie closed the phone, she turned to face Jason and his creepy friend, Carter. "Well, what did sis have to say, asked Jason?" "Oh just that her and Nick were going on a midnight cruise, somewhere romantic, so they could screw." "Is that where you were last night?" "Yeah! We enjoy cruising out into a quiet cove, and doing a three some." "Well I ought to belt you one for dumping me last night" Jason said. "I am not used to a girl doing that, just walking off, leaving me sitting at the table." "I am a different kind of girl." Answered Katie. "Right," said Jason,

"Look, we are all down here looking for the same thing. the money, so tell us did you find the money?" "I don't know what you're talking about." "Young lady, hear this" .said Carter. "The Richard's woman found in the house next door to Nick Jansen, said the same thing. That is what will happen to you if you do not cooperate." "Right, what will happen to me if I do?" shoot back Katie. "We might be inclined to just send you on your way." "Look, all that I know is that it is somewhere on the Keys." "Where, I don't know, you have the same information that we have." "It's buried at some mile marker, but no one knows where." "Other than that I don't know anything about it."

Carter looked at Jason, "We are wasting time, she knows something about the money or she would not be here, neither would her sister or Nick Jensen." Carter said, "Let me talk with her, see what happens." "I don't want her all messed up" said Jason, "I have plans of my own for her." Katie was scared. "Wait a minute Jason," she said as she moved towards him. "This doesn't have to be nasty. You are a good looking guy. You certainly don't look like the kind of guy that would have to force himself on a girl. Let's talk about this over dinner. I'll tell you everything I know. I'll tell you where we were last night."

Nick and Kristie stowed the equipment that they had bought aboard the boat. It took about an hour of cruising to reach Indian key and another fifteen to twenty minutes to locate and align the beacon. Nick carefully backed the Bay liner into shallow water as far as he dared. He and Kristie loaded the equipment into the dingy and went ashore. The sun was almost down, the light almost gone, just some red reflections in the sky. Once ashore,

Nick walked back to the highway, turned and sighted the beacon. He decided to try the easiest way. Flipping on the metal detector, he walked towards the beacon. Walking slowly, with Kristie holding the light, he listened for any kind of click. Nick walked, and listened, he heard nothing. Nick turned and walked back in the direction that he had from the road, except he moved over a foot. Kristie asked "How far did you walk the first time?" "I don't know? maybe a hundred and fifty yards." "Try a hundred,' said Kristie. "It said a hundred y. that might mean yards.' "Ok," said Nick, "let's measure it from the shore with the carpenter's tape we brought with us."

Kristie held the tape, as Nick, holding the other end, walked until she said, "Stop, that's 100 yards." Nick stopped, moved the metal detector around the area, but did not hear any beeps. "Ok, now what?" asked Nick. They read the instructions by the light of the lamp. "Maybe the alignment is off with the beacon" said Kristie. Nick said. "I just don't know." "What the hell is a Kennedy foot?"

Katie said to Jason, "I'll tell you what I know, which really isn't much, then we can have a cozy after dinner match. What do you say?" Carter said. Jason, "Don't be stupid. You can screw her anytime you want, I'll even leave you alone with her. I'll wait for you down at the bar." Jason, smiled. "No, I think I like her idea."

"Look, you want information from her, I either do it my way or no way," said Carter. "Who the hell are you to tell me?" "I'm running this operation." "No you aren't Jason I just got off of the phone with your partners They are tired of waiting, they want results, now I am making the decisions now. Here you call them," Carter flipped his phone over to Jason. Jason made the call, "Hey look, what's all of this about Carter being in charge here?" "Yeah, I know, but...but, Ok, we'll wait here for you after we're finished." Jason looked beaten. "Well Ok, Carter, but God, she has such a beautiful body." Carter answered, "I know I saw her twin sister, I can't wait to work on her."

Katie looked scared. "Come on Jason, don't let him do this." "Shut up, I'll decide, what's going to happen." Jason said "Too bad you are strange, Carter, we could have a nice threesome." "Not interested, Jason. You do your thing, then I'll do mine." Jason turned to Katie. "Ok, let's start with you on your knees." Katie started to cry.

Mean while on the beach, Kristie and Nick were searching for the treasure." I have been thinking about that," said Kristie. "Katie thought Kennedy was on some kind of money but she didn't know what it was." Nick said "It's a fifty cent piece!" "Wait go one hundred yards, east, and s. a Kennedy foot." "Could he have meant south fifty feet? Go south fifty feet!." Kristie looked at the compass, than measured fifty feet, she stood on the spot. Nick slowly walked back towards her. He could not hear a ping or click. "Damn! Well maybe we should dig." "The papers said something about down a fathom by half." "A fathom is six feet, let's dig down three feet."

Kristie put the lamps in a spot so that they would illuminate the area where they wanted to dig. Nick positioned the lamps so that the light could not be seen from the road. They started to dig. "Try to be quiet, sound carries, I don't want anyone getting too curious." Kristie said, "I am going to call Katie and tell her." She punched in Katie's number. No answer. "That's funny, I would think she would be waiting for a call."

They dug together, silently. The sand kept shifting back into the hole, so the work was slow. They kept digging, after an hour they were at three feet, but no sign of the money. Nick moved two feet to another area, nothing. "We'll dig one more hole, than start again tomorrow," said Nick. "This is tiring." He started digging again, the sweat was running down his face. Suddenly they hit something solid, Nick dug more, hit it again. "Oh Nick! We found it" said Kristie, "We found it!" "Let's see what we found," said Nick.

Jason walked towards Katie, he grabbed her, ripped her top off f her and forced her to her knees. He stood over her, unzipping his pants. Jason yanked Katie's head back by her hair, "Say ahhh" he said laughing. Katie was crying, she was scared, thinking to herself, I am not going to get out of here alive.

Suddenly, there was a loud pounding on the door. "Open this door, this is the police, open up now! We will break in the door!" "Shhh," Jason said to Katie. She leaned forward, opened her mouth and bit down hard on Jason. "Owww! Damn you bitch! "Katie hollered. "Help! Help!"

The door splintered, and slammed open and George Gabriel rushed into the room, pulling his gun. Jason was standing over Katie holding his crotch. Carter was over in the corner of the room. Katie hollered. "Look out, George.

He has a knife." George turned towards Carter, just as he threw the knife. It hit George right in his chest. He fired a shot as he fell.

Jason ran out of the room as Katie ran over to George. "Georgie! Georgie! Are you hurt?" "Georgie talk to me." Gabriel lay, blood soaking his shirt, he still held his gun. Carter holding his shoulder, started towards Gabriel. Katie grabbed the gun from George's hand, than she shot Carter, once in the chest, than two times in the head. Katie put the gun back into George's hand.

Georgie, tell me you are Ok, please, please." She picked his head up. Katie picked up the piece of clothing that Jason had ripped off of her, she pushed it into George's wound to stop the bleeding. "Come on Georgie, come on, talk to me." George looked up at Katie, "Oh God Katie, are you all right?" "I am fine Georgie, let me call an ambulance. Just wait right here." "No, No, don't leave me, stay here with me. Hold me, Katie, hold me." "Georgie it will be all right. I think the bleeding has stopped." Gabriel was having trouble breathing. He knew he was drowning in his own blood. He knew he did not have long to live.

He reached out for Katie, "Go home now, Katie he gasped, these people are dangerous. You are a beautiful, wonderful girl. The day we spent together was one of the best days of my life." George Gabriel, breathed his last breath, and died in Katie's arms. She gave him a kiss, and gently lowered his head. *What a shame, What a nice guy. Carter was dead over in the corner. Where the hell did Jason get too?* Katie looked around the room, went to the door and looked out into the hall. no one seemed to be coming, maybe no one heard the shots. She then quickly packed her belongings and left the room. Katie calmly walked to her car and drove off of the parking lot.

Back on the beach, Nick finally got the rusty lock to yield. He opened the first suit case. It was filled with hundred dollar bills, ,all neatly packed and banded. The smaller case held bonds and certificates. Nick looked over at Kristie. "Bingo!" Kristie smiled.

"Oh Nick, we're rich, we're rich." "We can't keep it Kristie, we have to return it to the FBI." "Why? They don't even know we have it, Nick." "Let's get this onto the boat. We can discuss it later" said Nick. They carefully covered the hole that they had dug. Then Nick dragged the two suitcases down to the dingy. "We better just carry one at a time. I don't want to risk losing any of these cases overboard." After putting one suitcase in the dingy, Nick left Kristie to guard the other and motored out to the boat. He than came back and they brought the other one aboard the Bayliner.

"Kristie, find somewhere to hide this stuff." "We don't want anybody to have it until we're ready for them to have it." Nick went back to the beach, found some brush and carefully covered all of the tracks that they had made. When he was finished, the beach looked as if it had never been disturbed.

We had better get the boat back into the cove, out of sight of the beach. They pulled into the cove and dropped anchor.

"We'll go back to Islamarado and pick up Katie tomorrow." Kristie stashed the money in the locker under the bunk in the aft cabin. "Nick, we could cruise the islands forever, we would never need a thing. We would not have a care in the world." "No, except how close the FBI is behind you" said Nick. "They don't even know we have the money, it you don't tell them," she answered. Nick let the conversation pass, no sense arguing over nothing. It wasn't their money, *True, no one knew they had it or where it was hidden, but is stealing previously stolen money the right thing to do?*

ust than, Kristie's cell phone chimed. "Hello., Katie?" "What's wrong?" "Where are you?" She listened. "My God! Are you all right?" "Where the hell are you?" "All right, keep coming south until you get to Indian Key. We'll meet on the highway." "Just as you come over the bridge into Indian Key, there is a bar called Mac's, you'll see the sign, we will be waiting for you inside. Be careful, Katie. Kristie closed the phone, and started crying. "What's wrong? What happened?"

They were waiting for Katie in her room, Jason and that man who molested me. George Gabriel showed up just as Jason was starting to mess with Katie. He burst into the room. The man killed George with a knife, but not before George shot him. He was only wounded, but Katie finished him off, with George's gun" "My God!" said Nick, "Where is Jason?" "Katie doesn't know, she got out of the room and to her car, now she is headed south."

Katie was driving fast down U.S. Route 1, she checked to see if Jason was following her. He left so fast and so much was happening, that she lost track of him. She didn't want to meet him, Jason was surely in a foul mood. Katie concentrated on her driving, this was a two lane road with water on each side, and she didn't want to miss the bar where Kristie and Nick were waiting. Katie thought, *I'll feel a lot safer when I am with Nick. My feelings for Nick are getting serious.*

A half hour later, Katie drove over the bridge into Indian Key, she saw the sign for Mac's Bar and pulled onto the parking lot. She moved the car over behind some palm scrub, so it wouldn't be noticeable from the highway. Katie hurried into the bar. It was an old time island bar, strictly for the locals on the key. It had a bare wooden floor, a bar in the middle of the room, surrounded by booths and tables. There were a couple of video poker machines over in the corner. Katie was looking though the darkness for Kristie and Nick

They were sitting in a booth in the corner. Kristie motioned to her, "Over here, Katie." She slipped in beside Kristie, gave her a hug and than started to cry uncontrollably. "Easy Katie, you are Ok now, you are with us, don't worry." "Oh God, Kristie, Georgie is dead, that sweet man is dead and it's my fault. It's my fault. He had a wife and a child, now that poor child does not have a father." "Calm down Katie." said Nick. "He was doing his job. Jason was wanted for murder." "That creepy man killed him," said Katie, "He threw a knife into George's chest." "George shot him before he feel and I finished the bastard with George's gun. I only wish I had shot that no good slime, Jason." "He was trying to force me to suck him, when George broke in." "I bit the bastard, hard." Nick started to laugh, than Kristie, soon all three were laughing. "This is just nerves, it isn't funny." "We know Katie, we know." "Let's get you back to the boat.

Where is your car?" "It's in the parking lot." "We'll hide it until we figure what to do. You girls should be very careful, Jason will be looking for the money, he is bound to show up here sooner or later. I just hope that we are gone by the time he and his friends get here." Nick went out to Katie's car, he drove down the highway about a half of mile. Right between highway marker 67 and 68 he found a secluded area between the road and the beach. He parked the car and covered it with some palm fonds. Nick went back to get the girls, and they headed down to the beach, pushed off the dingy, started the motor and went back to the boat. They climbed aboard the Bayliner.

Katie asked, "Can I take a shower?" "I feel really dirty Nick." "You would have to use all of our fresh water, why not take a swim to wash off the grime. The night is pleasant and the water is warm." "Ok" she said, stripping off her clothes and jumping into the water. "Last one in gets sloppy seconds". Rex jumped in with her, and soon all of them were all paddling around in the warm, calm water. Kristie said "Katie, I told Nick we could do this forever with all of money that we found. Wait till you see it how much we have." "So Nick, how about it?" "Katie, we really have to return the money, although this surely would be a pleasant way to live." "Come on Kristie lets, convince him we should stay and live the good life". The two girls swam over to him, grabbing at him, rubbing against him, "No fair," said Nick. They led him up onto the diving platform and inside the cabin. Than they used all their feminine wiles to convince him that they were right..

CHAPTER TWENTY FIVE

JASON RAN OUT OF the room, without looking back, *Damn, Carter probably killed that cop.* Jason went to his room, his hands were shaking, *God damn. What happened? This is bad shit. That cop was looking for me, could they connect me with Nancy's murder. If the cop was looking for me, and he is dead, the cops sure as hell will think that I killed him.* Jason, his hand shaking, poured himself a drink.

As he sipped the drink, he tried to get his thoughts together. *Carter is probably dead, there were three more shots, after I left the room. If Carter doesn't call, the partners from Miami will send some guys down here to take care of the loose ends, meaning me. I sure don't want to be here.*

Jason was thinking fast, *I have fake passports, I have plane tickets out of Key West. Ok, stay calm. Let me look at those papers that I took from Nancy. They say that the money is buried in the Keys, but they don't know exactly at which mile marker. I'll start with the lowest marker first and work my way south. One way or the other I'll find that stash. I have come too far to walk away.* Jason finished his second drink. *He thought, now if they find the bodies of Carter and the cop tomorrow or even this evening, they won't let anyone leave the motel. A cop was killed, they will be all over this place, and soon. I am leaving now. I am just going, I am not checking out.*

Jason pushed his things into a duffle bag, picked up the papers and left the room, lights still on, TV playing. He went out the back way to his car, started the car, pulled onto U.S. 1 and headed for mile marker 68, wherever that was. While Jason's was driving, the cell phone rang, he answered, "Yeah!" "Jason,

Sam here, we haven't heard from Carter, we can't reach him. Is he with you?" "No, I not sure where he is, there may have been some trouble." There was a long pause. "If he isn't with you there *is* trouble. We ordered him to stay with you." "Where are you, Jason?" "Uhhh, right now, I am on the road. I thought I would look for some of those mile markers, you know... see what I could find."

"You pull over at the first motel you come to, than call us. We are sending you help." Sam hung up.Jason thought, *Shit! Help, yeah, help to size me for a concrete coffin. I should go straight to Key West, I have a ticket and a passport. But I have to take a shot at that money. I had Laurie killed, I almost had Jensen's girlfriend killed. Then I killed Nancy. That's a lot of risk and work with no pay off.*

Jason crossed the bridge into Indian key, drove past a dive called Mac's bar. Farther down the road he saw it, *Mile marker 68! Damn! This could be the place.* Jason drove into the parking lot of a small motel about thirty yards off the road. *I'll stay here tonight, tomorrow I'll look around, see if I can find anything that gives me a clue about the money.*

Jason rose early the next morning. What a beautiful morning, the sky was clear, the Atlantic Ocean was calm and placid, the sun glistened off of the water, a warm, balmy breeze was coming off of the Gulf. Jason asked the desk clerk where he could get breakfast. The clerk directed him to Mac's bar. Jason drove the short distance, parked and entered Mac's to order a coffee and a pastry. "You have any bagels," he asked? "No." Jason finished the coffee and walked a half of mile to mile marker 68.Looking out towards the ocean Jason began pacing off to the east. He studied the paper. Find the red beacon. Standing on the beach he searched for the beacon.

Jason heard a small motor, of either an inflatable boat or a dingy. It was getting closer. He instinctively moved back into the sea grass and scrub out of sight. The skiff pulled up to the beach and a girl got out and pulled the dingy onto shore. Jason thought that she must be claming or fishing.

As the girl walked past him, Jason was stunned. *It's that bitch Katie! The one who had bit him last night*.He was still sore, where she had bitten him. The girl walked by without seeing him. Jason waited until she could not see him, than followed her. Katie walked up to Mac's, and went inside. After she had placed her order, she went over to play a poker machine. Jason quietly moved up behind her. Katie suddenly felt something hard pushed against her back.

"If you make a sound or move, I will put a bullet in your spine." muttered Jason. "Now, just calmly walk out of the door with me, tell that jerk behind the counter that you will pick up your groceries later."Katie, frightened, thought, *Oh no! That bastard Jason has found me!* Katie called to Mac, "I'll be right back." When they were outside, Jason grabbed her arm, "You bitch, I ought to kill you, just for biting me last night." "You would have, if I hadn't done that" said Katie.

"Ok smart ass, now we'll see who gets bitten. Call the other bitch, your sister." "Is Jensen with you girls?" Katie hesitated, "Is he?" asked Jason as he shoved the gun into her ribs. Katie nodded her head. "I should have known. I am going to put a bullet in that bastard" Jason muttered. "Call your sister, tell her what happened, get Jensen on the phone." "Than I'll do the talkng."

Nick Jensen opened his eyes to the bright sunshine, *wow, what a night. Those girls are dangerous. Man, this is like a dream, it is unbelievable.* He went out to the galley, where Kristie was cleaning up. Pouring himself a coffee, he asked "Where is Katie?" "She went to Mac's to get some beer and cold cuts. We thought we would have a picnic on the beach, it is such a beautiful day." Nick said, "I don't think that was wise. We don't know where Jason is, he could be heading this way. I was hoping we could get away from here, and back to Islamorada by noon or so." "Well, you know Katie," said Kristie. "She does whatever she wants to do." Kristie said, "While she is gone, I am going to change the sheets, and straighten the galley. Why don't you swab the decks?" "Aye, Aye captain," said Nick.

Kristie's cell phone beeped. "Hey Katie, what's up?" "What?" "Damn it, shit, darn. Nick you had better listen to this."

Nick grabbed the phone. Jason said, "I have that red haired bitch." "I know you have the money, if you want to see her alive listen to me. I'll meet you in Key West. I'll call you when we get there". "You be there with the money or you will find this little bitch will be gator bait." "I want that money, no more bull or somebody dies."

Jason walked Katie over to his car, "Get in, bitch, no bull shit." Jason snapped a handcuff on her wrist and one on seat belt. They drove south on U.S.1 heading for Key West.

Nick closed the cell phone, "Jason knows we have the money, he also has Katie. Let's get the boat under way, we have to get to Key West." Nick pulled up the anchor, while Kristie started the engines. They moved out of the cove into the open Atlantic. The farther out in the ocean they went it became choppy, but it still was a calm ocean. Nick checked the fuel gauge, and calculated that they had enough to reach Key West, but barely. He did not want to waste time getting serviced, he was extremely worried about Katie. Nick ran the engines a little faster.

"You really like Katie, don't you?" asked Kristie. "I mean, more than you like me." "I don't know, Kristie." "Sure you do, you just have to admit it. Don't worry, I am not pissed or anything." Nick said, "I wonder if I should call the FBI? What good is the money, if Katie is dead." "Well, you could run away with me," said Kristie. Nick gave Kristie a dark look. "Just kidding, Nick, just kidding." "I love my older sister, almost as much as you do."

Nick said nothing, just opened the twin mercury engines to full throttle.

Jason and Katie were passing through Marathon, when Jason's cell chimed. "Yeah?" He listened, "Well I am looking a little farther south in the Keys" "I'll be back in Indian Key in about an hour." Katie yelled, "He is heading to Key West." Jason back handed her across the mouth. "Shut up bitch," he said. Jason speaking into the phone, "It's nobody, just a slut I picked up. Carter? I found out that a cop shot him in the hotel. I think he came to arrest him, they must have found some evidence concerning those two women in Pompano." "Where? Ok I'll be there this evening."

A half hour later they crossed the bridge into Big Pine Key. They were a half hour or forty five minutes to Key West. Katie thought to herself, *I have to get away from Jason, he is becoming desperate. Whoever was on the phone really scared him. If they catch Jason before he meets Nick, he will probably kill me.*

Katie said "Jason I have to stop. I have a feminine problem that I need to attend to" "Ok, but I am coming in with you, I don't want any tricks." Katie said, "Oh that should be fun. Suit yourself. Does that mean I get to watch you pee," "Shut up," said .Jason as he pulled off the road at a garage. He yelled at the attendant, "Do you have a rest room?" The man pointed at a door around the side of the building

.Jason said, "No funny stuff, Katie, just walk naturally." They entered the rest room, it was not exactly the Ritz, but it did have an enclosed toilet. She asked, "Can you un cuff me and let me in the toilet, give me that much privacy." Jason looked around, checking that there were no windows. "Yeah! Sure" He was not anxious to watch her do what she needed to do. Katie reached for her handbag. "Not so fast," he said. "Let me see what's in there." "I just need this," she said she pulled the pink case out of her hand bag. Katie went into the enclosure, "Can I close the door?" "Yeah, Yeah! Just hurry!" "Ok! Ok! Man, this isn't my favorite thing to do either."

Jason stood at the door, looking outside. Katie quietly slipped the Ruger out of the case, as she took the safety off, she flushed the toilet. *Ok, Remember, what Georgie taught you,* Katie thought. Jason said, "Aren't you finished?" "One more minute, I have to fix myself a little."

Suddenly, the door banged open, Jason yelled, "I knew it, you bitch!" Katie aimed the gun at Jason's head, shot and missed. Jason quickly grabbed Katie's hand, twisting until the Ruger fell to the floor. Katie kicked Jason hard in the shin. "Ow! Damn it, I am going to kill you," Jason howled. Katie than aimed a kick at Jason's crotch. Jason was too fast, moving swiftly aside, he punched her in the side of the head with a fist. Katie was staggered, dizzy, she stumbled backward, her head hit the metal wall of the enclosure. She turned and aimed another kick at his groin. Jason put his gun under her chin. "Stop now or you are dead. Now!"

Katie still dizzy from the blow to her head, her nose bleeding, stopped struggling. Jason picked up the Ruger, he laughed, "This is perfect, I can use this to kill Jensen." "You lousy bastard!" Katie spat at him. He smacked her in the face again, splitting her lip open. "Now walk slowly out to the car and no funny business. I promise I'll shoot you and that dumb looking mechanic." They went to Jason's car and got in.

Jason turned to Katie, "Now, listen, anymore bull shit and I will kill you and dump you in a swamp. If I have to kill you, I can't trade you to Jensen for the money." "If I can't trade you, I'll just kill your sister and than I'll take care of Nick Jensen I will do anything to get that money, understand?" " Yes," Katie mumbled. "Good, now that we understand each other, call Jensen."

"When he answers, give me the phone." Katie called Nick, "Hey Nick, its Katie, here schmuck face wants to talk to you." Jason threatened to punch her, than took the phone. "Jensen, put the money into a suitcase, when I get into town, I'll let you know what to do next." "If you want to see this bitch alive, you will do as I say" said Jason. "Ok, said Nick, just don't hurt her" Later, Katie and Jason arrived at the edge of town, Jason said, "There is a McDonald's, I need to take a leak. If you want to come in and watch, that's OK, if not I am going to handcuff you to the steering wheel. If you cause any commotion, I'll come out and shoot you and anybody who tries to help you, got it?"

"Yeah, go ahead, I don't want to see anymore of you than I have too." Jason hooked her to the steering wheel and went inside. Katie thought *this is really amazing, all of this over money. People will do anything for money. If we don't give him the money, he will kill us. He has already killed Sara, Laurie and Nancy. George has been killed and the evil bastard, Carter. The trick is to give him the money without being killed ourselves.* Katie leaned her head back on the seat, the day was warm, the sun felt good on her body. She thought about *how good it felt to make love with Nick Jensen. That night on the boat under the stars had been wonderful. Katie thought, God I hope Nick doesn't get hurt, I don't care what happens to the money, I really think I am in love with him. That should go over big with Krisite, but you love who you love.* Jason came back outside, started the car and drove out of the parking lot. "Call your honey, tell him where we are, than give me the phone." Katie called Nick, "We're in Key West," she said.

CHAPTER TWENTY SIX

NICK'S CELL PHONE RANG, he answered. "Katie where are you? Are you all right? Put Jason on the phone,

Jason, where are you?" "I'm on U.S 1, just arrived at Key West." Nick said, "Meet us at the park n' ride lot off of U.S 1 on the west side. You should be there in ten minutes, we will be there shortly." "Hey! Just a minute, who is running this show?" "I am" said Nick, "You want the money or not? If you kill Katie, you still will not have the money.

The FBI is already here, so are a couple of your friends. Everyone is looking for you and the money. I am your best hope to get the money." Nick said, "I don't give a damn about the money, I just want Katie. If you hurt her, I swear, I will kill you myself with my bare hands."

"Now, here is what you do, Jason, meet us at the park and ride lot. I will be there at three p.m. you park at the back of the lot." "I will bring the suitcase, when I arrive, I will start walking towards you, Katie will start walking towards me, you can walk with her if you wish. When she has passed me, and I mean passed. I'll hand over the suitcase to you."

"Not so fast, Jensen, I want to look in that suitcase." "You can look in it with me, but only after Katie is safe.". "What makes you think that I wouldn't kill you right there?" "You might, but one of the girls will call the FBI." "I will hand the money over to you. Do it that way or I'll tell the FBI that you are here in Key West. This place isn't big enough to hide in, Jason." "All right, let's do it, When?" "We'll be there at three, this afternoon, that will give us twenty minutes, tops."

Nick and Katie, buttoned up the boat, than went up the street to a tourist shop that rented motor bikes." This is the best way to get around this island," said Nick. They hopped on the bike, Kristie holding on to Nick and sped off to meet Jason and Katie. Riding down the highway, they crossed the southernmost point of the continental United States and turned onto Duvall Street. Nick noticed a nondescript Ford with four men in suits cruising on the street. He had to laugh, those guys stick out like a sore thumb in this area.

Dodging the traffic of tourists and locals, Kristie and Nick slowly made their way to Truman Street. They went north a couple of blocks, than pulled into the park and ride lot. Jason and Katie were waiting in the car. Kristie was carrying the suitcase that she had bought the night before, and packed with the money. "Ok, Kristie, remember the plan." "I got it, don't worry, just be careful, don't let that bastard pull any tricks." "Don't worry, I came armed with my trusty 45."

Katie was sitting in Jason's car, when she saw Nick and Kristie, she jumped out of the car, Jason grabbed her. He twisted her arm behind her. "Ouch, you bastard, damn you." "Ok, Jason said Nick Don't get rough, take the cuffs off of her and either send her this way or you start walking towards me," Nick held up the suitcase, "I have the money."

Jason said to Katie, "Walk." He pulled out his gun. "No funny stuff, Jensen." Katie, crying, walked towards Nick, as she passed him, she reached over to kiss him. "I love you Nick, I love you." She hugged Nick. "Hey! What's going on?" said Jason. "Give me the bag."

Just then Nick flipped the case at Jason and pushed Katie towards Kristie, "Go! Run!" he yelled. "Go!" Nick pulled his gun out of his waistband. "Freeze Jason, stay right there." Kristie, waiting on the bike, said "Hop on Katie," and Katie jumped on the bike, and they both sped away.

Jason laughed, "You're not going to shoot anybody Jensen." Jason grabbed the suitcase, ran to his car and jumped inside, and sped out of the lot. Nick watched Jason drive off, and the dark sedan that followed him off of the lot with three men inside. I sure am glad they waited for Jason to take the money, Nick thought.

Nick pulled out his cell and called Biker. "Hey Biker, Jason and his friends have the money, you might want to check the airport." he closed the phone. Nick walked down to Duval street than to first avenue. The next sightseeing train, that he was planning to ride back to the marina, was not leaving for another thirty minutes. Nick walked over to Irish Kevin's and ordered a beer.

It was a warm afternoon, and the beer was cold. It was especially good and cold, now that Nick knew the girls were safe. Duval Street was full of tourists, some pale faced, some with a fresh sunburn, enjoying the wonderful weather, waiting for the sunset celebration on the square. Key West was one the few places in the world where you could watch the sunrise over the Atlantic, and the sunset over the Gulf of Mexico.

he bar was crowded with young college students, trying to entice the girls to lift their tops and give the guys a quick look at their boobs. The best offer so far was a free beer, but the girls were holding out for more. One girl said, "You want to play, you have to pay."

Nick's cell rang. It was Rob Biker. "Where are you?" "I'm having a beer in Irish Kevin's" said Nick. "Why don't you join me?" "I am waiting for one of the college girls to flash me." "Are you kidding?" asked Biker. "No Why?" "Come on over." "Where is Katie? Where is Jason?" Biker yelled into the phone. "Well, Katie by now is safely on board the boat. Jason is probably headed for the airport. Trouble was, it looked like he had a couple of his partners tagging along when he left."

"Ok, Nick, I am serious, where is the money? By God, Jensen I'll find that boat. When I do you are going to be in serious trouble. You'll get ten years for obstructing justice " "Bull! I don't have any money, you can't prove I ever did" said Nick. "The damn money is with Jason, why aren't you looking for him? Why do you care where Katie is, or me? I don't have any of the money, we gave it all to him. If you hurry, you might catch all of them fighting over the money at the airport. You may still be in time to get your cut." "Very funny, Jensen."

"Well everybody is suddenly looking for this money, that until a couple of weeks ago, no one knew where it was, or even bothered to look for it. Until that poor girl was mutilated and killed. Now, everybody is out to be the hero."

"Look Nick, you can help us, you should have notified me that you had the money. I could get you on obstruction of justice." "Screw you, Biker. I never wanted the money, first, I wanted to clear myself in the murders, second I wanted to get that bastard Jason. Where is Jason, FBI guy?" "He killed Nancy Johnson and had something to do with the cop being killed in Islamorada, find him." "We don't know, we have an APB on his car, but we haven't found it yet." "Good work," said Nick." There is only one road in and out, two lanes, this place isn't that big, what's the problem? I don't think he will be staying in town for the sunset. He took off just about fifteen minutes ago, like I said, check the airport."

Meanwhile, Jason had driven to the airport, parked the car, took the suitcase and hurried into the terminal. The dark sedan slowed at the entrance, two men got out and followed Jason inside the building. One was much larger than the other one, his name was Larry. The other one was smaller, but muscular and dressed very dapper. Larry called him Sam.

As airports go, Key West International wasn't very large or crowded. A plain concrete building, with service counters for three major airlines and maybe five smaller ones. It had the usual tropical decorative touches, bright colors, rattan furniture mixed in with the usual drab fixtures of an airport. Jason went to the ticket counter of his airline. "I need a boarding pass for the first flight out to Aruba or any other island, one that is leaving within the hour."

Jason showed the attendant his passport and ticket. "Yes sir, we have a flight to Aruba leaving in forty-five minutes." The attendant stamped his ticket, smiled. "Your boarding pass sir, Thank you." Jason walked toward the boarding area. Just then two of the men that had followed him to the airport approached him. "Hey, Jason, going somewhere?" "Hi Larry! Hi Sam, yeah! I was going back to Miami to deliver the money." "Man, it was a bitch getting hold of this money. I sure hope the reward is worth it. I just snatched it away from Nick Jensen at a parking lot in Key West."

"Really, said the larger man, let me see," and he grabbed the ticket out of Jason's hand. "Funny, the young lady must have made a mistake. This says you were going to Aruba. How about that?" Jason said, "Look Larry, I have the money, here in the suitcase." "Good, then let's step in there and take a look," he motioned to the men's restroom. As they headed to the rest room, Jason saw Sam slide his gun out of his belt. He jammed the gun in Jason's ribs. Inside the men's room was empty. "Check it out Sam," said Larry, as he took Jason's gun.. Sam looked around, and in the booths. There was an old man sitting in one of the booths. "Beat it old timer, scram, now!" The man hurriedly left the room. "It's clear, no one is here". "Good, watch the door, Sam."

Larry took the suitcase from Jason, opened it, looked inside. When Larry was looking at the suitcase, Jason slid Katie's Ruger out of his ankle holster. Larry looked at the money and closed the suitcase.

"Waste him, Sam." Jason turned with his own gun and fired at Sam, than Larry. Jason dove for the cover of a toilet booth. Sam was hit in the chest and went down. Larry, hit in the shoulder, returned fire, his shots ricocheting off of the metal booth. Sam, lying on the floor squeezed off a shot under the booth, hitting Jason in his left ankle. Sam fired, again, but missed. Jason jumping out of the booth and tumbling along the floor, fired three or four shots in Larry's direction. One shot hit Larry in the forehead. Larry was dead when he hit the floor. Sam had a huge hole in his chest and would last a couple of minutes longer at best. Sam, with his remaining strength fired his last shot at Jason, but missed.

Jason grabbed the bag and left the two dead men. He hobbled through the terminal, his ankle painful and bleeding, people were watching, A guard alerted by the shots, approached him.

"Halt right there sir! Police!" Jason quickly shot him twice in the face. The guard fell in his tracks, Jason headed for the boarding gate. Four men.

Entering the terminal, shouting, rushed after him, "FBI, halt! Or I'll shoot" said Biker. Jason ran for the plane, past the agent He turned at the walkway and fired off a dozen shots. Jason loaded in his last magazine of bullets. The agent hurriedly phoned the plane, "Close the door, now! Now!"

Jason hobbling down the hall, his ankle bleeding and burning with pain, shouted "Hold the plane! Hold the plane! Damit!" The flight attendant managed to shut the door just as Jason arrived, he turned, The FBI was right behind him. Jason raised his gun and fired off a fusillade of shots at the nearest agents. One of the agents fell dead, another was hit in the shoulder. The remaining agents all returned fire, emptying their guns. Jason a bloody mess, dropped the gun and suitcase and fell. Agent Biker looked at Jason and said. "He's dead.

Go check agents Strong and Jones .Call for some support here. Get an ambulance, Tell them to hurry, we have an agent down. Finally, after all these years, we have the money that Reggie Sanders hid from us. Give me that suitcase, I'm going to take it back to my office for safekeeping."

Nick started to order another beer, than he thought, *maybe Biker would look for the boat. I had better get back there. Biker didn't know what it looked like, but with Katie and Kristie on board, it wouldn't be hard to find in that marina.*

Nick went out into the late afternoon sun, man it was hot now. There was not much of a breeze, and the breeze is what makes this place livable, that and modern air conditioning. Nick started walking towards the east side marina, he kept a lookout for Biker, but did not think anyone was following him. Nick thought, *funny what money will do, Biker is after the money, as well as the mob guys. It isn't anybody's money, except for maybe poor Sara. He father wanted it for her. Sure, he had stolen it, but he paid his debt, and eventually paid with his life. Laurie and Nancy paid with theirs also. Reggie had just wanted his little girl to be comfortable. Biker would probably skip with it, unless Jason's partners get to it first. Nobody even knows how much money there it is. Even I don't, thought Nick, Kristie had counted and hidden it.*

Still walking, he approached the Marina. The beer and the afternoon sun were taking a toll. Nick was sweating and tired. He sat in the shade of a banyan tree to cool off. He just wanted to get back to the boat and get a cold beer and start for home. Nick entered the marina and walked towards the dock. Rex came running over to him, tail wagging.

Hey boy, "Where is Katie? Where's Kristie? "Oh...Damn! The boat was gone. The slip was empty, except for the dingy. Nick looked out to sea, but there was no sign of the Bayliner. He checked over at the fuel dock. "Yeah, they were here. They stocked up on food, and beer. Filled the water tanks, made sure they had gas". Nick asked,

"Did they say where they were headed?" "No, I asked them if they wanted company, but they just laughed and waved. The red haired girl said if you came looking for them to check in the dingy at the dock." Nick said, "Thanks." "Come on, Rex. It's just you and me. I think they left us." Nick went to the dingy. There was a package under the seat. He opened the package, inside was a note and some cash, a lot of cash. There was about one hundred thousand dollars, along with a note from Katie. "Sorry, Nick, I love you. Kristie was set on doing this. I wasn't going to go with her, but she was said she was going with or without me. I just couldn't leave my sister alone." Love Katie

CHAPTER TWENTY-SEVEN

AS THE BOAT CLEARED the marina, Kristie steered southwest, heading for the Dry Tortugos, She was a little nervous about cruising through the night, but Nick had shown her how to look for beacons and buoys .They would just take their time. Katie was having a second drink, Kristie said "Save it Katie, you'll get over him. It's just another guy. I need your help, if we are going to get to the Cayman Islands by daylight, so stay sober." Katie wiped her tears, "If you had loved him as much as I do, you wouldn't be doing this." "Oh yes I would, Katie. This is going to set us up for life. Guys are a dime a dozen."

Katie asked, "You think they are looking for us?" "No, maybe Nick, he probably doesn't appreciate being left at the dock, sort of holding the leash. He has to get home in the dingy." "Nick will manage. Meanwhile we can open an account with the cash and a Swiss account with the certificates at the bank in the Cayman Islands." Kristie said, "I counted a total of sixty million dollars in cash and certificates. I put five million cash in the suitcase, that we gave to Jason and I left one hundred thousand in cash in the dingy for Nick." "Nick and Rex should be able to make it home."

Katie said, "I think I love Nick, Kristie, I love him." "Easy Katie, we'll work it all out, just be patient." "Will we be Ok?" asked Katie? "I hope so" answered Kristie. "We have to be careful, I am going to need you to help me. I have to steer between Cuba and Mexico. I am not worried about Mexico, but I sure am worried that we will stray into Cuban waters and end up in prison, you know what will happen to us, not to mention the fifty million dollars." Kristie watching the compass turned the wheel to the southeast. "Now if we can squeeze between Cancun and the tip of Cuba, we will be headed right at the Cayman Islands". Katie said "It's getting dark Kristie, I'm scared." "Well Nick has a rifle down in the cabin, maybe you should load it just in case." As the night settled in, it was cloudy, no moon, very dark.. "Boy Kristie, it's dark, you think they can see us, you know, like other boats, especially big ones". "Stay calm Katie, Nick said all I had to do was follow the compass, and look out for the markers. Help me out, Katie"

They both saw the large boat approaching from their left, or port side as Kristie pointed out. Kristie slowed her speed. The other boat was getting closer. Were they coming at them or didn't they see them. She gave a short blast on the horn. The other boat did not acknowledge. "Katie, do you have that rifle loaded?" "Yeah, from what I can tell, it's kind of automatic. My ex boy friend had one of these and he taught me how to use it." "Good, I think we are going to need it."

Kristie looked over, at the other boat, now it was almost beside them, about twenty yards abeam. She could see three rather unsavory looking men on the other boat. "Hey, you want some company?" yelled one of the men, using the loud speakers. "What are you doing out here in the middle of the night?" "We can protect you. There are all kinds of bad and nasty people around here." "Let us come on board. We can have a party. Huh?" Kristie answered, "No thanks, we have to be somewhere by morning." "It is very dangerous to be out on the water at night. We can help you get to where you are going, There are three experienced sailors on board." "How many are on your boat? It can't be just you girls, No?"

Kristie pushed the throttle up and sped away. One of the men yelled," Damn it, after them, get them!" "It's just those two girls, that boat is worth a lot of money in Cuba, go get them." Kristie pushed the speed to full throttle, she was scared, they were speeding through the darkness, she could see very little ahead of her. Kristie wasn't paying attention to markers or buoys, she just wanted to get away. Kristie could see the other boat give chase, Nick's boat was pretty fast, but she was not sure if it was fast enough. *Maybe taking off without Nick was not such a good idea.*

Kristie had the Bayliner running at full speed through the inky darkness. The men on the other boat still chasing, tried to narrow the gap between the two boats. One of the men threw a line with a grappling hook at the girl's boat. The fourth try it caught on the gunwale. Two of the men started pulling on the line, trying to slow the Bayliner. Katie aimed the rifle and fired a shot, she missed. "Hey lady that was damn close." "Go away or I'll shoot again. This time I won't miss." The men laughed, "Hey these girls are feisty, I like that, they should be fun after we catch them." The men slowed their boat creating more drag on the Bayliner. "Damn it Kristie, what do we do?"

"Cut the line Katie, get Nick's fishing knife." Katie ran to get the knife. The other boat was getting closer. While Katie sawed on the rope with the knife, the men started pulling on the rope, while slowing the boat at the same time bringing their boat closer and closer. Kristie left the wheel, picked up the rifle and fired four quick shots at the men. There was a shout from the other boat, "Damn it I'm hit "said one of the men.

At that moment, the rope split and parted, the Bayliner leaped ahead, Kristie rushed to gain control of the boat. Katie picked up the rifle and fired a few more shots at the boat.One of the men fired five or six shots at the receding Bayliner. The shots missed. The men apparently giving up, started to turn back."Kristie are you Ok?" "Well, maybe if I knew where the hell we are" answered Kristie searching the darkness ahead. When she thought it was safe, she slowed the boat to three quarter speed. "Katie look at those charts, can you figure where we are?" "Not in the dark, I can't see anything around us." Kristie slowed the boat a little more. They ran that way until the dawn. The sun came up a big red ball, just over the horizon. Kristie said "Well, that's east and we are still heading south. I think we have to cut back a little to the east". Katie sat on the deck, tears running down her cheeks. "What is the matter with you?" "I miss Nick, I don't want to be running around shooting at people. I have had enough men trying to catch me. I want to go home and climb in bed with Nick." "Oh stop whining, I'll bet we are almost there." "Yeah, there will probably sixteen guys waiting for us including the cops and they will all want to kill us and take the money." "Oh please, look! Look! There it is, I bet that is the entrance to the harbor."

Kristie steered towards the opening of a sheltered cove. Minutes later they pulled into the harbor, of Grand Cayman Island. Kristie carefully steered through the traffic of the harbor to a marina. She and Katie docked at one of the piers, went to see the harbor master and settled in for the day. "Now, all we have to do is get a good night's sleep, freshen up and go to the bank in the morning." said Kristie. Kristie did not see the man, watching them from the dock. *He noted the two women, than walked across the plaza to the bar. Inside the bar he sat at a booth with three men, one of them had a freshly bandaged shoulder with his arm in a sling. He told the men what he had witnessed at the dock, and of the two lovely ladies. The three man listened, with great interest, slowly smiling.*

CHAPTER TWENTY EIGHT

NICK PUT REX IN the dingy and started the motor. They went out of the Marina, heading for home. He had a plan, thinking that he and Rex could get to Big Pine Key, spend the night in a motel. Than in the morning, they would gas up and try to make it to Indian Key by nightfall. If they stuck close to the shore, and the water was calm, it would be safe enough for the little boat. Nick had made sandwiches to take along, and he stopped for lunch around noon. He fed the meat off of the sandwich to Rex. Nick gobbled down the rest of the lunch, washing it down with a cold beer from a cheap Styrofoam cooler he had bought. He also had water for Rex. After lunch, they took a swim. It sure is different than the last swim, Rex did not make up for those beautiful girls. Nick wondered where the girls had gone. *I hope they went to the Bahamas, if they went due east from Key West, they could make Nassau in about four hours. I sure hope they didn't try to cruise through the night, that could be really dangerous. They were not that experienced. He had only taught them the basics, about the boat, just enough to make it to port in an emergency. I should have agreed to keep the money, later, I could have gotten them to agree to a sensible solution. Matt laughed, to himself, I wonder how much money Kristie put in that suitcase that we gave to Jason? Somebody sure is disappointed by now*

He and Rex set off for Indian Key in the little dingy. It was twilight as Nick approached Indian Key. He pulled up to the beach, about where he and Kristie had dug up the money. Nick and Rex went to get dinner. He walked up to Mac's. The owner did not say anything when he went inside with Rex. "We just want some dinner, what do you have?" "Well, we can rustle you up a pot roast, the missus fixed it this evening." "Sometimes the fishermen come in for dinner." "Great, I'll have two plates, one for me, one for my friend." Mac looked at the dog, "Sure, coming right up."

"Say isn't he that girl's dog?" "You know that gorgeous red head with the great body? What happened to her?" "She ordered groceries a day or two ago and never came by to get them." "Yes, he is her dog, I thought that I was going to end up with her, but instead I ended up with my friend Rex. She and her sister decided to take a boat trip from Key West, left me and Rex standing at the dock." Rex looked up from his plate at the sound of his name, but only for a minute, he was licking the plate of the remaining pot roast.

"We might need another plate of pot roast for my friend, he certainly is enjoying the missus cooking." Mac started laughing, "You bet, I'll tell her someone wants to pay complements to the chef." He went into the kitchen laughing. Nick finished off his dinner with a cold beer, while Rex had cold water. They spent the night in a small motel down the road. Nick got into bed and Rex climbed right up beside him, snuggling his large body against Nick. It sure is a big difference from my other sleeping partners.

Nick and Rex awoke early the next morning, they walked up the road, Nick searching the brush. At last he spotted the place where he had hidden Katie's car. Rex was excited when he smelled the car, he thought that Katie was inside. "No, I am sorry old man, I wish she was there also. Well at least we don't have to walk home." Nick drove to one of the boat yards and bought a boat trailer. He than drove to the beach and backed the trailer into the water and floated the dingy onto the trailer. He and Rex headed for Pompano Beach.

They arrived home about three hours later, they drove into the driveway, parked the car. Rex ran happily to the house, back, to Nick, back to the house, he was happy to be home. Nick thought, *I am glad to be home also. It will be good to get back to a normal life. All of that, trouble and all I got out of it was a bruised heart. I really had feelings for both of those girls. But I think I am in love with Katie. Oh well, I am a sadder but a wiser man.* He went into the house, stowed his things, opened a beer and crashed on the couch.

The sound of a truck, and Rex barking jolted Nick awake. He looked out to see what the commotional was. Jonathan and Sara were petting Rex, while trying to unload their gear. Nick went out to greet them. "Sara, Jonathan, boy is it great to see you guys! What brings you Home?" "Sara was feeling blue over her mother and aunt, plus she did not like Maryland in the winter." Sara said, "I needed to get home, there are too many loose ends concerning my mother."

"Well ,Sara, you will be pleased to know that they caught your mother's killer. He was killed in a shoot out with Gabriel. Sadly Gabriel was also killed. They got Jason for killing Nancy. Jason was killed by the FBI trying to escape with the money that we found. The FBI has the money and good riddance. I do have a small portion of it, Sara."Nick handed the packet of money to Sara, "Put this in a safe deposit box, don't spend it all at once. Put a couple of thousand in an account and leave the rest for awhile. The FBI may still be watching all of us." "I just want to get the house settled and get my life back together." said Sara. Nick asked Jonathan, "What are you're plans?" "I am going to enjoy the warm weather for a while, than maybe head back to college in the fall."

Later in the week, detective Davis drove into the driveway, he waved to Nick as he got out of his car. "Jensen, how are you?" "Just fine, detective, what can I do for you?" "I heard that you were back and I thought maybe you could clear up a few questions." "Sure detective Davis, ask your questions." "First, can you tell me where Kristie and Katie Ryan are?""I have not the faintest idea, except wherever it is, they are on my boat." "Do you want to come down to the office and file a complaint?" "No, no, I am sure they will bring it back when they come home." "So, you are expecting to meet them? Will that be soon?" "I don't know when that will be, detective, Are they wanted for anything?" "We think they have the remaining money, and have left the country." "Really?" "Jason Sanders has the money, I gave it to him in exchange for Katie." "It seems the guy that you thought was the innocent victim is guilty of kidnapping and possibly the killing of a police officer, whom I think was your partner."" So why aren't you looking for him, detective?"

"You think that you are pretty slick Jensen, I think you were in this up to your neck. I am betting that you sent those girls to hide the money and that you will join them later." Nick said "I gave the money to Jason Sanders in Key West. That's the last thing I know about the money. I'll take a lie detector test if you want." "Do you still have your warrant, Davis? Go ahead search the house. As far as I am concerned, you are one lousy bastard." "If you don't leave me alone, I am going to file harassment charges against you.

"Where is the money that I gave to Jason?" "He would have killed Katie, if I hadn't given it to him." The FBI has the money or at least a portion of it." "The FBI thinks that you gave Sanders a portion of the money and kept the rest." "Bull! I gave Jason every last dollar of that money. How much did they recover?" "Oh they recovered five to six million dollars" said Davis. "So, how much was Reggie supposed to have stolen?" "They estimated twenty to fifty million dollars, give or take a million." Nick Jensen laughed, "Yeah, that's what they told the insurance company." "Believe me Davis, they have what is left of the money that Reggie Richards left for his daughter, Sara." "What do you plan to do now, asked Davis?" "I am going to put in an insurance claim for my missing boat."

CHAPTER TWENTY NINE

KRISTIE AND KATIE DECIDED to get a room in the hotel. Kristie said to Katie, " I have spent the last week on this boat. I need a nice hot bath, with bath salts and perfume." "I am with you sis," answered Katie. "Do you think the boat is safe here?" "Sure, we are going to take everything to the hotel, there is nothing here to steal. We are in the Cayman Islands, it's English, you know, very proper."

Kristie and Katie gathered all of their baggage and walked to the hotel. Kristie went into the Cayman Hyatt, asked the clerk for the best suite that they had. "Yes Miss, that would be Suite 1560, the top floor. How long will you be staying?" "We have some business in town at the banks, I guess possibly a week." "Very good, Miss," he rang for the bellman, "Take these ladies and their luggage to room 1560." The bell man lead the way to the room and a half an hour later, Kristie was relaxing in her bath. Katie was watching TV. "Hey this place is fancy, she called into Kristie." "This is luxury, we each have a bath robe, they left us fruit and flowers." "Well get used to it Katie girl, because you and I are rich." Katie started to cry, "I wonder how Nick is doing, we should not have taken his boat and left him". "Oh please, Katie, stop blubbering, Nick is OK, He understands, this was the chance of a lifetime. No one knows we have a fortune. No one is looking for us."

"I am going to call Nick, said Katie, I miss him." "Don't you tell him where we are, you better not screw this up for us, Katie." "If you want to go to Nick, tomorrow, book a flight to Miami, but keep me out of it." Katie opened her cell phone and called Nick. He picked up at the third ring. "Hi Nick, it's

Katie, I'm sorry for leaving you that way. Are you all right? How is Rex?" "I miss you Nick, I love you, I do." "What? Kristie won't let me tell you where we are." "I don't know Nick. I can't leave Kristie just now, she needs me." "I don't care about the money, it's for Kristie, she is determined to keep it. I can't leave her until she is safe. I don't know what her plan is, she won't tell me." "Goodbye Nick, I love you, I'll be back, soon I hope."

" Katie I know just the thing that will cheer you up. Let's go shopping. We will buy some nice clothes, shoes, underwear, the works." "Come on Katie let's go." Kristie grabbed Katie's hand and led her out the door. Downstairs, they found an exclusive women's shop in the hotel arcade, and spent the next three hours shopping. The girls bought lovely silk blouses with matching skirts, shorts, tops, each picked outa business suit, they each selected four pairs of shoes and an assortment of lingerie. They paid for the purchases and instructed the salesperson to have everything sent to their room at the hotel. After Katie and Kristie returned to the hotel from the shop, there was a knock on the door. "Who is there asked Kristie?" "Bell man, I have the purchases that you made at the women's shop." Kristie opened the door, "Bring them in, thank you, by the way, can we get clothes laundered and cleaned at the hotel?" "Yes, Miss, certainly." "Good," said Kristie, taking her clothing out of the suitcase. She handed the clothing to the bell man. "Can I have it back tomorrow?" Kristie handed him a generous tip. "Yes, Miss, tomorrow. He walked away with the soiled clothing."

As Kristie started to close the door, someone pushed hard from the other side, the door flew open and the three men from the boat entered the room. "Get out of here," shouted Kristie, "What do you want? Get out!" Katie began hitting one of the men over the head with her handbag. "Grab that bitch! She's hitting me in the head." One of the three pulled his gun. "Ok! Ok! That's enough, you two broads sit there on the couch. We have a score to settle with you. You shot my friend out there on the boat and all we were doing was trying to help you." "Yeah, right. If you guys had gotten that boat, you would have thrown us overboard and sold the boat. What do you want?" asked Kristie. "We want your money, the bigger of the three said. We want all of it." Katie looked at Kristie, "Wha...What money? We came here to get money, we don't have any money. All we have is our boat." "You are Americans, all Americans have money. What are you doing here?" "Well we came on vacation, we are supposed to meet some friends here." "Look we just want to have some fun, you know?" said the man with the bandage. "We can go out and eat and drink and later the five of us can have a little fun, you dig?"

Katie said "Damn it Kristie, I told you we should not have come here." "What are we going to do, now?" Kristie said "I suggest we do just what they want, we'll go out, eat drink and later, well we will see what develops.

They don't look so dangerous." "Now that's more like it, we are just looking for money and a good time. You girls are on vacation, how about a little adventure" Katie said "I don't like this, I don't feel so good." "Come on Katie, lets go to dinner with the boys" said Kristie. "All right, let me fix my hair, I'll just be a minute."

Katie retreated to the bathroom, where she flipped open the cell phone and called Nick. When Nick answered, she started talking low and fast. ""Nick, it's Katie, listen to me, don't talk, we are at the Cayman Grand Hyatt, we are being robbed and maybe god knows what by three men who had followed us by boat, I can't explain now. We are going out to dinner, to stall them, than I don't know what is going to happen." "Help Nick!"

Katie hung up and went out to join the others. Kristie and Katie and the three men went to the cocktail lounge and ordered drinks. Katie whispered to Kristie, "What is the plan?" "I wish I knew" said Kristie, "Just play along, we will come up with something." Katie's heart sank, here we go again. *That damn money is going to get us killed.*

Kristie kept buying the men drinks, while sipping hers and splashing most of the drink out of the glass. The girls danced with the men and drank more drinks. The men became more and more unsteady on their feet.. The one with the gun said "I think it is time we took you ladies back to the room." Katie said "Come on let's keep dancing."

She pulled two of the men out on the dance floor. Katie started to dance suggestively, moving her hips and arching her back. Katie than removed her top revealing her lacy bra. The two men dancing with her began to move closer, to Katie each one trying to shove the other out of the way. Katie flipped her skirt up and spun around giving them a glimpse of her panties. The two men started pushing, than punching each other bringing the security bouncers to eject them, in the resulting mele, Kristie and Katie raced out of the bar and back to their hotel. They went to their room and called the hotel security. The hotel management promised that they would have security and the police patrol the halls for the rest of the evening. Kristie and Katie, after locking and bolting the door, pushed a chair against the doorknob. They felt reasonably save. I wish I had my gun, said Katie.

"That's how we got into this mess, you shot one of them," said Kristie. "Oh no, sister, we got in this mess because you are greedy and wanted the money. I could be home or cruising home with Nick if you had not decided to run with the money." "I told you either the police or gangsters would be waiting for us when we arrived here." "Stop worrying, every thing will be all right tomorrow, we will go to the bank, open a couple of accounts and go to the airport and fly wherever we want to, you'll see." "Yeah, first we have to live long enough to get to the airport." "Come on Katie, calm down, let's pack our new clothing in the suitcases that we bought." "We will be ready to leave tomorrow. We'll call the airline, make reservations tonight. In the morning we'll go to the bank, open the accounts, get a cab, come back here, get ourbags and go to the airport." "We will be on the plane heading for Paris with our money, we will be wealthy women." "Keep the faith big sister, than you can call Nick and do your thing."

Katie did not say anything to Kristie about the phone call to Nick that she had made earlier in the evening. I'll just keep that as my secret thought Katie. The next morning Kristie and Katie showered, dressed in the business suits that they had bought last night during their shopping spree before retiring for the night. They had breakfast in the hotel dining room. Then Katie and Kristie walked to the National Bank of the Cayman Islands.. "What are we going to do, asked Katie?" "Don't worry, leave everything to me," said Kristie. She asked for the bank manager and informed him that they wanted to make a large deposit. "Yes Ladies, of course, right this way to my office. Have a seat ladies, can I get you anything? Coffee, Danish?" "No thank you, we have had breakfast "answered Kristie.

"Well now," the manager addressed them, "Just what kind of deposit do you want to make this morning?" Kristie answered, "I want to deposit six million dollars in cash in this Cayman Island bank." The manager leaned forward, they had his attention. "Well that *is* a large sum of money." "Yes," said Kristie. "Also I want you to arrange to deposit these certificates in The Suisse Bank of Bern, Switzerland. I think they will total thirty million dollars." "As you wish, Madam." "May I see your passport for Identification?" Kristie produced her passport and Katie's also. She spoke to the manager,

"I want this to be two separate accounts, divided equally between my sister and I." "Yes Miss, certainly." After checking the passports and examining the certificates, he summoned his assistant. After giving him instructions, he turned to the two women. "That is quite a lot of money. Did you ladies inherit this kind of cash?" Kristie, giving the banker a look of disdain, answered "Sir, I came to this bank because I had heard that you were very discreet, I find that question offensive." "Yes, of course, I apologize, please forgive my manners." His assistant returned with the papers. "Please ladies, sign these documents. The first is a signature for the Cayman Bank and the other will be for the Suisse account. We will wire the money within the day." "You may use the Cayman account today, the Suisse may not be used until tomorrow." "Is there anything else that I can do for you?"

"Why yes, now that I think of it," said Kristie. "Can you arrange for someone to pick up airline tickets that we reserved last night? Could you have the tickets brought here by messenger? While we are waiting?" "Why, yes, of course we can." He summoned his aide once again, giving him the instructions. The aide hurried away to complete the task. Katie whispered to Kristie, "What are you doing? Where are you going?" "Trust me, big sis, you are going back to Nick, I am going to Paris and Nice, and every other place that I have always wanted to visit. We are both wealthy, we can do whatever we want to do." "What about those men? They could be are waiting for us." "Don't worry Katie, just listen to me and do what I tell you." Kristie said to the manager, "If you don't mind we will have that coffee while we are waiting, thank you." The manager poured coffee into two china cups.

Shortly, the aide returned with the airline tickets. After giving the tickets to the two women, he asked, "Will there be anything else, Miss?" "No, that will be all, thank you for your patience and courtesy, good day." Kristie and Katie left the bank and walked back to the hotel. "See Katie, I told you everything would be all right. We each have an account at the bank and the bulk of the Money in a Swiss account. They will never be able to trace it to us." "If you are smart, you'll go to Europe with me. We can live very comfortable."

"Yeah, well don't look now, but there are our friends again," said Katie pointing out the three men standing at the entrance to an alley next to the hotel. "Oh damn!" said Kristie. "Let's get into the hotel, they won't make any trouble in there". Suddenly the taller of the three men was beside Kristie, he pushed a gun into her ribs. "Keep walking and smiling, bitch. we are all going up to your room as guests."" So just act like there is nothing wrong, we are just a bunch of old friends." Katie and Kristie walked into the hotel lobby followed closely by the tall man and his two friends. The man moved Kristie gently ahead of him to the elevator. They all boarded the elevator, pushed the floor number, and the doors closed.

CHAPTER THIRTY

NICK JENSEN'S PLANE LANDED at the Cayman Island airport at 10:15 a.m. After Katie's phone call, he had dashed to the Fort Lauderdale airport and chartered a private jet to the Cayman Islands, leaving early that morning. Arriving at the airport, Nick rented a car and after checking the map drove to the Grand Hyatt hotel. Nick parked his car, close by the hotel, and walked to the Hyatt, entered the lobby and had the clerk at the desk call Katie and Kristie's room.

"There is no answer Sir, would you like to leave a message?" "No thanks, I'll wait for them." Nick walked away from the desk, sat in one of the lobby arm chairs. He had just picked up a newspaper that someone had discarded, when he saw the girls enter the hotel lobby. Before he could rise from his chair and rush over to greet them, he noticed a man following closely behind Kristie. It did not look natural, he was walking too close behind her. Katie had two men following her, although not as close. Nick held the newspaper in front of his face and watched all them get on the elevator and the doors close

Nick Jensen dropped the paper, went over to the bank of elevators and took the next one to the top floor. Careful not to be noticed, Nick got off of the elevator, but there was no sign of the girls. Nick began thinking of a plan to rescue the girls. Just than a bellman stepped out of one of the elevators and walked towards Kristie and Katie's room. Nick said "I'll take that for you, I was just going to knock on the door." The bellman hesitated, "I don't know, sir." Nick slipped the bellman a five dollar bill, "This is for you trouble. I don't mind taking the clothing into the room." ".Thank you, sir," the bellman took the five and left.

Nick Jensen knocked on the door, "Bellman" he said as he knocked. A man's voice answered, "Leave it at the door. "I am sorry sir, but I can't leave anything in the hallway, hotel rules, Sir." The door opened a crack, and the man reached his arm around the door, "Gimme." Nick pushed hard on the door knocking the man backwards. Once inside he slammed the door, turned towards the man, who had recovered his balance. Nick head butted the man, breaking his nose. Before the other two men could react, Katie picked up the fruit knife from the bowl and stabbed it into the arm of the man with the bandage. Kristie, reacting swiftly kicked the third man hard in the groin.

All three men were stunned and disoriented. Nick grabbed the gun from the man with the broken nose. "Ok, you three lover boys have a seat on the couch, hands on your heads. Move!" Katie ran over to Nick, "Oh Nick, am I glad to see you!" "That goes for both of us" said Kristie. "Where did you come from?"

I" called him when I was in the bathroom, last night. I knew he would come to my rescue." "He is like Superman, or Spiderman." Katie kissed Nick on the check. "I will thank you properly later, when we are alone." "Yeah, great" said Nick, "Who are these guys?" "Those guys are pirates and gangsters. They tried to steal the boat, now they were going to steal our money, and do whatever else they could get away with." The tall man looked at Nick,

"We just want to get out of here. Those two broads are trouble. Just let us go, we have had enough trouble the last two days." Nick said "Go ahead, leave, but I am keeping the gun, and I won't hesitate to use it." The three men rushed out of the room, one with a bleeding nose, one with a bleeding arm, and the other with a painful bruise. Kristie said, "I think it is time for us to leave. Thanks a million, Nick, I don't know what Katie's plans are, but I have a plane to catch." Katie said, "I am staying with Nick, if he will have me." Nick grabbed Katie and kissed her, "You bet!"

"I have a rental car down stairs, I can give you a lift to the airport. Katie and I will take the boat home." "Great!" said Kristie. "After all of this commotion, I want to get out of here, I don't want the cops starting to ask questions." The girls gathered their luggage, checked out the hotel while Nick stowed the bags in the rental car.. "Where is the boat asked Nick?" Katie said "I'll show you, come on, pulling on Nick's hand." Kristie said "Wait, don't leave me alone," following behind. When they arrived at the dock, the boat was gone. "Damn it! They stole the boat anyway" said Katie.

"Let's get to the airport said Nick, I have a feeling we have not seen the last of your three friends." While they walked back to the car, Katie filled all of the details of their trip to the Cayman's, including the boat chase. Nick said, "I don't know how you two girls did that. That is a dangerous stretch of water, especially at night." Reaching the car they settled in, started the engine and drove away

Around the corner the three men sat waiting in the car that they had carjacked. After leaving the hotel they went to an emergency health care facility, where they had their assorted injuries attended to. Leaving the medical building, in a foul mood, they accosted an elderly couple. Pushing the old man to the ground and forcing his wife out of their car, they drove off with the old man's car. They drove back to the hotel and waited for Katie and Kristie.

"When they show their face, we will get them this time. "They will pay for all of the pain we suffered. They are not going anywhere until we get what we want from them." Nick, and the two women drove past the car on the way to the airport. "There they are, follow them. Find a secluded section of road and force them off." Nick drove through the city and to the road to the airport.

The airport road followed the edge of the hills overlooking the beach. As Nick drove, he noticed a car following behind. Nick purposely pulled over at a convenience store to get a coffee. When he got back on the road, sure enough there was the same car. "Oh Oh, it looks like we have trouble," said Nick. "What now, asked Katie?" "It looks as if our three friends have managed to acquire a car and are following us." "What did you girls do to them?"

Kristie said, "Well they thought they were going to have sex at our expense, than steal our money. We offered to give them money, but that wasn't what they really wanted." Nick increased the speed, the following car kept pace. When they came to a stretch where the road twisted with sharp turns, the following car closed the distance. Nick let them come closer, closer, than as the other car pulled along side, Nick gave a sharp turn on the wheel, smashing a fender into the other car. The man driving the car, fought to control it, gaining control and racing alongside of Nick and the girls, he turned his wheels into their car trying to force them off of the road.

The two cars careened down the road trying to force each other off of the road at high speed. Nick said "Get down girls, I think they have a gun, hold on!" As the car with the bandits smashed into Nick, he braked suddenly, forcing the other car to move in front of them. Than Nick increased speed, smashing repeatedly into the rear of the gangsters car, sending it out of control. The last action forced the car's wheels to leave the pavement and into the soft sandy shoulder. When the wheels hit the sand the car spun completely out of control, leaving the road and crashing through to guard rail, speeding over the cliff landing on the rocks and beach below. As the car rolled over and over down the embankment, it exploded in a fiery ball of flame. Nick regained control of his car and continued on to the airport.

"I sure am glad that I picked up the insurance option" said Nick. The girl's, who until now were terrified, burst into laughter. Katie said "I wonder why they were so angry with us?" Kristie answered, "Well, you shot the guy on the boat, than you teased them on the dance floor, causing a fight with the bouncers. Later, you stabbed him in the hotel, then Nick broke the other guy's nose and I kicked the third guy in the balls, what's to be mad at?". The three of them were laughing as they drove into the airport parking lot.

Nick returned the rental car, made arrangements to pay his share of the damage to the car. Kristie produced the tickets to Paris at the counter and acquired two boarding passes. She turned to Katie, "I have our boarding passes, sis, are you ready?" Nick said "I want you to come home with me, Katie." She looked at Nick, "I want to also Nick, but I need to stay with my sister, Nick, she needs me." ""No she doesn't, not anymore, she is wealthy, she is ready to go to Paris." "Do you want to go to Paris, Katie?"

Kristie said to "Katie, go ahead, I'll be fine. I am going to see Paris and find me a sexy Frenchman." "Than I am going to Italy and find an Italian stallion. I am going to buy a house in Tuscany and a house in the Swiss Alps. You go with Nick, be happy." Katie looked at Nick, I can't, Nick, not yet. I love you, I do, but I can't leave Kristie like this, please try to understand. Wait for me for a while, please."

Nick answered, "I love you also Katie, but I do not understand why you have to go to Paris with your sister. You said you were tired of running, tired of finding someone waiting to steal your money or the police asking questions. I don't know if I can wait, or for how long. Come with me now." "I just can't Nick." 'When I am sure Kristie is safe and everything calms down, I'll be back . She saved me and helped me through my drug problems even though it cost her her marriage." "I can't leave her right now." "I'll call you, Nick." "Katie, I understand, but I don't understand. We will just have to take a chance and see what life brings us." Nick kissed both of the girls goodbye, picked up his bag and walked to the charter plane. As he left Kristie said to Katie, "That was stupid, Katie." Nick watched as the flight for Paris took off and disappeared in the distance

CHAPTER THIRTY ONE

THE FLORIDA SUN WAS hot, even for mid July, Nick was relaxing on the couch in the Florida room, with Rex lying across the air conditioning vent. Poor Rex hadn't been the same with out the companionship of Katie. Nick mused to himself, come to think of it, neither have I. Nick thought, *I don't have much luck, being in love. I loved Laurie, now I am sure I am in love with Katie, she leaves me for money. Odd, but money never meant a great deal to Nick. He had always lived comfortably and happy. Still the circumstances of the past few months had left him very well off financially.*

The past month Nick had sold his share of the landscape business to John Daly. He planned to use the cash to furnish offices and start a private detective business. Nick had arranged with Jake Lawson of Lawson and Lawson to do investigative work for them, beginning in September. He still needed a partner for the business, preferably one with cash to invest. Nick hoped that by September he would be ready to move on emotionally. *Money! It makes everyone greedy, it is so sad. Nick would rather have Katie by his side and just live, love and work everyday. Katie had not only been beautiful and sexy but she was also a lot of fun. Nick missed her everyday.*

Nick got another beer from the fridge, it had been a difficult week. He was finishing building the office space. Sara and Jonathan had returned from Maryland. Sara was living in her house and Jonathan was bunking in Nick's house. Jonathan spent a fee nights with Sara, but as far as Nick knew, they were both planning on returning to college in the fall, Sara wanted to get a degree and Jonathan was not sure of his plans. Nick relaxed and sipped at his beer, thinking about *Laurie, Katie and the events of the past few months. His life had changed completely. It had always amazed Nick how life surprises you from one day to the next. Just when you think you have everything figured out, life throws you a curve and you had better be ready for it.*

The only communication that he had received from Katie, was a letter, She wrote: *I can't reveal where we are, but Kristie has bought a beautiful villa on the Riviera. I am Enclosing a code for Sara to use, it is a Swiss account and it contains most of my share of the money. It really belongs to Sara. I will be returning to the U.S. If you still want me, I will do Anything to be with you. I love you. I hope to see you soon. Katie*

After Nick had finished his second beer, the progress of a rather large cabin cruiser making its way down the canal caught his attention. The boat slowed as it approached Nick's dock, he walked outside and asked the captain of the boat,

"Can I help you, are you lost?" "I am looking for Nick Jensen, is this his dock?" "Yeah, I am Jensen" "Well, I was ordered to deliver this vessel to you, I have the ownership papers, you just need to sign them and she is yours." "I don't understand" answered Nick. "That was my instructions" the captain produced the bill of sale and the title to the boat. "I am to leave this vessel at your dock, in your care." "Can you help me with the lines?"

Nick after helping the captain fasten the lines, went into the cabin and signed the ownership papers. The man left in an inflatable boat tied alongside. "Good luck" he said to Nick, smiling.

Nick looked around the plush, richly furnished main cabin. This boat must be 60 feet, I am going to need a bigger dock. Nick walked through the boat, investigating every cabin. The ship had a spacious main cabin, a well equipped galley. There were two sleeping cabins. Nick thought this ship can sleep eight easily.

When Nick opened the door to the master suite, there was Katie sprawled naked on the king size bed. "Hi Nick, welcome aboard, I missed you." She said softly. Katie sat up on the bed, stretching her arms out to Nick. "I hope I am not too late. Do you still love me?" "Do you still want me?" Nick appraised Katie for a full minute before he spoke, "Hi partner" Than he rushed into her arms.

THE END